An Act of War

Gordon Wallis

Table of Contents

Prologue.

March 20th, Undisclosed bush camp, 60 kilometres north east of Palma, Cabo Delgado Province, northern Mozambique.

It was 5.00 am when 48-year-old Mozambican national Joao Quintas first stirred. Even at that early hour, the air was hot and heavy with humidity and this was further compounded by the cramped confines of the makeshift grass hut in which he lay next to his sleeping lover. He brought his left hand up to his face and rubbed his eyes as the familiar feelings of despair and anguish grew in his mind. The training session the previous day had been brutal and he had pushed his unit of men long into the night, only stopping when complete exhaustion had taken over. It had been only then, after prayers to Allah the almighty, that the group of 50 men had eaten and finally slept. The meal had been prepared by the group of 8 young girls they had kidnapped from a remote village some 60 kilometres to the west. The remaining residents of the village had been brutally massacred and their bodies dismembered with heads and limbs scattered around and discarded to the jackals and the flies. Although the girls had been raped several times after their capture, Joao Quintas had since ordered they be left alone and allowed to concentrate on their new jobs of cooking and gathering wild fruits for the men under his command. He knew very well that an army cannot operate on empty stomachs. And this *was* an army. The men were not only Mozambicans. Several were from Tanzania, Uganda and there was even one of Arab descent in their ranks. As their leader, Joao Quintas had driven them hard in their training and preparation and he felt certain they were fit and ready to carry out the grand plan that had been the focus of their training over the past year and a half. The day when this would take place was soon and the pressure he felt was overwhelming at times. But this pressure had been alleviated by the regular doses of speedballs. A powerful mixture of heroin and cocaine, he had spent the past 4 years addicted to the cocktail of drugs. It had started, as it had done with many of the disenfranchised youths in the north of Mozambique, when the control of the passage of these drugs had fallen into the corrupt security forces of the army and the police.

As a major transit conduit for the global trade, Mozambique's biggest export was heroin, and this was not likely to change in the foreseeable future. For those in control, the drugs were freely available and could be had in such massive quantities; there was no real disruption to the lucrative trade. The skimming had been going on for years and it would continue as long as global demand was there. It had also resulted in the majority of the disenfranchised young men who were affiliated with their group becoming addicts. But this was a minor issue, as more importantly, it had enabled the shady group to which they belonged, Al Shabaab, to fund their weapons and equipment. A somewhat ragtag and loosely organized outfit, their leadership was secretive, fragmented, and unknown to the greater world. But this had not prevented them from causing untold havoc in the Cabo Delgado region. Their campaign of terror had been running smoothly with random and brutal killing having taken place for some time now. Their momentum was growing, as was their focus, and the recent discovery of massive LNG gas reserves in the region had bolstered their determination. Of course, there had been setbacks. The storming of Mocimboa Da Praia, south of Palma had resulted in failure, but it had brought global attention to their cause and they were now known as a force to be reckoned with. Altogether there were six similar units of men scattered strategically around the area now, and all were in touch and communicating with advanced solar powered satellite equipment. Massive stashes of arms and ammunition, including RPG rockets and mortars had been secured and cached, and very soon their most brazen and ambitious operation would take place. Although their ideology had been questioned, ridiculed even, the world would know very soon that they meant business. For too long they had been branded a simple, drug-crazed youth movement with no real direction, rebels without a cause who posed a minor threat. But this had changed recently and they were about to make world headlines.

Joao Quintas lifted his skinny, coffee-coloured arm and wiped the sweat from his forehead. The terrible cravings had begun as they always did, and he needed his morning fix. That short snort of the drug and all of the worry and fear would magically disappear. He glanced at the battered steel trunk that held his worldly belongings and saw the open bag of white powder atop it. Lying next to it was the burnt spoon and syringe, but this was something he chose to ignore.

No, the spoon and the needle are only for the time after the work is done. Not for the day. Not for the day. But as the craving grew, so his temper flared. It was the same every morning. As Joao Quintas shifted his body, he disturbed his lover who still slept next to him. 22-year-old Darwesh Gonzalez snuggled his head further into Joao's shoulder and hummed quietly as he dreamt. This angered Joao who sat up suddenly and struck Darwesh on his face with the back of his hand.

"Get up, you filthy pig!" he snarled in his native Portuguese. "Get up and get out of my hut!"

Darwesh shrieked in pain and shock as he was awakened. He

scrambled to his feet and his naked body shook with tears.

"Please, master..." he whimpered. "Please can I have one snort?"

"Bring me tea!" growled Joao "Then we will see about your morning treat."

Hurriedly, Darwesh gathered up his clothes and made his way out of the small exit. Although Joao Quintas regarded himself as a straight, heterosexual man, he had found comfort in the company of Darwesh for the past 3 years. The regular drug taking had smoothed off the dreadful feelings of guilt and shame, and he placated himself by the thought that once the Jihad was over, he would settle down with a woman. But for the moment he was a man on a mission. As were the other five similar groups of men strategically placed around the town of Palma. Although the plan had been loosely put together at first, it was now becoming a reality and all of the weapons were ready, as were the men. The strategic gas wealth in the north of the country would be theirs and there would be no way to stop them. As dictated in the Koran, the infidels would be maimed and killed, and their objectives would be accomplished. Joao Quintas took the large, razor-sharp blade from its sheath where it lay on the mud floor near his mattress. He dipped the point of the blade into the open packet of powder and brought it up to his nose.

After two loud snorts, he shook his head and sneezed as the potent chemicals began coursing through his veins.

"Ahhh..." he exclaimed loudly. "Yes, that's better."

It was as he was dressing in his green fatigues that Darwesh returned with the tea. By then he too had dressed and as usual, he appeared sheepish and nervous as he approached. The small grass walkway between the two men's huts had been specially built to allow nocturnal access. The fact that the two were lovers was a secret that Joao would take to his death. Joao Quintas grunted as he took the steaming enamel mug and looked at the pathetic sight of his servant lover.

"Go ahead..." he said as he took a sip. "Don't use too much!"

Most of the men in the camp were addicts. This was an evil that Joao accepted as being part of their mission which was for the glory of Allah and the good of the people. The drugs gave the men unlimited energy and took away any fears they might have. Added to that, they made the men forget their families and focus solely on the reason they were all there. When they were on the drugs they had no qualms about killing in the most brutal fashion. In fact, it was entertainment for them and they actively enjoyed it. But it was Joao himself who controlled the distribution of the drugs among the men, and it was his responsibility to make sure there was enough to keep them going at all times. But having control of the movement of the illicit cargo from the north to the south gave him an almost unlimited supply. It would never run out. There was simply too much money involved for it to stop. *No,* he thought as he watched the skinny young Darwesh crouching and sniffing from the blade. *The plan will go ahead and this time the world will know the existence of Al Shabab.* Darwesh Gonzalez stood up and blinked repeatedly as the drug began to take effect.

"Are the men ready for the parade?" asked Joao.

"Yes, master," said Darwesh.

"Good," said Joao thoughtfully. "I will be there to inspect them in 10 minutes. The time for our mission is soon. I will give the men a morning show before we start our training. Make sure you are filming when I do so..."

"Yes, master," said Darwesh in a slightly effeminate voice. "May I go now?"

"Yes. Go now, and be ready for me when I come out..."

It was 10 minutes later when Joao Quintas made his way through the forest down towards the small clearing near the main camp. The men stood in formation, all wearing their green fatigues with belts of ammunition across their chests. In their hands they held the AK47 assault rifles they would carry into battle. Many of them wore head scarves which covered their faces and exposed only their eyes. Those eyes were fiery and their spirits charged with religious fervour and speedballs. Here were 50 extremely dangerous men and every one of them looked up to their leader. Joao Quintas made a spectacle of the morning inspection, walking slowly among the rank and file, studying each man's face and picking at any loose clothing as he walked. The men stared directly ahead, they were too afraid to look him in the eye. *Yes.* He thought. *I have trained them well.* It was only when the inspection was over and he was truly satisfied, that he made his way over to the small anthill that served as a pedestal of sorts from where to address them. Slowly, and with a great show of theatre, he climbed up and looked down at his men.

"My brothers," he said in his native Portuguese. "Our training has been long and hard. For months, and in some cases years, you have waited patiently while diligently following the path of the righteous and holy. Your hard work and dedication have not gone unnoticed. But today I stand here to give you news that will please you greatly. The day of reckoning is upon us! Within days we will march and our attack will commence!"

He paused to gaze down at the men and saw with satisfaction that they were smiling.

"The weapons we need have been transported and stashed in strategic locations around Palma. Our brothers in the five other similar units scattered around Cabo Delgado are ready, as we are. The day is soon, my brothers. Soon we will rain hellfire down onto the infidels that have captured our region and stolen our resources. Soon we will claim what is rightly ours and it will be all thanks to the mercy and blessings of Allah!"

"Allahu Akbar!" shouted the men in unison, their excitement building.

Joao Quintas smiled and paused to allow the men their moment of joy.

"So, to celebrate this auspicious occasion, and to bring you some entertainment, I have decided to set one of the girls free!"

A murmur of confusion rippled through the ranks of men, but they stood enraptured as their leader went on.

"Darwesh!" shouted Joao, turning his head slightly "bring one of the girls!"

As if on cue, there came a whimpering sound and a rustling of leaves in the forest behind the anthill. Within a minute, two figures emerged from the dappled morning shade. Darwesh Gonzalez led a young woman. She couldn't have been more than 19 years old and her clothes were filthy and torn. With her hands bound behind her back, she stumbled along as tears ran down her chubby face. Her afro hair was in disarray and her body juddered with sobs. The men, still slightly confused, watched and waited in their ranks. Joao Quintas stepped down from his anthill podium as the pair arrived nearby. He smiled as he walked towards the sobbing, pathetic sight of the woman.

"Now, little dove," he said, pausing to smile at the waiting men. "Today is your lucky day. You have been chosen to be set free. Free to fly into the forest and sing from the branches as you should. Are you not happy?"

The woman stood there with Darwesh positioned behind her.

Although she understood, she could not bring herself to answer, let alone lift her gaze.

"Little dove!" shouted Joao "I asked you a question! You are being set free! Are you happy?"

Still, the woman would not respond and simply stood there shaking and staring at the sandy soil at her feet. Joao Quintas turned and smiled at the congregated men who were mesmerized.

"The little dove has lost her voice, my brothers!" he shouted. "I will help her find it."

A murmur of excitement rippled through the crowd as he removed his blade from the sheath on his belt. He grabbed the woman's hair and pulled her head back violently. As he did so she shrieked and staggered on her feet. The blade sliced through the thin rope that bound her wrists behind her back and her arms fell forward. With her head still pulled back at an obscene angle, Joao Quintas spoke again.

"See!" he shouted, "I have freed you, little dove! Fly! Fly away now!"

At that moment he stabbed the woman in her right buttock. The blade travelled through her tattered clothes and then a good 4 inches into her flesh. Her body stiffened at the sudden shock and her scream pierced the morning. The blood-covered blade made a squelching sound as it was pulled from her flesh and Joao Quintas kicked her forward with a boot to her lower back. With one hand clutching her backside, the woman ran forward into the clearing in a lopsided and duck-footed stagger. She wailed as she went but showed no sign of stopping.

"Fly away, little dove!" shouted Joao as he sheathed his blade and lifted the AK47 that hung from his shoulder. With the gun at hip level, he waited until the woman had run a good 30 metres before he began firing.

Using random, single shots, he pulled off 10 rounds and the dust was kicked up around the screaming woman's feet. The rank and file began to cheer and roar with bloodlust as she went. Finally, Joao Quintas brought the butt up to his shoulder and aimed. The bullets blew great chunks of flesh from her body as she ran. Her right shoulder exploded in a red mist of shattered bone and meat, quickly followed by her side and thigh. Still, the woman ran, although now zigzagging from side to side. The men jeered and whistled, their drug-addled brains filled with a savage fervour of hatred and barbarism. Finally, one of the bullets smashed into the woman's spine in the centre of her back and she was thrown forward to land in a cloud of dust.

"The little dove was unable to fly!" shouted Joao with a broad smile. "Let us finish her, my brothers. Shoot!"

The morning air was filled by the rabid screaming of the men and a cacophony of gunfire as the dead woman's body was ripped to shreds by hundreds upon hundreds of bullets. The butchery continued until all of the magazines were emptied and what remained could barely be recognized as human.

Chapter One: London, February 1st 2021.

"Is that Mr Jason Green?" inquired the woman's voice on the phone.

Her accent sounded upper class British with a hint of South African thickness. I picked up on it immediately.

"Speaking..." I replied.

"Good morning, Mr Green..." she said. "My name is Amanda Coetzee, I'm calling you from the London offices of the Jackson Advisory Group. I have been asked by Colonel Jackson to set up a meeting. He would like to see you as soon as possible."

The name sent my head spinning. It was one I had not heard in many years, but the simple mention of it brought back a flood of memories from my past. Colonel Callum Jackson was a notorious figure from the top brass of the Rhodesian Army. Born in Northern Rhodesia in 1950, he had been only 16 years old when he joined the Rhodesian Army and had been placed in the Rhodesian Light Infantry. Court-Marshalled and expelled from the army soon after for killing a fellow trooper in a drunken bar brawl, he had travelled to South Africa before returning to Rhodesia a year later and joining the army once again. Tough and uncompromising, he had risen through the ranks rapidly and single-handedly led the raid on the Mozambican town of Manica that had been a resounding success at the time. Having moved to South Africa after the war, he formed the shady mercenary group that went by the name of Private Military Outcomes or PMO. This venture had made him an extremely wealthy man whose services were used extensively by governments and private entities throughout Africa. At one stage he had well over 500 hardened ex-military personnel on his books. A number of my own friends had joined this group after the war seeking to make their fortunes quickly and retire. Some of them had tried to convince me to join them at the time, but I had chosen the move to London and subsequent civilian life. I had seen enough of war and the prospect of becoming a professional soldier of fortune was a career path I had not been willing to take. More recently, the Colonel had formed the Jackson Advisory Group or JAG, which was involved in lucrative demining and high-level security contracts around the globe. I recalled a confrontation I had had with the man all those years ago.

At the time he had made a decision on the deployment of troops near the Limpopo River. I had been vehemently against this and had made my objections clear. This had rattled him and his dislike of me had taken root. Being far superior in rank, his orders had been carried out and had resulted in the loss of three men from my own unit. The man was a cold, hard operator with little regard for human life. The call had caught me off guard and I had to think on my feet.

"What is this in connection with?" I asked.

"I'm afraid I'm not at liberty to discuss that, Mr Green."

"I see..." I replied, feeling annoyed. "Please tell Colonel Jackson that I'm busy at the moment and will not be able to meet him."

"Very well, Mr Green," she replied evenly. "The Colonel will be having meetings in his suite at the Savoy Hotel over the next two days. You now have my direct number. If you change your mind and are able to meet him, you can contact me at any time and I will set up an appointment."

"I'll keep that in mind..." I said.

"Thank you, Mr Green," she replied. "Good day."

I placed the phone on the table and stood up from the desk where I had been working. *My, my... Good old Jacko. Always was a mean son of a bitch. What on earth would he want from me? More importantly, how did he get my private number? Crafty old fucker. Well, screw him. He can sit at the Savoy and drink tea and eat scones to his heart's content.* I lit a cigarette and walked over to the large bay windows that looked down on the urban sprawl of North London. The sun shone its pale, late winter glow down onto the landscape and I tried to focus on the tasks I had set myself for the day. But I soon found I was completely unable to concentrate. My curiosity was fast getting the better of me. *Why the hell would he choose the Savoy? That's the very hotel where Robert Mugabe would stay while in London. It must be to gloat. He's probably booked the very same room as the dead tyrant and he'll be lapping it up. Yes. It would appeal to his sense of humour. That's gotta be it. Anyway, fuck him. Let him enjoy his stay. One thing's for certain, he won't be seeing me any time soon.*

But just two hours later I made the call.

"Ah, Mr Green," said Amanda Coetzee, "I was hoping to hear from you."

"Yes..." I said. "I realise I have a few hours free today. Please tell the Colonel I'll be there at 3.00 pm this afternoon..."

Chapter Two.

The black cab pulled into the porte-cochère in front of the world-famous establishment that is the Savoy Hotel in the City Of Westminster, central London. The impeccably uniformed doorman stepped forward and opened the rear door as I paid the driver.

"Good afternoon, sir," he said. "Welcome to the Savoy."

"Thank you..." I replied as I climbed out of the vehicle and made my way towards the perpetually revolving doors at the entrance.

The interior was as plush and luxurious as one would expect, with gleaming chequered black and white marble floors and subtle art deco lighting. Square Corinthian pillars topped with elaborate gold-leafed scrolls stood in perfect symmetry throughout the lobby and luxurious leather furniture and heavy mahogany tables sat between magnificent flower displays and babbling fountains. I made my way directly to the grand reception where I was greeted by a rakishly thin middle-aged man in a black suit and tie. His skin was so pale it was almost translucent and his demeanour oozed with unapologetic snobbery.

"Good afternoon, sir," he said with a thin voice and a condescending smile.

The man was eyeing my black jeans and leather and sheepskin jacket with obvious distaste.

"Jason Green to see Colonel Jackson," I said unsmilingly.

"Ah, yes..." said the man as he lifted a telephone. "One moment please, Mr Green."

The man blinked and turned his head in an effeminate manner as he spoke into the receiver in a hushed tone. I turned to look at the clientele as he did so.

Relaxed and wealthy looking, there was a mixture of old and young of all races and I noticed an Arab family exiting the lifts followed by an entourage of anxious-looking helpers.

"Excuse me, Mr Green," said the receptionist, "Colonel Jackson is expecting you. There will be a porter coming to show you the way to his suite."

"I'm sure I can find it myself," I said. "You worried I might steal the silverware?"

The man winced visibly and turned a bright shade of pink as he dropped his gaze to his computer screen. I chuckled to myself as a young man approached and greeted me warmly.

"Good afternoon, sir. I'll show you right up."

I winked at the haunted-looking receptionist before following the young porter across the vast foyer to the lifts. The suite was situated on the 5th floor with a view over The Thames with the London Eye to the right. The front room had been converted to a temporary office and I was greeted by the woman who had called me as I walked in. The time was exactly 2.58 pm and I checked this on my watch as I sat down to wait. Colonel Callum Jackson was a stickler for punctuality and I was pleased to have made it on time.

It was at 3.00 pm on the dot when the phone rang on the desk and the lady motioned me into the main area of the suite. The room was plush with high pressed ceilings and richly decorated panelled walls. To the centre of the room, behind an antique rosewood and ormolu desk sat Colonel Callum Jackson. Leaning back and facing the windows in a plush leather chair, he clutched a ream of papers in his right hand which he studied through a pair of spectacles that sat on the end of his nose. He wore a crisp white cotton shirt that was open at the collar revealing a red and blue paisley cravat. His now grey hair was short-cropped and his barrel-like chest and broad shoulders were still full and solid as a rock. I could see the man was still physically fit despite his advancing age.

Behind him, mounted on a large three-legged easel was a map of Africa. Without looking at me once, he spoke.

"Jason Green..." he said in a booming voice with a deep sigh. "Take a seat."

I pulled a chair out from in front of the desk and sat down.

"It's been a while, Colonel. I have to say it came as a surprise to get the call this morning."

"Yes, Green," he said as he removed his spectacles, placed the papers on the desk, and swung his chair around to face me. "It has been a while..."

The man's face was red and flushed with the obvious signs of good living and prosperity, but his cold blue eyes were still as angry and piercing as ever. In an instant, he looked me up and down and nodded at what he saw.

"You look fit, Jason..." he observed. "I believe you're doing well."

"And somehow you seem to know a lot about me, Colonel," I replied. "My private number for example. How did you get it?"

The man laughed as he sat back in his chair.

"Green..." he said as his face became serious once again. "Do you really need to ask me that question? We have our ways. You of all people should know that."

"I guess you're right," I said as I looked him in the eye. "So, why am I here?"

"How about a drink?" he said reaching for the Baccarat decanter to his right.

"Sure..." I replied.

"Laphroaig Single Malt Scotch..." and he removed the stopper and poured a couple of liberal tots into two crystal tumblers. "30 years old."

"Sounds expensive," I said.

"Very..." and he pushed the glass towards me, "£850 a bottle."

The whisky was sublime, it tasted of creamed peat smoke tempered with lime and sea salt. Colonel Callum Jackson closed his eyes as he took a long sip from the tumbler and savoured it. After what seemed an eternity, he placed the glass on the desk and glared at me.

"You are here because I need good people, Green."

"I'm not a mercenary, Colonel," I said firmly. "If I had chosen that route, I would have joined your PMO group after the war."

"Jason..." he said with a sigh "Private Military Outcomes is a thing of the past. We are a legitimate and transparent operation now. The Jackson Advisory Group has multiple contracts around the world. Demining, security and humanitarian work."

I smiled at his last words.

"Why am I here, Colonel?" I said as I glanced at my watch.

The man had noticed this and I could see it had angered him immediately.

"Seeing as you are in a rush, Green," he snarled, "I'll get straight to it."

The man stood up and I saw again that despite his age, he was fit and trim. He brought up his right hand and pointed to the east coast of Africa on the large map behind him.

"This is the Cabo Delgado province of northern Mozambique," he said. "In 2012, one of the biggest global discoveries of liquefied natural gas, or LNG, was made here in the Rovuma Basin just off the coast. Since then, western majors like Total, Exxon Mobil, Chevron and BP have all jumped on the bandwagon and entered the Mozambique LNG industry. These gas projects are estimated to be worth $60 billion in total. It is predicted that Mozambique could well become one of the top ten LNG producers in the world."

"Sounds like a good thing for the country," I said. "Especially in the north, which is poor and marginalised compared to the south."

The man glared at me, then continued.

"This is the town of Palma..." and he pointed to a specific spot on the map. "It is planned to make this place a major LNG manufacturing hub. There will be thousands of skilled workers based there and it is envisaged that this development will drive the rapid advancement of a shit hole country that ranks right at the bottom of the United Nations Human Development Index."

Colonel Callum Jackson swung his chair around, sat down once again and continued.

"But as is always the case in Africa, there are problems..." he said. "The central government in Maputo only has a fragile and precarious control over the territory and borders of the north. The Mozambican army is a fucking useless bunch. Couldn't organise a piss up in a brewery! More recently since 2017, the militant Islamic movement, Ansar al-Suma - known locally as Al-Shabaab - has been active in Cabo Delgado. It now poses the biggest security threat in the country, with some of the northernmost parts now almost ungovernable. To date, over 700 000 people have been displaced."

I nodded as I listened and the man paused to take another swig from the tumbler.

"My company has been contracted by the French firm, Total," he went on. "Given the situation in the north, foreign companies with considerable investments in the LNG industry now feel threatened, especially at this critical stage when they are making final investment decisions. With the piss poor protection offered by the Mozambican army, they feel a lot more comfortable doing business under the watch of a professional organisation. And that is my business, Jason."

"Understood..." I took another sip of the liquid nectar. "But how do I fit into all of this?"

"I'm looking for good men," he growled "Good men who know the country and the people. And you have experience in Mozambique, Jason."

There was a long pause as I saw the half-smile form on his face. The man had clearly done his research well.

"The contracts are short and highly paid," he continued. "One month on, two months off. Luxury accommodation and all travel and living expenses will be provided."

Colonel Callum Jackson sighed deeply and tossed a large sealed envelope across the desk towards me.

"I have plenty of work here in London..." I said, looking him in the eye.

"Not at this pay rate, you don't..." he replied with a cold smirk. "Take the file, Jason. Read it thoroughly. I expect an answer by 3.00 pm tomorrow."

The arrogance of the man got my hackles up. However, my natural curiosity already had the better of me. I picked up the envelope and stood up to leave.

"Always a pleasure seeing you, Colonel..." I said as I opened the door.

"3.00 pm, Green..." he boomed, "tomorrow!"

Chapter Three.

I began reading the many documents in the envelope on the way home in the taxi. As expected, they were thorough to the point of being pedantic and detailed every single aspect of the contract and the work expected should I take the job. There was page after page of photographs, aerial maps, and listings of the specific duties involved. The position was for head of security for JAG within the framework and workings of the Total Palma site and compound. Every aspect of security as far as travelling to and from the site and the general surveillance of surrounding areas was to be attended to in addition to the monitoring and guaranteeing of the safety of all employees and subcontractors involved.

The accommodation was to be in a hotel in the coastal town of Palma in the centre of the Cabo Delgado region some 15 km from the actual Total site. I skimmed through the photographs and saw immediately that it was a charming old Portuguese port town with palm tree lined streets and an attractive bay with clear, blue waters. Not wanting to waste any time on the finer details of what was expected from the position, I paged through the pile of papers until I found the section that dealt with the actual contract I was to sign if I took the job. I was most interested in the remuneration and what it involved. I recalled Colonel Jackson's sneer when he had boasted that my current pay rate was nothing like what I would earn with JAG. It turned out he was right. The pay was a staggering $1 600.00 per day with all travel, food and accommodation taken care of. My eyes widened as I read the figure once again, but there was no mistake. That was the amount they were offering. *Holy shit!* I thought. *This is certainly an extremely lucrative contract for the old bastard if he can afford to pay that kind of money for security. Jesus, it must be worth millions!* I put the papers on my lap and stared out at the dreary grey weather as we drove into north London. *That is a life-changing amount, Green. Make no mistake.* The freelance nature of my work with the insurance company allowed me to dictate the working conditions of my duties in London. There would be no problem should I decide to take the Colonel up on his offer.

But there was still a mountain of paperwork to go through and I would certainly need to do my own research on the area and the implications of what he had told me. *Well, you can do that when you get back home. Take a good look at it, do some independent research and make an informed decision based on that. Despite the money, you certainly don't need any unwanted shit in your life, Green.*

It turned out that there was a vast amount of research needed and it was 11.00 pm by the time I had completed reading the papers and scouring the internet for news and other articles on the prevailing situation in northern Mozambique. With production due to start in earnest in 2024, the area had become a hive of activity with the various companies positioning themselves for the bonanza. But there had been a great deal of consternation within local communities with many people having been evicted and relocated after the discovery of the LNG. *Not all happy days and sunshine, Green.* This would partly explain the disturbances that were mushrooming in the area. Intensifying attacks near the gas site on the Afungi peninsula were making the major players increasingly jumpy, and understandably so. Because of this, the US Department of State had designated Ansar al-Sunna Mozambique, which it referred to as ISIS Mozambique, as a foreign terrorist organisation. What made this armed force so significant was that the movement had orchestrated a series of large scale and targeted attacks. In 2020 this had led to the temporary capturing of the strategic port of Mocimboa Da Praia in Cabo Delgado, south of Palma. Although the town had since been retaken by the Mozambican army, the insurgents had simply vanished into the bush and surrounding jungle, and little had been done to capture them. There was no doubt that the Islamist insurgents were increasing the scale of their activities in Cabo Delgado. A lack of governance or a proper security response by both the Mozambican government and southern African leaders made this a case of high political risk for the LNG industry. The escalation of the insurgency could potentially jeopardise the successful unlocking of Mozambique's resource wealth. So far, the main LNG installations and sites had not been targeted, but the attacks in Mocimboa Da Praia had brought the turbulence dangerously close to some of the installations. The Mozambican armed forces were clearly stretched beyond the point where they could protect the local communities and reports of beheadings and other such atrocities were being received from random remote locations in the north every week.

By the time I had finished my research, my eyes were stinging and I yawned deeply as I stood up from my desk. The lights of North London twinkled below in the drizzle and I found myself in a difficult and infuriating state of indecision. I lit a cigarette and walked back to the pile of papers. I flipped through them until I found the actual contract I was to sign if I was to take the job. The number that had surprised and shocked me was there in bold black and white. *$1 600.00 a day! That's a fortune, Green. You do four months and it's pretty much two hundred grand in the bank. That old bastard, Jackson is right. You know the country. You know the customs and the people, and you know how things work there. You'll be set up in a fancy hotel and have zero expenses. A bit of sunshine and loads of beer and seafood. Sounds good on the surface of it. One thing is for sure, it's certainly not too good to be true. They've made* *no bones about what's happening on the ground in the region. Probably best to sleep on it, Green. Your life here in London is quite satisfactory even if the work can be tedious. Sleep on it.*

But sleep was something I found difficult that night, and I tossed and turned as I battled to put the events of the day out of my mind. I awoke at 6.00 am sharp the following morning feeling annoyed and nursing a mild headache. But my mind was made up. I would take the offer the Colonel had made but I would only agree to one month at a time. I was not prepared to sign up to an ongoing project that I might not enjoy or get any satisfaction from. This would give me the upper hand in negotiations and although I knew it would infuriate him, I felt sure he would agree to my terms. In my mind, I heard his booming voice as I had left his office at the Savoy Hotel.

"3.00 pm, Green," he had said, "tomorrow."

Well, I thought. *I'll keep you waiting, old boy.*

It was at exactly 2.55 pm that afternoon when I called the number his secretary had used to contact me in the first place. It came as a surprise to hear Colonel Callum Jackson answer the phone instead of his secretary.

"You took your fucking time, Green!" he growled "Speak to me..."

"I'll do it, Colonel," I said, "But I have terms I would like to discuss."

"10.00 am, tomorrow..." he replied. "Be here..."

Chapter Four: March 18th, Pemba, Mozambique.

The LAM Mozambique Airlines Embraer 190AR jet banked steeply to the left over the sparkling turquoise waters of the Indian Ocean as it descended and prepared to land. Having just been roused from slumber, I blinked repeatedly to stop my eyes stinging from the vibrant colours and the almost blinding brightness of the tropical scene spread out below. I pulled my sunglasses from my pocket and put them on as I reached for the plastic water bottle I had stashed in the front compartment of the seat. I had caught the Emirates flight from Heathrow to Dar Es Salaam via Dubai and had only managed to sleep a few hours having forgotten my sleeping pills. I had cursed myself when I had realised this and although I had tried, the pharmacy at Terminal 3 in Dubai had refused to give anything other than herbal sleep remedies. My fortune changed, however, at Julius Nyerere International Airport in Tanzania. With a $20 bribe handed surreptitiously to the salesman, I had managed to buy a month's supply of my usual brand of sleeping pills from the pharmacy there. The flight from Dar Es Salaam to Pemba was short so I decided against taking one of the pills and had fallen asleep anyway almost immediately after boarding the one-and-a-half-hour hop to Pemba. The passengers on the flight were a mixed bag of races and all appeared to be on business rather than pleasure. This made sense given the tensions the region of Cabo Delgado was experiencing.

One man sitting near the window on the opposite side of the aisle had intrigued me. He wore tight jeans and a faded AC/DC shirt that was stretched to the point of splitting over his squat, barrel-like frame. His muscular arms were hairy, deeply tanned, and covered in tribal tattoos. I had noticed him sitting quietly staring at the rear of the seat in front of him as if he was in a trance. His balding, chestnut hair was closely shaven and his grey streaked beard looked like a tangle of steel wire. On the one occasion he had looked at me, I had noticed his piercing green eyes were bloodshot and tired looking. I put him in his late fifties and wondered what he might be doing in this remote neck of the woods. I had seen him drinking a cup of tea soon after take-off and had noticed his hands shaking slightly. I turned my gaze to stare out of the window once again and saw the changing hues of the crystal clear water below as the plane approached the shoreline.

Soon enough we were speeding over a multitude of rusted tin-roofed buildings and palm-lined streets as the small jet descended and prepared to land. The aircraft touched down with a series of bumps and I immediately noticed the tarmac of the runway was faded to almost white by the blazing tropical sun. The engines howled as the air brakes engaged and we trundled slowly towards the squat, 1970s cream-coloured building that was the Pemba airport terminal. Here I would be met by a representative from JAG and be introduced to my second in charge, following which we would both be transferred by light aircraft north to the town of Palma where the LNG extraction plants were under construction. I took a deep breath as I stared out at the blinding light that sparkled off the tarmac and I watched the palm trees on the perimeter of the airport swaying lazily in the breeze. *Africa, Green. Could be worse.* The passengers stood before the plane had come to a halt and began removing hand luggage from the overhead compartments. The two stewards reprimanded them from their seats but the majority ignored their instructions and continued regardless. I watched through the window as a small stairway was driven up to the front door of the aircraft. The letters 'LAM' were emblazoned up the side of the stairwell and I saw the paint on the sides of it had begun to peel and blister. By the time the seatbelt sign was turned off, the majority of passengers were standing and readying themselves to exit the aircraft. Just then I noticed that the man I had been watching earlier was still sitting quietly, staring blankly ahead of him. I felt a twinge in my legs as I stood and ducked under the overhead compartment to step into the aisle. I retrieved my rucksack and pulled it over my shoulder as I joined the queue of impatient passengers waiting to disembark. Finally, the door was opened and we began to make our way out of the plane in single file.

The heat hit me like a double-decker bus as I stepped out of the door and into the blazing midday sun. Combined with the oppressive humidity, it was as if I had just stepped into a giant foundry. Even the handrail burned as I made my way down the steps towards the waiting bus. Initially, it came as a shock from the crisp air-conditioned interior of the aircraft and I had to remind myself that this was the tail end of summer in the tropics and we were not that far from the equator.

By the time I reached the bus and stepped inside, I was sweating and the interior of the vehicle smelled of dried fish and body odour. I stood clutching a greasy chrome rail and awaited the rest of the passengers. It was some 10 minutes later that I walked into the interior of Pemba airport. The darkness was overwhelming at first and I removed my sunglasses as I followed the other passengers towards the immigration desks. My visa had been prearranged by the Jackson Advisory Group and was already plastered in my passport taking up a full page. My passport was quickly stamped and I stepped through the immigration hall and into the baggage reclaim area. The room was spacious and stark, unlike many other coastal towns, and I put this down to the lack of tourism since the troubles had begun in the area. Indeed I had read that the world-famous Quirimbas Archipelago of islands that peppered the coastline was now virtually abandoned and the tourist facilities almost completely bankrupted. *Nothing like an Islamic insurgency to fuck things up, Green.* With the air conditioning in the building struggling to keep the heat out, I stood quietly in the corner of the room and waited for our luggage. It took a further 10 minutes but eventually, the reclaim belts began moving and the bags started coming through. I had decided to travel light and only had one piece of luggage. I had brought a few items I thought I might need, but it had been made clear that all equipment, including weapons would be supplied by JAG. Eventually, I spotted my bag and stepped forward through the impatient crowd to retrieve it. The customs staff could not have been more disinterested in the passengers and I stepped through into the arrivals hall without a second look from them. Desperate for a cigarette, I made my way immediately towards the exit but it was then that I noticed the man holding the laminated card with two names on it. He was tall and thin with a shock of ginger hair, the skin on his arms was burnt pink and his face covered with freckles. I put his age in the late twenties. He glanced at me as I approached and I nodded in acknowledgement. The laminated card had two names printed on the front. J. Green and C. Van Der Riet. I pulled the pack of cigarettes from my pocket as I approached him and spoke.

"Jason Green..." I said offering him my hand. "Pleased to meet you. Seems you're waiting for someone else, I'll be outside having a smoke."

"No problem, Mr Green..." he said with a knowing smile. "Welcome to Pemba."

I stepped from the relative cool of the arrivals hall and walked out onto the shaded pick-up point beyond. The small airport car park stretched away to the perimeter of the grounds which were surrounded by lush vegetation and palm trees that were an almost luminous green against the perfectly blue sky. I could smell the sea salt in the air and the humidity washed over me like bathwater. A group of taxi drivers who were congregated on the opposite side of the tarmac called out to me in a mixture of Portuguese and English. Their black faces shone with sweat and their wide smiles were perfectly white. I held up my hand and shook my head to indicate I would not need a ride as I lit the cigarette and they soon returned to their animated and loud conversation.

"Well..." I whispered to myself as I exhaled a plume of smoke into the still air. "Looks like you're back in Africa, Green. Good to be back."

I stood quietly smoking for the next five minutes, wondering what the next month would hold for me. The briefings I had been given had been extensive and detailed to the point of almost being ridiculous. I put this down to the work ethic of Colonel Callum Jackson and I knew full well that my duties would be painstaking and thorough. It appeared that every part of the Jackson Advisory Group had his fingerprints all over it, and I expected nothing less. Being in charge of security for the duration of my contract, my responsibilities would be for the safety of all employees of Total both at the gas plant and in the town of Palma. In my bag, I had a ream of paper detailing my day-to-day duties and various other security protocols. I recalled feeling that I had gone back to school when I had first got started studying them all. I had no idea who I would be working with having been told that all introductions would be made on-site and the handover procedure from the existing head of security would take place a day after the initial briefings and familiarisation tour. The contract was 'wet', meaning that alcohol consumption was permitted after working hours. This, it seemed, was the only respite from what would be a very busy time indeed.

The Colonel was paying top dollar but he had made sure he would get his pound of flesh in return. I was under no illusions about that. It was as I was walking over to a concrete sandbox to crush out the cigarette that I saw the tall ginger JAG representative step out through the exit doors. Walking next to him was the man I had been watching on the plane. Short, stocky and powerful looking, his muscular arms held two heavy-looking leather bags and his face was dark and serious.

Both men walked up to me and the short man dropped the bag from his right hand and thrust it towards me. His grip was firm and energetic and he smiled as he looked up at me and spoke.

"Mr Green," he said in a thick Afrikaans accent, "my name is Cecil van Der Riet. My friends call me Stompie. I believe I'll be working for you as your second in charge here in Cabo Delgado. It's a pleasure to meet you, sir."

Chapter Five.

—————◆—————

"Jason Green, pleased to meet you, Stompie" I replied. "And seeing as we'll be working together for the next month, I think you'd better call me Jason."

"No problem, sir, err Jason..." he said, looking somewhat surprised.

His green eyes were as bloodshot as I had seen them on the plane and I wondered if perhaps he had partaken of a few too many drinks the previous night.

"Right..." I said to the man who had met us, "I believe we're to be flown to Palma?"

"That's right, Mr Green," he replied, offering his hand. "My name is Colin. I'm one of the pilots for JAG and I'll be flying you guys up to Palma today. The JAG hangar is situated at the far end of the main airport complex. I'll drive you down there now and we can get going. The current head of security up there is waiting to meet you."

I looked at Stompie who blinked and nodded.

"Sure..." I said, "let's go."

The three of us crossed the road and walked into the slightly ramshackle looking car park. There were a series of parking rows with faded shade cloth awnings and we stopped at a cream coloured

Toyota Land Cruiser with the letters JAG emblazoned along the side.

"Well," said Colin "here we are. Please load your luggage in the back and we'll take the short drive to the hangar."

Stompie and I did as instructed and I climbed into the passenger seat in the front. Despite the shade cloth above, the fabric of the seat burned my skin and the interior of the cab was like an oven.

I turned to watch Stompie climb in the rear and noticed his shirt was soaking wet around his armpits. Still, the heat did not seem to bother him, he appeared completely unfazed by it. Colin started the engine and we drove off into the blazing sun taking a right near the exit. It appeared the crude strip road had been recently made and this was confirmed when Colin spoke.

"Our hangar was specially built when JAG got the security contract up in Palma for the gas company. We have a fleet of two Cessna 172 Skyhawks and three Jet Ranger helicopters."

Once again I was reminded of the staggering amount of money involved in this contract. The cost of the aircraft alone would have run into millions.

"And how are we getting to Palma today?" I asked.

"Today we'll fly in one of the Cessnas," replied Colin. "We have a small private airstrip up there, it's only a short hop of 250 kilometres."

I nodded as we trundled along the perimeter fence of the airport complex and I savoured the cool blast of the air conditioning coming through the vents on the dashboard. Soon enough I noticed a brand new hangar structure up ahead. It stood out from the rest of the buildings on the property in that it was freshly painted and tidy looking. There were several administration buildings nearby along with satellite communication dishes and several similar land cruiser vehicles.

"That's the hangar up ahead," said Colin as we approached. "The Colonel had to arrange special permission from the Mozambican government to build it here within the airport complex."

"Why did he not simply build the base at Palma?" I asked.

"JAG needed the facilities here at the main airport in the Cabo Delgado province," he replied. "We have frequent international arrivals and the main fuelling facilities are here. Palma is so remote, it takes a good 10 hours to drive depending on the condition of the road. At the moment it's pretty washed out with the rains."

"Makes sense..." I said quietly as we pulled up into a shaded parking spot near the administration buildings.

"Well," said Colin, "if you gentlemen are ready we can leave right away. The plane is already on the skirt and waiting."

I glanced behind me at Stompie who sat with a blank look on his face. He nodded at me with wide eyes and I wondered then if he was afraid of flying. *It might explain his strange behaviour on the previous flight.*

"Sure..." I said, "let's go."

The three of us climbed out of the vehicle and Stompie and I busied ourselves retrieving our luggage from the rear. Once done, we took a walk up a paved concrete pathway around the buildings towards the front of the giant hangar building. There were several JAG staff all wearing either khaki shorts and shirts or overalls branded with the company logo. The aircraft stood on the concrete skirt to the front of the hangar. Freshly painted in blue and white livery, it glinted in the sun and I watched as Colin pulled the aviator sunglasses from his top pocket. To the left, the open hangar doors revealed the brand new fleet of Bell Jet Ranger choppers within. Modern, hugely expensive, and fast looking, I wished at that moment that we were taking one of them up north rather than the Cessna. It took less than 2 minutes to load the small cabin of the aircraft and climb in after which the chocks were removed and pre-flight checks were done. The temperature in the tight space was chokingly hot and I wiped my forehead as I waited.

"It'll cool down once we get moving," Colin assured us as he handed me my earphones.

Stompie donned his own pair of earphones as the engine was started and the entire body of the small aircraft juddered with vibration.

"All set?" said Colin into his microphone.

I turned to look at Stompie who nodded and gave the thumbs up.

"Yup," I said, "let's get going..."

The small aircraft trundled towards the end of the runway which was surrounded by a rusted fence and palm trees with their fronds blowing lazily in the slow breeze. After what seemed an eternity, we reached the end and Colin stopped the plane to get clearance from the tower. Although I knew he was South African, he spoke briefly into his headset in fluent Portuguese. The crackled reply came almost immediately and it was clear that we now had permission to take off. The engine revved as he swung the plane around to face the South and pushed the throttle to full. The aircraft lurched forward and the roar of the engine was deafening in the cabin. Soon enough we were speeding back towards the main terminal building we had arrived at earlier. The wheels left the faded tarmac as we were parallel with the building and I felt the familiar sinking feeling in my stomach as we gained altitude. I sat back in my seat and stared out at the small town of Pemba to my left. The mustard coloured dirt roads were lined with palms and the tin roofs were yellowed and rusted red from the salty sea air. Even from that low altitude, I could see that the town was charming and the faded colonial splendour was still evident. The water in the port was crystal clear and faded to a deeper blue as it stretched away. Colin executed a steep left turn once we had left the town boundary and the aircraft tilted heavily until we had fixed a course to the north.

"We'll be heading up the coast today to Palma," he said into his headset. "You'll see some of the islands to our right as we go. They're pretty much deserted now what with the trouble in the region."

"How long is the flight?" I asked.

"It'll take us just over an hour and twenty minutes..." he replied.

I stared out to the left at the carpet of green that was the interior of the north of Mozambique. As we gained altitude it appeared thicker and more impenetrable than it had done from ground level. It was nothing short of a jungle that stretched away as far as the eye could see. With the town of Pemba now behind us, and having reached cruising altitude, Colin turned and smiled as he spoke.

"Now," he said "Is anyone thirsty? I think there'll be some ice cold drinks in the back there."

I turned in my seat to see Stompie had already placed the cooler on the seat next to him and was rummaging around inside.

"We have Cokes, Fantas and bottled water," he said. "Looks like some sandwiches as well."

Colin and I opted for bottled water and a packed sandwich each. They turned out to be freshly made ham, cheese and lettuce and were delicious.

"Not bad at all..." I said between bites.

"They're getting better at it all the time!" said Colin.

The three of us were silent as we ate and drank. To the right, the Indian Ocean stretched away in magnificent indigo while to our left, the steaming, flat green jungle of landmass reminded me of a 1970s shag carpet. I found myself wondering about the character of the man I would be working with for the next month. *Stompie van Der Riet. An Afrikaner for sure. Puzzling fellow. Looks like he's been through the mill a few times. Certainly tough. Not to be messed with. I'm sure you'll get to know him in due course, Green.* With the sandwiches finished, Colin started the conversation once again. He explained that we were flying over the Quirimbas National Park at the time but the terrain below was similar all the way to Palma. He spoke of a rough coastal road that used to run between the two towns near the coast but explained that it had long since fallen into disrepair. I mentioned that it seemed to me that there was little to no sign of human habitation below. He replied saying that there were clusters of villages but these were scattered and mostly covered over by vegetation. He did mention that there were a few tiny fishing outposts along the coastline but these were mostly run by individual families who owned boats and were few and far between. At one stage he pointed out a dhow that was moored off the coast, bobbing in the waves below."It's a vast area of mostly untouched bush, basically," he said. "There are a few settlements with illegal mines and the odd store but really, it's pretty wild down there."

I stared down at the landscape and pictured the sweaty humidity and rough, sandy terrain beneath the lush canopy of trees.

"What about wildlife?" I asked.

"Oh it's there," he replied. "Much more so than in the south where it was poached out years ago. Even the Chinese logging companies haven't made it this far north yet. But, I'm sure you know, it's only a matter of time before that'll be exploited."

"Yup," I said quietly, nodding my head, "I know..."

The aircraft droned its way north for another 40 minutes until I saw Colin cut the revs and begin his descent. I had become sleepy in the cool comfort of my seat and I yawned and took a drink from my water bottle to wake me up.

"Almost there," said Colin, "we'll be landing in five minutes."

Suddenly I was alert and awake and looking forward to what the rest of the day would bring. I knew there would be some introductions and perhaps a partial site tour. There would be a thorough process of familiarisation the following day along with endless briefings. But none of this bothered me in the slightest. It would be a short but extremely well-paid stint in the bush and I was looking forward to it. The air that howled through the open window panels warmed as we lost altitude and finally I saw the tiny town of Palma up ahead. Set in a natural bay, only 32 kilometres from the Tanzanian border to the north, it appeared to be a sleepy tropical paradise. Surrounded by pristine beaches and untouched coral reefs, the troubles the region was facing seemed bizarre and absurd. *Don't fool yourself, Green. There's a very good reason you are here.* As we approached I saw the runway set inland in an area of thick jungle that had been recently cut away.

"You say the colonel had this airstrip made?" I asked.

"Correct," said Colin. "It's a bit rough but it serves its purpose. There's a small hangar and two helipads as well."

I nodded as we descended further until we were skimming over the trees in our approach. I turned briefly to look at Stompie who sat impassively staring into space.

That's it, I thought. *He's afraid of flying. Hell, each to their own.* The pilot had been right when he had described the runway as rough.

The small aircraft bounced and lurched as we touched down onto the compacted dirt strip and I held on to the door handle to steady myself. Finally, the plane slowed and Colin turned it to face the rudimentary hangar and workshops that were set against the surrounding tree line. Two black men in khaki overalls approached the plane before the engine was cut and stood nearby waiting. It appeared to me that arrivals at the airstrip were a regular occurrence and I knew that whatever procedures were in place would be quick and efficient. Colonel Callum Jackson would have made sure of that. Finally, the engine stopped and the propeller jerked as it became still. Colin and I opened our doors and climbed out followed by Stompie a few seconds later. The two men stiffened upon seeing us and saluted in unison.

"Good afternoon, gentlemen!" bellowed one of them. "Welcome to Palma!"

The two men wasted no time retrieving our bags from the aircraft and ushered us towards a car park set among the trees at the rear of the hangar. The afternoon was stifling and the insects in the trees hissed and clicked loudly. Soon enough we arrived at the car park and I saw 3 identical land cruisers parked in the shade. One of the men carrying out bags spoke quietly to Colin who nodded in understanding.

"My instructions are to take you straight to your hotel," he said. "The security team you are replacing are waiting for you there."

"That's fine," I said, "let's get moving."

Our bags were quickly loaded into one of the vehicles and we climbed in with Stompie in the back seat as before.

"It's a bit of a rough road to the town but we'll be there in 10 minutes," said Colin as he started the diesel engine. "I'm told the management housing compound at the gas site is full and you'll be staying at the hotel."

"That's right," I replied as we pulled off down the dirt track. "Is the hotel any good?"

"It's excellent," said Colin as we approached the gate, "Best seafood in town."

The drive took us through a maze of forest and muddy fields until finally, we arrived at the outskirts of Palma. The tar road we met was no better than the bush track we had just left and Colin had to swerve to avoid the numerous potholes. The buildings were mostly grass reed thatch walled dwellings with galvanized tin roofs. Clumped together in tiny yards with swept sand boundaries, children were running around and shouting as they played football and climbed palm trees. I stared out at the scene and what I saw was a place of contentment and peace. There were women with brightly coloured sarongs in African designs. Walking in sandals, they carried loads of food and other items effortlessly balanced on their heads and they smiled as they went about their business. There were groups of men sitting outside the tiny general stores drinking beer. They too appeared happy and laughed and waved as we drove past. Soon enough we left the high-density township area and entered the town of Palma itself. Here the buildings were of the old colonial style and the streets were more ordered and lined with trees that were trimmed in the Portuguese style of old. I noticed a few modern-looking shops and government buildings with fresh coats of paint. An uncommon sight in Mozambique. All in all, my initial impressions were that it was a pleasant seaside town with a relaxed atmosphere and an easy-going population who went about their business with a typically slow pace common in Africa. We passed a busy market that was bursting with fresh fruit and produce and I smelt the fishmongers' stalls before I saw them. It seemed food was plentiful and the people happy and content. It was also somewhat outlandish to imagine that there was an Islamic insurgency happening in the region. We continued up a gentle slope through the wide streets in the glare of the afternoon sun until we reached the highest point of the town. It was only then that I saw the true, rustic beauty of the place.

The quaint colonial buildings spread out below us in orderly streets until they reached the harbour. Numerous brightly coloured fishing boats and dhows bobbed around on their moorings in the crystal clear water. On either side of the harbour were wide sand beaches that stretched out as far as the eye could see within the bowl-shaped bay. Tall palm trees were scattered along its white sands and I was immediately struck at how litter free the place was. I knew from experience that the cities of Beira and Maputo to the south were heavily overpopulated and spoiled by litter.

Here was an idyllic tropical paradise nestled into the natural harbour. Untouched and unspoiled by big business, it stood as a reminder that even in extreme poverty and hardship, there was a certain charm and beauty.

"Well," said Colin nonchalantly, "that's Palma, quite a pretty little place."

"Certainly is..." I replied.

"We'll be at the hotel in two minutes..." he indicated as he made a left turn in front of the main municipal building.

As we drove I found it hard to take my eyes from the peaceful and picturesque scene to my right. I knew the LNG gas processing plant was 15 kilometres to the north and I wondered how the inevitable inpouring of investment and subsequent development would change the place. *For so many years it's simply existed here. More than likely with very few people coming and going. Well, it seems that's about to change, Green.* At that moment I could not have imagined just how things were about to change.

Colin drove up the tree-lined avenue until we reached a hill that was thick with all manner of trees. Winding our way around a few tight corners, we reached a high wall painted in the same colour as the sand of the beach. We drove along this for a good hundred metres until we came to the gatehouse.

The thatched structure had a guard station built into the wall and a large, ornate steel sliding gate. Painted on either side of the wall were the words 'Hotel Cabo Delgado'

"Well gentlemen," said Colin as he hooted the horn to get the attention of the guards inside. "Welcome to your home for the next month."

Chapter Six.

It was only when the shrieking screams of bloodlust had simmered down that Joao Quintas spoke.

"Cover the body of the little dove," he said with a smirk. "We march towards Palma tomorrow but the flies are already gathering. We don't need them bothering us."

With that news, the men cheered once again and several of them ran towards the pile of shredded meat that had been the young girl. The loose grey sand was easy to shift and before long, what was left of the body was covered with a thin layer of it. Once done, the men gathered in their ranks once again in front of the anthill. Joao Quintas climbed up once again and readied himself to address the men.

"My brothers," he said slowly, his eyes burning with religious fervour. "As you heard me announce earlier, the time has come and we will leave this place at sunrise tomorrow. We will march through the day and then rest for the night and the following day. Awaiting us is the cache of arms our brothers have hidden. Great piles of weapons and ammunition which we will uplift and move to the outskirts of the town of Palma during the night. Our fellow fighters are ready and will be doing the same so we have a well-coordinated operation. This time there will be no mistakes. We will attack simultaneously from all sides and we will move through the town until we have seized control. There will be further briefings closer to the time, but I want you to know one thing. Your faith and hard work will be rewarded with a great bounty and we *will* prevail. This time, the entire world will know our name."

Joao Quintas paused as he stared at the men, looking them in the eyes individually. Once satisfied, he nodded and raised the AK47 into the air with his right hand.

"Allahu Akbar!" he shouted.

The rank and file of the men followed suit, raising their own weapons high in the air as they shouted their response.

"Allahu Akbar!" they shouted again and again, their voices rising in volume and their eyes glowing with drug-induced intensity. It was a fearsome and disturbing sound that seemed to drown out everything else. Joao Gonzales knew then and there that they were ready.

Chapter Seven.

T he guard stepped from the small door in the wall and smiled as he recognised the vehicle. He quickly walked to the centre of the gate and pulled the handle towards the guardhouse. The ornate gate moved on a set of steel wheels on the railing and revealed a vast tropical garden stretching up the hill within. Green lawns rolled between lush beds of blooms with water sprinklers quietly turning in the afternoon sun. The droplets of water on the lush foliage glittered like diamonds as they dripped onto the rich soil of the flower beds and there were teams of gardeners raking leaves and collecting coconuts from the lawns. To the centre of the garden at the top of the hill, was a large thatched structure surrounded by palm trees. It stood two stories high. The dried reeds of its roof curled down over the eaves like a schoolboy's haircut and a driveway of red concrete pavers wound up through the palm trees and giant strelitzias of the gardens. Colin waved at the smiling guard as we passed through the gate.

"Obrigado..." he said through the open window.

The driveway climbed up to the left of the giant thatched structure and it was only then that I saw the parking lot. There were several vehicles, mostly off-road 4X4 sedans and pickups parked near the immaculately maintained flower beds which were filled with glistening variegated bromeliads and birds of paradise. My first impressions were that we had landed in a veritable Eden and if the accommodation was anything like the entrance, we were in for a very pleasant stay indeed. Colin pulled up next to a bright orange Land Rover which seemed somehow out of place with the other standard coloured vehicles. I noticed a British Army sticker on the rear door panel as we pulled up next to it. I quickly put it out of my mind as I noticed two young men in white uniforms approaching the vehicle. Clearly hotel porters, they wore wide smiles and one of them greeted us in English.

"Welcome to The Hotel Cabo Delgado..." he said.

We climbed out of the vehicle and made our way up a winding path up towards the entrance to the double-storey structure.

The pathway was lined with cashew trees, delicious monsters and bright red and yellow heliconias, all of which were thriving in the moist, humid air. Finally, we arrived at the stairway that led up to the shade of the reception area. We walked into the cool interior and I immediately noticed the overhead fans whirring above, circulating the air in the vast space. At that moment I saw two white men stand up and make their way over to us. They had been sitting at a table at the far side of the space near a swimming pool. The men looked like they meant business and I knew then they were part of the security team we were to replace.

"Mr Green?" said the taller of the two.

"That's me..." I said offering my hand.

There followed a series of greetings between us all when the senior of the two introduced himself as Smith.

"Well," he said, " I think I'll introduce you to the hotel manager and let you get your luggage into your rooms first. Then perhaps we can meet back here for a beer and a quick briefing?"

"That sounds fine," I said glancing at Stompie.

At that moment we were approached by a tall Portuguese man who introduced himself as Rogerio. Dressed in black trousers with a crisp white shirt, he told us he was the general manager and politely welcomed us to his establishment. It was clear to me that the contract the hotel had with JAG was extremely lucrative and we would be treated very well indeed. Rogerio proceeded to personally escort us to our rooms with our luggage following behind in the hands of the porters. Our rooms were adjacent to each other and set in a wing of the hotel towards the rear of the grounds. Rogerio spoke as he walked, pointing out the various facilities and features of the hotel. The rooms were all thatched and set in lush gardens similar to the front of the establishment.

There was a covered walkway leading down past the rooms and Rogerio paused as he walked and pointed out one particular room with heavy steel bars in the windows.

"That is the hotel armoury..." he said. "Your predecessors will hand over the keys tomorrow as everything in there belongs to JAG."

"I'm sure that will all be covered during the final handover tomorrow," I said.

"Yes..." said Rogerio. "The room was specially modified for this purpose. A bit of added security makes a real difference."

I knew there was a larger armoury at the main LNG gas site but the fact that there was a second one at the hotel was news to me. Finally, we were shown our rooms and Rogerio walked me through the various facilities within. Spacious and airy, the room was cool and fitted with all of the modern fittings one would expect to find in a top hotel in any big city. It was clear that the owners had spent a great deal on the construction of the hotel and were now geared to cash in from the many workers and contractors that would be visiting the region while working for the gas sites. All in all, it was a pleasant environment which far exceeded my expectations for a remote fishing town on the coast of Mozambique. *This will do very nicely indeed,* I thought as I surveyed the space. With my bags placed on the rustic wooden furniture, I stepped into the bathroom and quickly washed my hands and face. The room came with a modern key card locking system and I stepped back out into the stifling heat of the afternoon. There I found Stompie and Rogerio waiting for me in the shade of the walkway.

"How's your room, Stompie?" I asked.

"Excellent, very lekker," he replied happily. "Better than I expected."

"Good," I said turning to Rogerio. "I think we can make our way back to the reception to meet the others."

"Certainly..." he replied.

We made our way back up the walkway and into the huge thatched structure that was the main hotel area. The two men waiting at a table nearby were drinking beer from tall frosted glasses.

"Gentlemen!" said Smith, "I hope you're happy with the accommodation?"

"Very nice indeed," I replied.

"Yes..." he replied. "We've been very happy here. Although they have a superb compound at the gas site, we prefer it here, and it's only 20 minutes up the road anyway."

At that moment I turned to look at Stompie who was standing to my left. He stood there silently staring at the glasses of beer on the table and seemed to be in some sort of trance. I cleared my throat as if to break the moment but then Smith spoke.

"Well, why don't we head upstairs and have a chat?" he said. "You gentlemen look like you could use a cold drink. There's a great view over the harbour and a nice sea breeze. Shall we?"

"Sure..." I said nodding, "let's do that."

The men led us through the dining room to a stairway near the far side of the lower level. The nearby swimming pool had a rockery and a fountain in amongst the surrounding tropical foliage. The stairs were fashioned from cut poles and the rustic theme of the place continued to the smaller, upper level. There we found ourselves on an open-sided deck with low tables and chairs and expansive views of the harbour and the town on either side. As promised, there was a steady breeze and a smiling barman stood behind a wicker counter awaiting our orders.

"Now, gentlemen," said Smith, "what can I get you?"

"I'll have a beer please," I said, "Manica if they have it."

I glanced at Stompie who was standing to my left staring out at the ocean.

"Yes," he said suddenly, "yes, I'll have a beer, please."

We took a table at the ocean side of the deck in the shade of the overhanging thatch roof. The chairs were comfortable and the breeze was pleasant as we awaited our drinks. They arrived soon after and the glasses were frosted and the beer ice cold. It stung my throat pleasantly as it went down. *Ah, yes,* I thought. *I could get used to this. And being paid $1 600.00 a day to boot. Not too shabby, Green. I think you're onto a winner here.*

At that stage, I had no idea how dreadfully wrong I was.

Chapter Eight.

———◆———

It was 8.30 pm when Joao Quintas finally returned to his grass hut after having eaten and bathed using the hot water that had been dropped near the back of his hut by Darwesh. This nightly routine had been consistent for the past three years and Joao knew that very soon, Darwesh would arrive with a steaming kettle of sweet tea. The rest of the men who were camped down the hill near the clearing would be resting now, even though they were all thrilled by the news that the assault on the town of Palma was imminent. Joao had sent an extra-large package of the white powder cocaine and heroin mixture as a reward for their hard work and dedication. He knew the men would be pleased by this and it would help them to rest before the long march through the bush the following day. The daily radio contact with the other splinter cells of fighters had been made as usual at 3.00 pm and the word was that the plan would go ahead without fail. There would be another brief conference call that was scheduled for 8.00 pm the following night. This was to confirm that the various militias were in place and had recovered their respective caches of weapons. If everything went to plan, and there were no hiccups along the way, the raid on Palma would take place on the evening of the following day. The six separate groups of fighters would storm the town at exactly 11.00 pm using the element of surprise to confuse the residents and security forces. The barrage would continue through the night and only when the sun was rising over the ocean, would the men make their way triumphantly into the town.

But once again Joao Quintas was feeling jittery and anxious. The steady doses of speedballs he had snorted throughout the day were starting to wear off and he was now craving the needle. He turned his head and looked at the burnt spoon and syringe that lay atop the old metal trunk to his left. It was a sight he loved and loathed in equal measure. A guilty pleasure of sorts. Something he knew he really should not be doing, but did anyway. This was very much like his love affair with young Darwesh. Although Joao was a cruel and sadistic soldier, he knew he had a soft spot for the young man and the combination of the needle and the company of Darwesh was a great comfort to him in his darkest hours. It was not long after that he heard the soft rustling in the grass walkway and the crunch of the swept sand under bare feet.

"Master, it is I, Darwesh..." said the shaky, effeminate voice. " May I enter?"

"You may..." said Joao quietly.

As usual, the robed figure of Darwesh appeared through the doorway, hunched over and lean in the yellow glow of the solar lamp. In his right hand, he carried the enamel teapot and he smiled nervously as he stood upright.

"I have brought your tea, master..." he whispered, his eyes flicking towards the spoon and needle on the trunk.

"Sit down," said Joao with a sigh, "pour two mugs of tea and light a candle to heat the spoon..."

Darwesh Gonzales did as he was instructed and sat down on the crude wooden stool near the trunk. With a slightly shaky hand, he lit the candle that stood in the wax-covered bottle. Once done, he carefully poured two cups of sweet tea into two chipped enamel cups. Using a stained cloth, he wiped the base of one cup and carefully handed it to Joao who had taken a seat on a stool nearby.

Joao took the cup and slurped from it noisily then blew softly into it to cool the hot drink.

"Prepare the spoon..." said Joao quietly.

Darwesh smiled as he dipped the blackened spoon into a cup of water, half filling it. Next, he squeezed a few drops of wild lemon juice into the spoon. The citric acid would help to break down the heroin component, making it easy and effective to mainline it into the veins. Slowly and methodically, he dipped the blade of Joao's knife into the open packet of powder and carefully tipped it into the liquid in the spoon. Next, he lifted the spoon and held it steadily above the candle. It took only a few seconds for the mixture of drugs and water to start to boil, fizzle and darken in the spoon. Both men watched as if in a trance. Darwesh lifted the syringe from the top of the trunk and carefully stirred the bubbling liquid in the spoon with the needle as it thickened and turned black.

Finally, some 40 seconds later, the mixture had reached the right consistency and he placed the spoon and its contents back onto the top of the trunk. Satisfied his servant had done the job correctly, Joao Quintas pulled the belt from his combat trousers and wrapped it around the bicep of his left arm several times. He pulled it tight until the veins showed proud. Now ready, he looked up at Darwesh who sat patiently waiting.

"Give me the needle..." said Joao, his voice shaking with anticipation.

Darwesh did as instructed and handed the syringe to Joao. Slowly and carefully, Joao opened and closed his left fist until he had chosen the vein he would use to inject the drugs. Without pausing, he plunged the dirty needle into the vein and the sharp pain he felt was like a harbinger of things to come. Next, he depressed the plunger, injecting half of the contents of the syringe directly into the vein. Finally, he let the belt drop from his arm and sighed deeply as he rested the back of his head against the grass wall of the hut. The sudden and almost violent rush of euphoria was immediate and overwhelming. Instantly his mouth became dry and his skin flushed with an otherworldly heat as his limbs became heavy. As heavy as lead. The overwhelming rush continued as the powerful concoction raced through his veins into his brain and body. Joao Quintas let out a long sigh as his body slumped and fell to the bed to his right. He was entering that blissful state he had been craving all through the day. The state that alternated between drowsiness and wakefulness during which normal mental function became hazy and dreamlike.

Seeing his master now in his happy place, Darwesh Gonzales gently took the syringe from the limp hand of his master and lifted the same belt he had used to expose his veins. He took the same stool as Joao had been using and repeated the process on himself. It was less than a minute later when he too slumped and fell slowly next to Joao. Both men were now comfortably numb and completely oblivious to the outside world. The lovemaking would happen, but that would be much later. It would be when the initial effects of the needle were starting to wear off. Then the ritual would begin again and continue through the night. This is how it had been for as long as he could remember.

Chapter Nine.

S tompie and I spent an hour on the top deck of the hotel chatting
to the men we were to replace. They seemed comfortable and
happy to have finished their stint at the site and were looking
forward to returning home for their respective breaks. We learned
that they would return after a month to take over from us once their
holiday was over and our stint was done. They were on the same
salaries as we were and were clearly pleased with the high paying
jobs they had landed. It was decided that the formal briefing and site
tour would take place the following morning and that our meeting
that day was to be more of a social event rather than a working one.
I for one, was happy with this arrangement as I was sleep-deprived
and knew I would have a clearer head the following morning after a
good rest. We sat drinking cold beers and staring out at the ocean as
we chatted comfortably, discussing the quaint town and the various
restaurants and dining options. I was somewhat curious as to the
character of Stompie who sat quietly, seeming to listen more than
he spoke. It seemed he was a guarded person, unwilling to give too
much away to strangers. Seeing as I was to be working closely with
the man for the next month, I decided to find out more later during
the evening.

"Well, gentlemen," I said after finishing the dregs of my beer, "I
think I am going to retire to my room, do some work and take a
shower before dinner. Will you be here this evening?"

Smith explained that they had prior arrangements to dine at the

Total compound that evening, but would meet us for breakfast the following day before the handover.

"That's fine," I said, standing to leave, "Stompie, shall we meet at the restaurant downstairs at say 6.30?"

"Yes sir, err Jason..." he replied. "I'll see you downstairs at 6.30 sharp."

I thanked the men and shook hands with each of them before heading downstairs and making my way to my room.

My bones were aching from the uncomfortable flight. *Fucking Colonel Jackson can afford to pay $1 600 a day but can't fork out for business class seats. Tight arse.* By the time I got to my room, it was 4.15 pm and I headed straight into the shower. Once done, I lay down on the bed in the breeze of the air conditioner and dozed off with Sky news on the flat-screen television in front of me.

It was 6.00 pm when I awoke with a start and for a few seconds I was unsure of where I was. It quickly came back to me and I lay there thinking about the events of the day. *Seems fine so far, Green. The hotel is great, the people are friendly and the town is very pleasant. Yes, so far so good.* I sat up on the edge of the bed and stretched. I was feeling rested and refreshed from the brief sleep and used the next 20 minutes to unpack my clothes and set up my laptop on the desk near the window. As I worked I noticed a few guests making their way to and from their rooms. Finally, I dressed and stood outside the door to smoke. The evening was darkening and the sky overhead had taken on the rich orange and red hues that can only be associated with an African sunset. There were songbirds squabbling in the palm trees above and a great quiet had settled over the hotel grounds. It was a warm kind of peace that was impossible to find in the hustle and bustle of London. It was that perfect golden hour of the late day when the night was approaching and calm had returned to the land. Feeling happy and satisfied, I walked back into the room to grab my phone and shut down the laptop. There was much to do but it could wait until after dinner. For now, my focus was to get acquainted with Stompie Van der Riet and try to glean some information about the man I would be working with. Until then he had seemed something of an enigma. Although he was working under me, I had decided that a friendly working relationship would be essential to a smooth operation and I knew it was important that we establish a working bond at the very least. I stepped out of the room and locked the door behind me. The first stars were starting to show through the fading red streaks of the sunset as I made my way up the covered walkway towards the main building. It was exactly 6.30 pm when I walked to the restaurant to find Stompie sitting at the bar. He had showered and was wearing a black t shirt that was stretched tight over his tough, barrel-like frame. He turned in his seat as I approached and smiled.

"How are you doing, Stompie?" I asked as I took a barstool nearby.

"I'm great thanks, Jason. Much better after a shower. Was a long flight to get here. Can I order you a beer?"

"Please... Manica."

We sat talking quietly for the next 20 minutes. It turned out that Stompie Van Der Riet had been working in private security in Afghanistan for many years. This had changed when the Americans had pulled out and he had since found work in Iraq. On hearing about the contract for JAG in Mozambique he had promptly resigned and taken the job. The reason was clear and simple. The money was more than double what he had been earning in Iraq and there had been no quibbling over it. He had spent his early years in the South African Defence Forces and had done over 18 months in the Angola conflict before finally leaving and working in private security around the world. This high paying job was dangerous but it paid extremely well and all of this information helped me to build a picture in my mind about the character of the man I would be working with. Gruff in nature, grizzled looking and certainly a no-nonsense type, I found him likeable although I was still convinced there was something about him that was hidden. It was as if he was slightly damaged in some way. Perhaps it had been some kind of personal issue but I decided to keep the initial conversation light and to discuss only his professional background. I in turn told him mine, and it came as quite a surprise to learn that I had been in the Selous Scouts during the Rhodesia conflict. Our conversation continued amiably until a waiter approached and offered us menus at around 7.15 pm. After browsing the selection, I decided on the fillet steak and Stompie chose the prawns. I had not noticed it at the time, but in the short 45 minutes we had been sitting at the bar, he had drunk 4 beers. The MacMahon lagers were served in 1-litre bottles and it was only when we were making our way to our table near the pool that I realised this. *A heavy drinker? That might explain his state earlier on the plane to Pemba. His red eyes and drowsy appearance. Still, as long as he's composed in the morning there is no problem with that. It's a wet contract after all. Keep an eye on it anyway.*

The meal was served under the stars with the sound of the ocean in the distance. The food was excellent and we washed it down with another beer and ended with chocolate ice cream.

We both lit cigarettes as the plates were cleared and I sat back feeling full and satisfied.

"Well," I said as I exhaled a plume of smoke. "I'm looking forward to a smooth and easy month. I hope we can work well together."

"I'm sure it'll be fine, Jason..." he replied somewhat nervously. "We'll get the job done."

"Hmm, I'm not ready to retire just yet," I said glancing at the bar. "How about we head back inside, have one for the road?"

"Sure, let's do that..." he agreed happily.

We took the same bar seats. There were several guests in the dining room all involved in hushed conversations and eating their dinner. Stompie and I spent the next 20 minutes chatting about our pasts and getting to know each other. It was then that I saw her. She was short and slim with thick auburn hair that hung down to her middle back. She wore tight blue jeans and a brightly coloured, loose cotton shirt. She arrived and sat two seats away from us, and I watched her out of the corner of my eye as she ordered a vodka lime and soda. She had a wistful look on her face and what seemed to be a permanent half-smile. As we spoke I noticed Stompie turn and look at her, but our conversation continued immediately after. The woman sat there sipping from her tall glass and then opened her brown leather tasselled handbag and took out a packet of cigarettes. In the dim light of the bar, I could see that she wore thick layers of make-up. I put her age in her mid-forties and I wondered what she was doing in such a remote neck of the woods.

"Excuse me, barman," she said after lighting up. "Could I have an ashtray please?"

The woman smiled briefly at the two of us as the ashtray was handed to her and Stompie and I continued with our conversation.

But it was only five minutes later, while Stompie was describing the working conditions in Afghanistan, that I saw her rolling her eyes. Clearly, she was eavesdropping and something he had said had caused her to do this. Choosing to ignore her, I pressed him to continue with his story. He went on to talk of the routines he would work under while there, transporting white-collar workers and lawyers to and from their offices. He then went on to describe the working conditions in Iraq. This was different to the previous contract in that he was transporting journeymen and blue-collar workers to and from oil installations. This was not unlike what we would be doing in Mozambique. Stompie had seemed to relax and open up somewhat and I listened attentively as he spoke. But it was as he was telling me about an incident towards the end of a contract, where his convoy had been involved in a fracas with armed bandits, that I noticed her laugh and roll her eyes once again. By then this had annoyed me and I decided to introduce myself rather than leave her sitting nearby listening in to our conversation.

"Evening," I said with a smile. "How are you doing?"

"I'm fine thank you..." she said in a posh English accent. "I take it you chaps are here working for JAG?"

Stompie turned in his seat to follow the conversation.

"That's right," I said, "we arrived today."

The woman nodded and smiled sarcastically as she took a deep draw from her cigarette.

"I thought so..." she said, exhaling a cloud of smoke.

Feeling somewhat confused by her attitude, I decided to break the ice further and introduce us both in the hope that she would go away. I stood up, walked around behind Stompie and offered her my hand.

"Jason Green," I said with a warm smile. "Pleased to meet you."

The woman dropped her gaze as she looked at my hand but she paused for a split second too long. It was long enough to appear rude but I kept my hand extended. Eventually, she rolled her eyes once again and took my hand.

"Penny," she said, "Penny Riddle."

"This is my colleague, Stompie Van Der Riet," I said gesturing towards him.

Stompie stood up jerkily and offered his hand to the woman. His eyes were wide and it was as if he had sensed the tension of the past few minutes.

"Pleased to meet you, Penny," he said in his thick Afrikaans accent.

The woman shook hands with Stompie and I immediately noticed that she was somewhat dramatic and animated in her demeanour. At first, I thought she might be drunk but her eyes were clear. Standing closer to her, I noticed once again the thick layers of make-up she wore. She was not unattractive, in fact many would have found her quite beautiful. But there was something strange about her I couldn't put my finger on. She annoyed me intensely. This was unusual in itself and I immediately put it down to fatigue from the travelling and the long day. I decided then to make my way back to my seat and continue my conversation with Stompie. I had, after all, been polite and introduced us both. I had hoped she would appreciate that and perhaps leave us alone. But sadly that was not to be. As I sat down she spoke once again.

"So..." she said. "How long is your sentence?"

"Our sentence?" I asked with raised eyebrows.

"Your contract with JAG."

"Oh, I see," I said. "We're here for a month at a time. Working in security."

Once again she nodded and smiled while regarding us in a somewhat disparaging way. This only served to annoy me further but I smiled and continued the conversation.

"And you, Penny," I said, "what brings you to northern Mozambique?"

"Oh, I'm with a German aid agency," she said proudly. "Schauspiel für Kinder."

"I'm not familiar with their work," I said. "What is it you do?"

Penny Riddle rolled her eyes as if to imply that we were both ignorant for not understanding the name of her employers. Once again this infuriated me but I kept smiling.

"Schauspiel für Kinder..." she said in an exaggerated German accent, "Drama For Children."

Feeling somewhat confused, I let the information sink in before I spoke once again.

"I see..." I said, "So you're out here in Mozambique teaching kids to act?"

Suddenly Penny Riddle burst into a loud bout of animated laughter. Had it not been so quiet in the bar, I would have been deeply embarrassed by the outburst.

"No darling..." she said finally, her voice drawling with affected attitude. "We do a lot more than teaching kids to act. There are life skills lessons, gender studies, and drama among many other skills. I've been here for a year now with Aggie."

This statement served to do nothing but confuse and irritate me further. All the while Stompie Van Der Riet sat staring at the woman in wide-eyed amazement. *Holy shit, Green. You've found a right fucking nutter here. Teaching village kids in Africa gender studies and drama. What a fucking idiot.* But the conversation was yet to be closed and I fully intended to do just that.

"Aggie?" I asked politely. "Is this someone you're working

with?"

Penny Riddle burst into yet another fit of highly animated laughter that lasted just a few seconds too long.

I glanced at the barman who stood frozen and as wide-eyed as Stompie.

"No darling," she replied finally. "Aggie is my Land Rover. Her full name is Agatha. She's orange in colour, parked outside in the parking lot."

It was then I remembered seeing the strange looking vehicle as we had arrived at the hotel. At the time I had quickly put it out of my mind but it had appeared somewhat unusual. *Your theory is confirmed, Green. Jesus Christ. The woman is a fucking lunatic.*

"Ah, yes," I said, "I did see that vehicle when we arrived."

"Gorgeous isn't she?" said Penny, beaming from to ear with a clown-like look on her face.

At that moment I realised that our stay in Palma may not be as smooth and easy as I had hoped. Deep down I prayed silently that she was simply visiting the hotel and was not actually staying there. The few minutes I had spent in her company had been enough to last a lifetime.

"Very nice," I said "Early '80s model if I'm right."

"My, my, Mr Green!" she blurted out loud. "You are a very clever boy!"

Fuck me! What a nightmare! I thought to myself. It was then that I knew I had to end the bizarre exchange and leave before it got any weirder. I made the first move to cut it off as quickly as possible.

"Well Penny," I said nodding to the barman for the tab, "it's been a pleasure meeting you. I think I'll head off to my room."

"Oh!" she exclaimed. "Are you staying at the hotel as well?"

"Yes," I replied, the feeling of doom growing rapidly. "We're both here for the month."

"Oh, how super!" she said, more animated than before "Me too!"

Fucking great, I thought to myself. *You'll be wise to stay clear of this one, Green.* At that moment Stompie turned to look at me. It was as if he was in a state of shock. Somehow the presence of the strange woman seemed to have damaged him even more than a lifetime in a semi-military environment. I quickly signed the tab and stood up to leave.

"Good night, Penny," I said quietly.

"Good night JAG darlings!" said Penny with a wave as we both left the bar.

Stompie and I made off in stunned silence down the walkway until we had reached the halfway point.

"Bit of a strange one..." I said under my breath.

"You can say that again," he replied shaking his head.

"Well," I said, putting her out of my mind "It was good chatting to you, Stompie. I'll see you in the morning."

"6.00 am I'll be ready, Jason."

"I believe our meeting is at 8.00 am," I replied as I reached my door. "Let's meet at 7.30 in the restaurant so we're prepared for the others when they arrive."

"Perfect..." he replied, "I'll see you then. Goodnight Jason."

It was only as I entered the room that I realised how tired I was.

I stripped off my clothes and stood under a cold shower for a few minutes before drying off and lying on the bed. The events of the day went through my mind as the cool air from the air conditioning blew over my body. By then the fatigue had overtaken the memory of Penny Riddle and I slowly drifted off into a much-needed sleep.

Chapter Ten.

———◦❦◦———

It was 5.00 am when Joao Quintas first stirred. During the night he had awoken three times and had injected himself and Darwesh each time. They had had sex at around 2.00 am as usual and eventually collapsed into each other's arms afterwards. At first, he was confused as it felt like any other day, but he soon remembered that this was the day that he and his men would march through the bush to the weapons cache that had been hidden near the town of Palma. The responsibility he felt weighed on him like a tonne of bricks and the dreadful feelings of fear, shame, and anxiety had returned with a vengeance. More than that, this morning he felt scared. Terrified even, and he desperately needed something or someone to vent these feelings on. He lay there thinking as he reached for the grimy plastic bottle of water that stood near his mattress. As he did this he disturbed Darwesh who was still in a drug induced, semi-comatose, slumber next to him. The skinny young man groaned softly as he turned over and this infuriated Joao intensely. With a clenched fist he struck the sleeping man on the side of his face. Darwesh's scream was like that of a young girl and he leapt up naked, shaking from head to toe.

"Get out of here you filthy creature!" hissed Joao through clenched teeth.

Great rivulets of tears ran down the young man's face as he gathered up his clothes and crouched to leave the hut. As he did so,

Joao caught sight of the man's parted buttocks and dangling scrotum. The sight came as a sudden reminder of the depth of his depravity and he felt the bile rising in his throat. With his right foot, he booted the man in the backside causing him to scream once again as he was propelled out of the low door of the hut into the still, dark morning. With his head pounding and his skin creeping and itchy, Joao Quintas reached over and dipped the blade of his knife into the bag of white powder. He brought the covered tip of the blade up to his nose and sniffed loudly. The powder burned as it always did and he slowly lay back to allow the drug to take effect.

Chapter Eleven.

———————◈———————

"Morning, Jason," said Stompie as I walked into the restaurant.

"Stompie," I said as I pulled up a chair at his table. "Hope you slept well?"

"Very well, thanks," he replied.

I looked around the restaurant hoping that the woman from the previous night, Penny Riddle, was not there. Thankfully she wasn't. The last thing I wanted was for her to embarrass Stompie and me on the day of the handover. It had just gone 7.30 am and I had slept like a log. I had awoken at 6.00 am and showered before browsing the news on my laptop and going through the ream of papers from the JAG offices. This was the day we were to take over the security of the gas plant and I wanted to be prepared. The list of responsibilities was huge and I knew full well that Colonel Jackson would want his pound of flesh. The day would entail a briefing in the restaurant followed by a tour of the armoury in the hotel. This would be followed by breakfast and then we would all proceed to the LNG site some 15 km north of the town of Palma. There we would be introduced to the team that would be working under us and a familiarisation tour would take place before the official handover later in the afternoon. If everything went according to plan, Stompie Van Der Riet and I would be in charge of the site by 3.00 pm. From then on, we would be on call and on duty every single day of the length of our stay. The team working under us was comprised of over 150 general guards and scouts who would report directly to us through a general manager we were yet to meet. I knew nothing of this man other than that he was a Mozambican national who had been educated in Portugal and had been trained by JAG. I had only seen a picture of the man but I knew from his profile papers that he was highly respected by everyone under him. This would be a distinct advantage given most of the local guards would be Portuguese speakers and communication would be difficult. I put this man's appointment down to thorough planning by Colonel Jackson. A nice touch. Stompie poured me a cup of coffee from a flask that sat in the centre of the table and spoke.

"Well," he said "today's the big day. Hope it goes smoothly."

"I'm sure it will," I replied as I lifted the cup. "We'll be done by 2.00 pm."

I looked around the restaurant to see several guests at the tables. I was starving hungry but I knew we would be eating with the men from JAG so I avoided looking at the buffet which was set at the far side of the restaurant near the pool. The appetizing smell of bacon and sausages drifted through the warm morning air.

The men arrived at 8.00 am on the dot and greeted us cheerfully as they arrived. Accompanying them was a huge black man dressed in green camouflage. He must have been close to 7-foot tall and he was completely bald. His shoulders were broad and powerful and although his face was kindly and handsome, he had a definite air of authority about him. I put his age in his early forties.

"Morning, gentlemen," said Smith. "This is Louis Santos, otherwise known as Sarge. He's the general manager of the JAG security team and will be working with you as your 3rd in charge. "

Both Stompie and I greeted the man and shook hands with him. His grip was cool and firm and he smiled as he greeted us in perfect

English with only a slight Portuguese accent. It was quickly decided that we should all sit down for breakfast before the tour of the hotel armoury. We made our way to the buffet and loaded our plates before sitting down to eat. Once done, coffee was served and the briefing began. Smith explained most of what I already knew but I did not object as I wanted to be sure that everything was in order and fully understood before they left the following morning. The conversation flowed amiably until it was decided that it was time for us to view the hotel armoury. The five of us made our way down the back wing of the hotel until we reached the heavily secured room I had seen the previous day with the hotel manager, Rogerio. There were several heavy-duty locks along with a complicated alarm and access codes, but finally we were able to open the door and step inside.

The room was wide with high ceilings and the walls were lined with steel shelving. The selection of weapons was extensive for a private security operation. There was a selection of sub machine guns, handguns, flash grenades and boxes of ammunition stacked along the walls on the shelving. To the centre of the room was a table that had two modern drones atop it. These were powerful, fully loaded DJI Matrice models with thermal and zoom cameras. I knew by looking at them that they would have cost over $12000.00 each and once again I was reminded of the staggering amount of money involved in this contract.

"This is only a small section of the weapons and equipment we have at our disposal," said Smith. "The main armoury at the gas site has at least 10 times this so you'll have no shortages."

"Impressive," I said as I looked over the AR-15 assault rifles. "Clearly the Colonel wants to be prepared for any eventuality."

"Oh yes," said Smith with a smile "That is definitely true."

With the tour of the hotel armoury complete, we made our way out and the keys and codes were handed over to me then and there. Next, we were led back through the hotel and out to the car park where we would be given our vehicles. It came as no surprise to see they were identical to the ones we had used the previous day. Standard Toyota Land Cruisers, modern and almost unbreakable. Smith and I climbed into one while Stompie, Sarge and the other man used the second. The drive took us out of the hotel grounds, through the gate to the bottom of the hill and then right through the town heading north up a coastal road. We soon left the town's outskirts and the familiar thick green jungle that made up the common vegetation of the coast enveloped us. Although maintained and graded by the gas companies, the dirt road was rough having been well used and damaged by the heavy rains that were still persistent in the area. We passed several heavy vehicles of all descriptions on the journey and I was informed there was a huge truck depot not far inland where the majority of the trucks and tankers were based.

It was some 15 minutes later when we climbed a small hill and upon reaching the crest I saw the expansive gas sites stretching out near the coast below us. Although the Colonel had explained the size of the discovery, nothing could have prepared me for the vast scale of it all. Huge tracts of virgin land had been cleared and bulldozed flat and the various boundaries established. The site was made up of four vast sections, each of them self contained and secured with hundreds of prefab buildings and steel structures within them. Smith pulled over and stopped the vehicle on the crest of the hill to allow me to take it all in.

"Pretty impressive isn't it?" he said quietly.

"That it is," I said letting out a low whistle. "Which one is the Total site?"

Smith informed me that it was the nearest one on the right before engaging gear and heading on down the hill towards the massive installations. The further we travelled down the hill, the rougher and muddier the road became. This was due to the weather conditions and the hundreds upon hundreds of heavy vehicles that plied the route daily. Each site was a hive of activity with uniformed workers moving around like ants. It took a further 10 minutes of rough driving until we arrived at the impressive gates of the Total gas site.

"Well," said Smith, "here we are."

Within minutes our gate passes were handed over and we made our way into the relative order and sanity of the interior of the site. There had been attempts at beautification with grass having been planted and stunted palm trees along the verges. What was immediately apparent to me was the high security that was evident everywhere. One could not drive more than 30 metres before meeting armed and uniformed guards who seemed to be placed everywhere. Soon enough we arrived at the headquarters of JAG which was a squat white building with very few windows, a massive air conditioning unit and multiple satellite dishes atop it. Smith pulled up at the parking lot and the wheels of the land cruiser left muddy streaks on the tarmac. Before we had even alighted, a gardener rushed forward to wash the vehicles and spray the tarmac.

Stompie's vehicle pulled up alongside and the five of us met at the stairs of the building before heading inside.

"Well Jason, Stompie," said Smith "These are our offices. This is the hub of our operations here in northern Mozambique. All of our communication equipment and our main armoury is here. It's pretty sophisticated given our location but as I'm sure you know, JAG are sparing no expense and our principals are very happy with our work so far. So, if you're ready we'll head inside now and get on with the handover."

"Sure," I said. "Let's get on with it."

The rest of the morning was spent in a blur of site tours, meetings, briefings and instructions. Every single aspect of the running of the site was covered over and over again. Both Stompie and I were familiarised with our new offices and the various pieces of equipment within. It soon became apparent that my days would be filled from 8.00 am to 4.30 pm with a series of daily incident reports, subsequent investigations, and deployment of guards and scouts whose jobs were to infiltrate the surrounding area and gather intelligence on any suspicious events. Then finally I would have to make a detailed daily report to both the site bosses and the JAG offices in Durban, South Africa. It was clear that the giant oil companies were extremely concerned about the prevailing situation in the region and took their security very seriously indeed. There was a brief respite from the barrage of information when we were taken to the managers' canteen at the north end of the site. There we met with the engineers and other senior staff, most of whom were French nationals. It seemed they had brought in a chef as the food was superb and all washed down with ice-cold bottles of Perrier mineral water. Although every single building on the site was air-conditioned, the heat outside while making our boundary and facility tours was oppressive and deeply unpleasant. By the time we got back to the JAG offices, our shirts were wet with sweat. It was exactly 3.30 pm that afternoon when Smith announced that the handover was complete.

"I know you gentlemen will be fine here," he said as he handed me a black briefcase filled with cards and keys. "Now, shall we head back to the hotel?"

It had been a long day and there had been a great deal to take in. I drew a deep breath and looked at Stompie who had been quietly listening most of the day. Clutching several files under his muscular arm, he nodded and spoke.

"I think we're good to go..."

"Good," I said turning to face Sarge. "I agree with Stompie. We'll handle it just fine, and if there are any issues we can always turn to Sarge."

The big man smiled widely with perfectly white teeth in his huge, rotund head.

"Any time, Mr Green," he said in a deep, booming voice. "I'm at your service 24 hours a day."

Unlike the majority of engineers and contractors who lived in a plush compound within the gas site complex, Sarge lived in a house on the outskirts of the town of Palma. Feared and respected in equal amounts by those who worked under him, he was an integral cog in the security machine that kept the site safe. In the short time that I had known him, I had grown to like him and was quite happy to have him as my 3rd in charge.

"Well," I said, standing to leave, "let's head back to the hotel."

Chapter Twelve.

Joao Quintas was dog tired. The time had just gone 12.30 pm and he and his band of militants had been marching solidly since 6.00 am that morning. Already they had covered over 25 km making their way in single file through the difficult and sometimes impenetrable terrain that was the interior of northern Mozambique. Walking in single file, carrying their weapons and all of their kit, the men pressed on through the thick undergrowth, avoiding routes that would be naturally expected by any military patrols of reconnaissance outfits. The men walked silently and steadily, not stopping for breaks at any time. This was partly because they were all dosed up with large amounts of speedballs or 'bola' from the large packet Joao had sent to them after they had eaten in the early hours. The drug imparted the strength and stamina to do this in the stifling heat and appalling humidity that was at times overwhelming. Straggling behind him and battling to keep up was Darwesh Gonzalez. Still sulking from the beating he had received that morning, he had kept his distance throughout the day knowing full well that his master and lover was stressed and agitated. Still, the mission was on and any signs of weakness would be dealt with brutally so he pushed on through the pain. The other men were much stronger but Joao would not allow them to see the weaker man at the rear of the column.

It was exactly 1.00 pm when a whispered message was sent up the ranks of men that it was time to stop for a much-deserved rest. The men halted in a grove of msasa trees at the foot of a low hill and sat down in the shade to drink the cloudy, brackish water from their bottles. Already they had covered almost half the distance to the rendezvous and the arms cache. The man they were to meet was a scout for one of the gas companies who had been recruited and paid off almost a year ago. His disaffection with his employers had been identified early on and he had been convinced to join the ranks of the insurgents as a mole. A mole specifically placed within the security apparatus of the gas company who would impart vital information on the operations and the movements of their security networks. Hidden at the rendezvous, in a long-abandoned quarry, was the cache of weapons. Joao Quintas had not laid eyes on this cache as yet but he had been assured that it was there and all was in order.

Whether this was true or not would be revealed later that night when the rendezvous took place. This was just one of the many worries that had played on Joao's mind constantly through the long day. On three occasions he had stopped and paused to snort yet another huge dose of the speedball concoction. It was the only way he could keep up as he was not as fit as the rest of the men. Feeling some pity for his bedraggled lover, he had left small piles of the white powder on leaves placed in the footpath that had been left by the men who had marched ahead. Joao Quintas had turned occasionally to check on Darwesh and on more than one occasion he had seen him stopping to take a dose. *At least he will keep up. Only Allah knows this march would kill him without it.* The break at the foot of the heavily forested hill lasted for 40 minutes and thankfully Joao felt rested enough to send the signal that the march should continue. Using a GPS device to map the way forward, he told one of his runners to inform the man at the head of the column to commence marching in a specific direction. There were numerous open glades that they would have to avoid in case of any aircraft or drones flying overhead. Their informant at the gas company had told them months before that these high tech devices were being used and they posed a significant threat to the operation. Should even one of the six units of men that were to attack the town of Palma be discovered, the entire operation could quite easily collapse and their objectives would be foiled. This was to be avoided at all costs and the hardships they would endure staying in the cover of thicker vegetation would be more than worth it in the end. They had also avoided any pockets of civilians and villages. Although few and far between in this remote region, they were there and were also a significant threat as the villagers might inform the authorities of their movements. There had been far too much hard work and gut-busting preparation put into the plan for it to be scuppered at the last moment. And Joao Quintas was not about to be the one responsible for that failure. *No, that will not happen on my watch.* It was 3.00 pm as they were making their way through a heavily forested low lying glade criss-crossed with small rivulets that Joao stopped to once again take a snort of the powerful cocaine and heroin mix. Not seeing he had stopped, Darwesh arrived and was immediately spooked to see he had almost stumbled across his master. He backed away quickly but Joao was too tired to care.

"Do not go," said Joao. "I can see you are tired as well," he said wiping the sweat from his face. "Come here, have some of this."

Seeing his master had forgiven him, Darwesh smiled and approached the squatting figure of Joao.

"Thank you, master," he said, "I hope you have forgiven me for whatever I did wrong."

"Hmm," said Joao as he snorted half a gram of powder noisily up his left nostril from the tip of his blade.

He dipped the blade into the bag once again and held the knife out to Darwesh.

"Hurry," he said. "We must not fall too far behind the other men. They are counting on us."

It was 5.00 pm when the sun was starting to set and the blistering heat of the day was beginning to subside, that Joao called another halt to their march. The time had come for another break and a quick briefing before they continued. Ahead of them was the single most dangerous part of their march. The area ahead and up to the rendezvous point was more populated than the country they had just left. There were numerous human settlements and small villages. In fact, it had been nearby where they had kidnapped the girls who were now cooks and slaves for the men. The message had been sent to the front of the column that the men should gather for a briefing where instructions would be given on how to move ahead. Although the darkness would fall at roughly 6.30 pm, they would need to move through the night to reach their rendezvous point. This would be difficult and dangerous but it had all been planned. The sky was clear and the moon would rise early which would be a great help in the many kilometres ahead. It was some 15 minutes later that the men all gathered in a natural basin at the foot of another hillock. Still buzzing from the massive dose of bola, Joao waited until they were all seated before he spoke.

"My brothers," he said quietly "I know you are all tired from the march today. We will rest here for 20 minutes. Use this opportunity to bolster your determination. We are almost there and you have done very well to get this far. I have instructed Darwesh to distribute some more bola to get you through the final hours. Soon we will be able to stop and rest for 24 hours. Then, my brothers, we will rain hellfire on the infidels who have stolen our land and resources."

The men let out a subdued cheer as they took in this news.

"Darwesh!" said Joao, reaching into his top pocket. "Take this to the men. They have earned it."

Darwesh Gonzales stepped forward and took the bulging plastic bag from his master. He wasted no time in distributing it evenly through the rank and file of waiting men who were more than grateful for the boost it would provide. It took less than 10 minutes for each of the men to receive and take their doses and a calm quiet descended on them as they sat in the shade of the trees. All were wearing the green camouflage uniforms which blended perfectly into the environment. *Yes.* Thought Joao. *Now they are ready for the final push.*

But it was at that moment that Joao saw the young boy. He couldn't have been more than 9 years old. He appeared in a clump of rocks in amongst the trees not 50 metres ahead of the men. In his left hand he held a homemade catapult made from wood and an inner tube from a car tyre. Until then the boy had no idea of the presence of the men. He must have strayed from a nearby village and was more than likely hunting birds for the family pot that evening. The very fact that he had strayed so far from his village was unusual. The local villages were well aware of the presence of the insurgents and were terrified of running into them. It was Joao who saw the boy first and his eyes widened as he did. He paused and watched to make sure the boy was alone. He was. Slowly he raised his forefinger to his mouth in a silent signal for the men to remain quiet. Then he slowly pointed ahead towards the boy. The men turned in unison and almost immediately the atmosphere became electric with tension. Once again, Joao Quintas raised his finger to his mouth to silence the waiting men.

Then he pointed at his own chest to inform them that he would deal with the young intruder. The very fact that he was there was testimony to the danger they were all in. Not only that but should the young boy see them and then escape, he would inform his parents who would in turn alert the authorities to the presence of the men in the area. This was something he could not allow to happen.

Joao Quintas raised his hand slowly instructing his men to remain silent where they sat. Moving like a cat, he crouched down and slowly made his way towards the boy who was waiting near an outcropping of granite rock.

Stealthily and silently he moved through the brush and long grass, his men silently watching from behind. Joao Quintas knew this was an opportunity to once again demonstrate his cruelty and brutality. He knew these displays served to charge the men and radicalise them further into the cause. The boy would be easy to catch and dispose of and he would do it in front of them. The young boy had travelled over 5 kilometres to get to the hill. He had had success there hunting birds in the past although he had been sternly warned by his parents never to venture too far from their tiny village. Still, he intended to bag a great booty of birds for the pot that night. Something which always pleased his mother who battled daily to put food on the table. Already he had shot two purple doves, fat specimens that made excellent eating with the stodgy millet meal his mother prepared every night. But his parents would be all the more pleased if he could return with 4 or 5 birds and although it was getting late, he was determined to get his quota. The boy stopped near the trunk of a msasa tree that grew out of the base of the rock and sat down, catapult at the ready. If he waited there quietly, he know that soon, one or more of the fat feathered creatures would arrive and perch on the branches above. Then he would take the shot. He had been practicing all his young life and now he regarded himself as a master hunter. Certainly the best in the small village he called home.

Joao Quintas made his way slowly up the hill towards the base of the tree where the boy was waiting. He paused on two occasions to confirm the boy was alone. As far as he could see, he was. Keeping to the left within the tall grass, he moved like a snake, weaving his way forwards and upwards as he went. He paused regularly to watch the boy who was preoccupied with the upper branches of the tree he sat under. Behind Joao, the men watched in an enraptured silence.

But it was when Joao had sneaked to within 10 metres of where the boy sat that he was spotted. The boy yelled out loud as he leapt to his feet and made ready to run, but it was too late. Joao Quintas darted forward like an attacking leopard and caught the boy from behind by his tattered t shirt. Before he could scream, Joao cupped the lower part of his face with his right hand and lifted him clear off the ground. The boy thrashed and kicked wildly and his muffled screams were frantic as Joao made his way back down the hillock towards the waiting men who were already hissing and clamouring with bloodlust. With a wide grin, Joao arrived at the small clearing and made his way to the centre of where the men now stood.

"Look what I have found, my brothers," he said through clenched teeth. "A little antelope has strayed from the herd. This was a terrible mistake as there are many dangerous predators in the bush."

The men let out another subdued cheer as they anticipated what their leader was about to do.

"Now the way of the wild dictates that these small antelopes who stray from the herd are often never seen again," said Joao, knowing that this display was firing the men up. "I will now put the little antelope in a safer place."

No longer able to contain their fanaticism and primal bloodlust, the men began to chant and stomp their feet in anticipation of what was about to occur. The young boy's muffled screams grew louder as he kicked and thrashed with his loose limbs. But it was to no avail and Joao Quintas held him easily. Slowly, and with a great show of pomp and ceremony, Joao reached behind his waist and drew the razor-sharp blade from its sheath. Without hesitation he drew the blade across the boy's throat, slicing easily through the stretched skin and instantly severing his windpipe and the veins and tendons of his throat. The blood cascaded down over his filthy and tattered shirt and pumped out in great gushes. Within seconds, the boy's violent thrashing began to wane as the lifeblood left his body. The hissing and jeering of the men grew in volume until Joao had to reprimand the men in a fatherly way. Standing near the back of the crowd, Darwesh Gonzales felt a stirring in his loins at the sight of the spectacle.

His arousal grew and grew until he had to physically rearrange his underwear to accommodate his throbbing erection. The very sight of the killing had stirred something primal and overwhelming inside him, and he knew then that the love he felt for his master would never fade. He would serve him forever. With the young boy's body now hanging limp in his arms and a pool of blood at his feet, Joao Quintas released the body and watched as it fell. With wide, crazed eyes, he looked up at the men and spoke.

"This, my brothers," he hissed "is what we will do a thousand times over when we reach the town of Palma."

Chapter Thirteen.

It was some 40 minutes later when we all gathered in the lounge area of the Hotel Cabo Delgado for the official handover. Sarge sat to my left while Stompie was on my right with the other two men on the far side of the table. Looking pleased with the events of the day, Smith called a waiter over and offered a round of drinks. Stompie and I opted for a beer while Sarge ordered a Sprite. It was when the waiter had left to collect the drinks that Smith spoke.

"Well that went a lot better than I thought," he said, looking pleased. "I think we'll have a drink with you then we must get back to the compound. We have a farewell dinner to attend there."

Both men pushed their car keys across the table towards us.

"We are being collected in ten minutes and I guess the next time we'll see you is after a month."

"Hope you enjoy your break," I said. "It's well deserved. The workload here is heavy."

"That it is," said Smith. "Heavy, but manageable."

The drinks were served and we spent the next 10 minutes chatting cordially with our predecessors. Eventually, their driver arrived and we stood to shake hands and bid them farewell. The three of us watched them make their way past the reception and down towards the car park. Once they were out of sight, we sat down again to finish our drinks. With the vehicles handed over, we were now officially in charge of the JAG security operations in Palma. I glanced at my watch as I finished my beer to see it had just gone 4.30 pm.

"Well, gentlemen," I said, "I think I'll head to my room and do some work. I'll be back here at around 6.30 if you'd like to join me for dinner."

Stompie nodded in agreement while Sarge told us he would be heading home for the night.

"I'll see you at the offices at the gas site tomorrow morning, boss," he said. "I usually have dinner at my house in town."

I stood and bade farewell to my new colleagues before making my way through the restaurant and back through the lush gardens towards my room. The amount of information I had processed and the weight of the responsibilities were more than I had expected. There would be endless paperwork added to my daily duties. I knew that with time, I would adjust to this new environment and settle in, but initially it seemed slightly overwhelming. I decided to sit down at my laptop and craft a daily schedule that would make the tasks clearer and set out for both Stompie and me. With some sort of structure, the various duties could be parcelled out evenly and the coming days would at least have some sort of routine. Colonel Jackson was a hard man to please and I was determined not to give him any reason to complain. *No, you'll crack it, Green,* I thought as I opened the door to my room. I immediately sat down and opened my laptop to get to work.

Chapter Fourteen.

It was 9.00 pm and the moon had risen high in the sky when Joao Quintas and his band of men arrived at the rendezvous point. The journey had been arduous and back-breaking but the men's spirits had been lifted by the killing of the boy and the regular doses of bola that had been handed out. The final 10 km had been made in darkness and progress had been painfully slow, but finally, they arrived at the point on the handheld GPS that had been planned for them. To Joao, it looked like any other random location in the familiar rolling bush and forests of the region but the technology did not lie, and he double-checked the device to make sure. *No, this is the place. We wait here and rest as instructed.* To the right of where the men had gathered was a clump of acacia forest. This would provide decent cover and a place where the evening meal could be prepared by the women who had been force-marched through the day. Some of them were sobbing quietly from their torn feet and bruises but all had made it alive. Now they would cook for the men as they rested. This break would last for 24 hours and unless he heard otherwise during their pre-planned communications, the assault on Palma would begin the following night. Using a series of whispered instructions, Joao herded the men towards the shrouded canopy of the trees to settle and await their contact who would lead them to the arms cache. There were so many unknowns. So many weak links in the chain that if broken could throw the entire operation into disarray and failure. *What if the man did not appear?*

What if he had been found out by his superiors at the gas company? So many questions and so many things that could go wrong. The pressure Joao Quintas felt was overwhelming and he squatted down to snort another dose of bola as the men made their way over the rest site. It was some 45 minutes later when he saw the slim figure of Darwesh making his way towards him in the moonlight.

"Master," he whispered. "The women have prepared some food. Shall I bring you some or would you like to eat with the men?"

"Tell them I will join them soon," said Joao grimly. "I am awaiting communications from the others and we are still to meet our contact. I will remain here until everything is settled, then I will come."

"Very well, master," said Darwesh as he backed away and turned to walk back to the camp.

But it was a full and agonizing hour later before the mobile phone in Joao's pocket vibrated finally. The code word was quickly conveyed and the caller hung up immediately. This came as a huge relief but there was still the vital rendezvous with their contact that was yet to happen. Feeling somewhat helpless, Joao once again dipped his blade into the shrinking packet of bola and snorted a small pile of the stuff. He sat there for the next 40 minutes, slowly rocking back and forth in his position as he waited for the signal. When it came it was almost inaudible in the distance. But the whistle of the nightjar was distinctive and unmistakable. Joao opened his eyes and blinked as they became accustomed to the darkness. The night was silent apart from the steady whistling of the crickets and the rustle of the breeze in the leaves. The bird call sounded again and this time Joao responded. He pursed his lips and whistled the same call in reply. Almost immediately the call of nightjar responded. This was repeated a few times as Joao stood up, his excitement and elation building. The calls continued until there was absolutely no doubt. Their contact had arrived at the rendezvous. He had succeeded and now he would be led to the hidden arms cache. The two men met in an open glade between the trees. It had been six months since they last laid eyes on each other but they embraced warmly as they met.

"My brother," said Joao, "you have come as promised. Is everything in order?"

"Everything is well," said the man, his teeth showing in the moonlight. "The weapons are near and everything is to go ahead as planned."

Chapter Fifteen.

It was 6.00 pm by the time I had finished my work on the laptop. I sat back and yawned as I stretched my arms above me. I had created a schedule that conformed to the existing daily protocols for the JAG operation at the gas site. To me, it made more sense than the one the previous crew had been working with. My way would run a lot smoother and would save time and effort. The reports would be completed every day by 4.00 pm and would be sent off to the JAG headquarters in Durban in good time. Feeling pleased with my progress, and finally fully confident in the task ahead, I stood up to take a shower before meeting Stompie in the bar for dinner. I watched the news on the television as I dressed then locked the room and made my way up to the main hotel area. Stompie was sitting in his usual spot at the bar and he turned to greet me as I arrived.

"Any sign of Penny Riddle?" I asked with a smile as I sat down.

"No..." he replied, scanning the area. "Thankfully not."

I ordered a beer and lit a cigarette as I waited for it to be delivered. I noticed the strange custom of the barman leaving the top on the bottle after opening it. It was something I had only ever seen in Mozambique. Stompie and I chatted quietly as the guests arrived for dinner. A few men took seats at the far side of the bar but were engaged in conversation almost immediately. Stompie and I spoke about what we would be doing the following day at the gas site. I explained I had created a draft schedule for him to look at.

Seemingly happy with my plans, he ordered a fresh beer and poured it into the tall glass. It was then that I noticed his speech was ever so slightly slurred. At first, I thought I was mishearing him but after some more conversation, I was in no doubt. The man's speech was definitely slurred and I could only put it down to drink. Still, he appeared alert and steady but I also noticed his eyes were slightly bloodshot as well. *Perhaps he's had one too many, Green. I'm sure the food will sort that out.* A waiter arrived soon after with a set of menus. We browsed the selection and made our orders immediately. I decided on the creamy mussel pot followed by crayfish while Stompie went for the pork chops.

I ordered another beer as we waited and before long, we were summoned to our usual table near the pool. The evening was warm and there was a pleasant breeze coming in from the ocean as we ate. I watched Stompie as I ate and felt sure his speech had improved with the food consumption. *Could be a blood sugar issue?* Once again we finished with chocolate ice cream and sat back to smoke. Then I suggested we both head to the upper deck to finish our drinks before retiring.

"Let's head upstairs to the deck and finish our drinks there," I suggested. "A nice view of the ocean in the moonlight."

"Good idea, Jason. Let's do that."

Carrying our glasses, we made our way up the rustic stairway to the top deck. It was only when we arrived that I saw her. Penny Riddle was sitting facing the ocean with her legs up on the balcony. She must have been up there all along and it was something of a surprise that we had not heard her from below. Casually slumped in her chair, she clutched a glass in her hand and was clearly having some quiet time. By then it was too late as she had seen us both arrive. My heart sank immediately as I heard her voice.

"Ahhh!" she said loudly. "It's the JAG darlings. Have you come up to admire the view? Come over and join me."

I looked at Stompie who appeared to have immediately sobered up at the prospect. But it was too late, we were unable to leave politely by that stage.

"Evening, Penny," I said as I walked over to take a chair.

Stompie remained silent as he took his chair nearby. The moon had risen over the ocean and the stars above gave a spectacular display with no city light spoiling the view. There was the smell of salt in the breeze and a calm quiet had descended over the charming town of Palma spread out on either side. Had it not been for the high pitched, shrieking laughter of Penny Riddle, it would have been a very pleasant half-hour. Her questions were inane and many as she rattled off a barrage of theories and made idle conversation while rolling her eyes and cackling away.

It was just before 9.00 pm when I could take no more and stood up to excuse myself.

"Well I have a long day tomorrow, I think I'll retire. Have a good evening."

Stompie sat forward as I left but made no move to leave. I decided he would do so in his own time or at least until she had driven him crazy. It was a relief to be out of her company and I was full and feeling tired from the events of the day. *A night of good sleep and you'll be ready for whatever the day brings, Green. Time to rest, put your feet up and watch a movie before crashing.* The breeze ruffled the fronds of the palm trees above as I made my way down the quiet covered walkway to my room. I passed the armoury knowing that I would be visiting that room in the morning before heading to the gas site. It was standard procedure for all security men to be armed while on duty. Stompie and I had decided to carry hand guns as they were easy to conceal and move around with. We would meet at the door of the armoury at 6.30 am the following day before breakfast. Despite the evening being relatively cool, it was a relief to enter the interior of the room and I wasted no time getting horizontal and using the remote control to switch the television on. Finally, I was in control and on top of the situation, and I felt confident I would handle the job easily enough. It had been a good start to the contract and I was already earning good money. London seemed a distant memory and I was happy to be where I was. *Yup, you'll be fine*. It was half an hour later when I fell asleep with the bedside light still on.

Chapter Sixteen.

The old stone quarry was situated less than a kilometre from where the men were camped. Joao Quintas and a group of five other men accompanied their contact through the thick undergrowth to the site. It had once been used by the road contractors many years before but had long been abandoned and fallen into disuse. There was an old strip track that led directly to the outskirts of Palma. This had also been long forgotten and had the men not known of its existence, it would have been virtually invisible having been covered by vegetation over the years since it was last used. This would be the route the men would take when the time came for the attack. It was an ingenious plan. Six separate teams of fighters all strategically placed around the town would attack at once. This would cause maximum confusion and terror and the barrage would continue through the night. Joao felt his excitement rising as the man in front shone his torch into the jagged rocks of the quarry below.

"Follow me," motioned the man. "It is well hidden near the bottom."

The men made their way carefully down the rocky sides until they had reached the stagnant pool of water at the bottom. The millions of mosquitoes that bred there buzzed about their ears and the water smelt putrid. The moon above caused the small body of water to look like a perfectly flat sheet of silver. The man in the lead made his way around the pool to a pile of rocks near the far side. He waited for Joao to arrive and then spoke.

"This is it. The weapons are hidden under these rocks."

"Remove them," Joao instructed the men.

Immediately they got busy removing the rocks while Joao stood nearby watching proceedings. It soon became clear that the team who had brought the cache had done an excellent job of concealing it. It took a full half-hour of back-breaking work to remove the rocks but finally, they were presented with a store of weaponry packed into steel crates.

The pile was equivalent in size to two large motor cars. It had been covered with multiple layers of tarpaulin to protect it from the elements. Joao illuminated his torch as he instructed the men to open random crates for inspection. It was as he had been promised. Better even. Apart from at least 100 replacement Kalashnikov AK47 rifles, there were boxes containing thousands upon thousands of rounds. Then there were the RPGs and mortars. All had been stacked with military precision and expertly hidden. Joao Quintas felt his spirits lifting as he surveyed this great hoard of killing equipment. He crouched down to open yet another crate and found it to be full of grenades.

"Our brothers have outdone themselves," he said quietly. "Allahu Akbar."

Finally satisfied, and knowing that there were now very few impediments that could stop the great event from happening, he stood up and spoke again.

"Cover the weapons with the tarpaulins and a few rocks," he said. "We will return with the other men tomorrow to uplift them and move them closer to the track. For now, we all need to rest. We have come through hell, but we have prevailed so far and will do so again."

The men made their way out of the old quarry and through the bush back to where the others were camped. Joao Quintas gathered them together to make the announcement. The news was received with cheering and blessings to Allah and Joao Quintas basked in the glory of his achievements. Although he lacked much of an appetite, he forced himself to eat and finally he made his way some 50 metres from the other men to the camp that Darwesh had prepared for him. That night, he lay there in the dappled moonlight on the leaf-covered ground. Darwesh had already brought the steel trunk and the knowledge that the needle and spoon were safely inside was a comfort. But Joao Quintas was deeply unsettled. The craving had returned as it always did during the night. Soon, Darwesh would bring his tea and they would begin the ritual of injecting themselves once again. Darwesh would be camped nearby and he too would be of comfort to him. But at that moment, the terrors had returned in full force. He stared up at the stars above as his fears grew.

Chapter Seventeen.

It was at 6.30 am on the dot when I stepped out of my room and made my way up the walkway to the hotel armoury. Stompie Van Der Riet was waiting for me at the door as promised. I greeted him and although he sounded fresh and rested, I noticed his eyes were still bloodshot. I quickly put this out of my mind as I went through the procedure of opening the highly secured door. We stepped inside and busied ourselves choosing the weapons we would carry whilst on duty. I chose a Glock G45 compact with a magazine capacity of 17 rounds. I loaded and holstered it as Stompie did the same with a Ruger LC9. Once done, he looked up at me with his bloodshot eyes and nodded.

"You happy with that?" I asked.

"Yup," he replied "All good."

"Let's get some breakfast before we head off to the site," I said, walking towards the door.

The restaurant was quiet at that early hour and we ate a breakfast of cereal followed by an omelette and coffee. We would take two vehicles to the gas site and move in convoy on the way there. Once there, we would meet Sarge and get on with the day's work. I felt rested, refreshed and confident in our abilities to do the job. My work on the laptop the previous day had made things a great deal clearer in my mind. Once there, we would do a tour of the site and introduce ourselves to the team of guards working under us. I felt it was important that they knew exactly who it was they were working for. Even at that early hour, the heat of the day had begun and by the time we reached the parking lot there was a thin film of sweat on my skin. Stompie and I climbed into our respective vehicles and headed off down the driveway towards the large, ornate gate. The guard smiled and saluted as we left the hotel grounds and we made our way down the hill towards the town. Once there we made a right turn heading north towards the gas sites. The route was familiar and I took a slow drive with Stompie following closely behind me.

It took less than 15 minutes to make it up the gentle slope of the hill to the peak where the gas sites stretched out clinging to the coast below us. On my right was the drop off while on the left was the thick, jungle-like vegetation common to the Cabo Delgado region. The road had dried up somewhat and the journey down the hill towards the sprawling gas installations was easy. I arrived at the Total gas site and the boom was lifted before I had even driven up to the gate. This was something that bothered me immediately and I made a mental note to look into the entry procedures later that day. We arrived at the JAG offices to find Sarge waiting for us near the entrance. His towering frame and easy smile was welcoming and I greeted him as Stompie and I made our way into our new offices. The front of house staff greeted us and I ordered coffee and called a meeting between Stompie, Sarge and myself immediately. Having printed out my new schedule for the daily work programme, I handed a copy to both Sarge and Stompie and told them to look over it. While they did so, I set up my laptop and began perusing the pile of papers and reports that had already arrived on my desk. It took less than 5 minutes for Sarge to announce that the new schedule was far better than the one the previous team had used and he nodded eagerly upon seeing its benefits. The three of us spent the next 15 minutes drinking coffee and discussing the plans for the morning tour and the meet and greet session. I decided that it would be prudent to summon the guards and scouts who were on hand to gather in front of the offices where we would meet them. I had decided that I would introduce myself and shake hands with each one of them in an effort to familiarise them with the new management team. With that instruction, Sarge left to organize the meeting while Stompie and I decided to make a perfunctory tour of the perimeter of the installation on foot.

The vast gas site was comprised of an oblong section of land that had been bulldozed, cleared and sealed with palisade fencing topped with razor wire and multiple cameras. The control room for this surveillance equipment was situated in a small office down the corridor from my own office and was manned 24 hours a day. Contact between the staff who manned these cameras and ourselves was open 24 hours a day and any unusual events that warranted our attention would be reported either by phone or radio immediately. Stompie and I set out on foot and walked the boundary of the giant site.

By then the sun was blazing above us and the only respite from the heat was the constant breeze that blew in from the Indian Ocean nearby. Teams of engineers, builders, and other contractors were busy at work within the site and there was a steady stream of vehicles arriving as we made our tour. It was at 11.00 am when the guard inspection was ready and Stompie and I made our way out to greet the men. Accompanying us was Sarge who walked up and down the ranks of men as we greeted them and shook hands. The men were cheerful and seemed happy to be working. Of course, there was another contingent who would be working the night shift and I made arrangements for us to repeat the process later on in the day with them. By the time we had finished this task it was nearing lunchtime and I decided to leave the tour of the armoury until later that afternoon. Lunch was served in the managers' canteen and as it had been the previous day, and the food was excellent. Stompie, Sarge and I made our way back to the JAG offices and began our tour of the armoury straight after lunch. The main armoury was a carbon copy of the one at the hotel and of particular interest to me were the drones. The DJI Matrice models were state of the art machines capable of so much more than the average consumer model. They were to be flown regularly and sent inland during both the night and day to film and record any happenings below. I found the inventory was up to date and everything accounted for after a stock take that took less than an hour.

Next, we were called outside once again to meet the scouts who were responsible for gathering intelligence in the surrounding areas. This would entail travelling many kilometres into the bush and visiting remote villages on their duties. Their instructions were to be kind and benevolent to the locals in the hope that any suspicious activity would be quickly reported back to us. There were 10 men on the team who would go out for 3-day shifts. All were in cell phone and radio contact with the JAG offices and were a vital cog in the security machine of the gas plant. I took my time meeting these men and talked to them at length using Sarge as an interpreter. Most were ex-military and accustomed to the country and terrain. Once again, they appeared cheerful and happy to meet their new bosses. By 3.00 pm that afternoon I had built up a clear picture of the day-to-day running of the facility and all that was left was to conduct a tour of the managers' compound and to meet the guard crew who were to take over that night.

While the incident reports were being handed to me I was informed that the guards from the night shift were waiting for us outside. Before heading out, I finished my own daily report and emailed it to the JAG head office in Durban. A printed copy was taken by a runner to the main offices of Total and I stepped out once again into the heat of the late afternoon to meet the night shift crew.

The process of meeting and greeting the guards was repeated and as I had done before, I met and spoke to the men. It was 4.30 pm by the time Stompie and I had finished and I called a meeting in my office to wrap up the day. As far as I could tell, it had gone smoothly and I was pleased with the arrangements so far. Before heading back to the hotel I sent off a quick email requesting tighter entry checks at the main gate. I knew the senior staff at the JAG offices in Durban would take this request seriously and my suggestions would be implemented the following day. It was at 5.10 pm when we finally walked out of the offices and bade farewell to Sarge who had his own vehicle parked outside.

"Thank you, Sarge," I said. "I'll see you tomorrow morning."

"See you then, boss," he replied with a smile.

The sun was starting to set over the mainland as I drove out of the giant complex and turned right to reach the main road to Palma. I was pleased with my work and felt more comfortable than ever about the task ahead. 20 minutes later I pulled into the parking lot of the Hotel Cabo Delgado and walked up the stairs with Stompie on the way to our rooms. Before parting, we made a plan to meet at 6.30 pm as usual for dinner. I showered and sat at my desk afterwards to browse the local websites and news channels for any reports of disturbances in northern Mozambique. There was nothing and it appeared that the region was enjoying a period of relative calm. This was good news for me and my team but I knew it was no reason to let our guard down. The situation remained volatile and dangerous, and only a fool would sink into a false sense of security. We were there for a very good reason, and I would never forget that.

It was 6.23 pm as I was preparing to meet Stompie in the bar for dinner that my phone rang.

The number was recognised and I answered it immediately. The man on the line was from the control room at the gas site. There had been a security breach in the north west quarter of the gas site and a section of the palisade wall had been cut. The guards had arrested two men and were requesting we come down to assess the situation. Not a minute later there was a knock at the door. Stompie was standing there freshly showered and looking somewhat anxious.

"I've just had a call from the site, Jason," he said. "They need us down there right away."

"Yes," I replied "they called me as well. Let's go down there now. We'll come back later for dinner."

The two of us headed up through the reception. On the way, we ran into the manager, Rogerio, and we informed him that we would be back as soon as possible. As expected, he promised to keep the kitchen open as long as it took for us to finish our work. The sun had almost set and was throwing great purple streaks across the clouds above the ocean as we drove out of the hotel grounds and made our way back to the site for the second time that day. Stompie and I travelled in my vehicle seeing no reason to take two cars. By the time we reached the site and made it to the JAG offices it was dark and the moon was rising over the ocean. We climbed out of the vehicle and were led around the back of the building to the holding cells. There we found the guard who had made the arrests. Thankfully it turned out that the intruders were nothing but a pair of young opportunists. Neither could have been over 17 years of age and armed with a pair of pliers and a hacksaw, they had attempted to gain entry through the fence in the north west quadrant. From their swollen faces and sullen expressions, I could tell that they had already received a beating from the guards. This was not unusual in Africa and I had been expecting this. It did come as some relief, however, to note that the two youngsters were nothing but petty thieves, probably after stealing whatever they could get their hands on. They posed no major threat to the operation although any breach had to be taken seriously. As I stared at them, Sarge arrived looking flustered and alarmed. He too was relieved to see the intruders were of no real significance.

After sharing a joke or two, I told him to inform the local police to come and take them away. I then instructed the maintenance crew to repair the damage they had done to the fence immediately. Finally, with the whole unfortunate incident wrapped up, Stompie and I left at 7.25 pm and headed back to Palma with Sarge following in his vehicle behind us.

"Looks like it's gonna be a busy month..." I said as I lit a cigarette.

"It certainly does look that way," Stompie replied in his thick Afrikaans accent.

Stompie and I finally finished our dinner at 9.00 pm that night. The kitchen had been kept open specially for us and the manager, Rogerio, had told us that it was a fairly common occurrence that the JAG teams would be called back to site after hours. The food was good and we retired to the bar afterwards for a final beer. Thankfully the common area of the hotel was virtually deserted and we settled down on our usual stools at the bar. It was then I noticed Stompie's hands were shaking slightly. It was even more evident as he poured his beer into the frosted glass. Saying nothing, I poured my own and pretended not to have seen this. My immediate thought was he needed a drink; something akin to the behaviour of an alcoholic. If this was the case, it might present a problem for our working relationship going forward. Still, I kept to my own and kept the convivial conversation going. I did notice that he drank his beer very fast indeed, and I had drunk only half of my own when he ordered another from the barman. I decided I would sit with him for a while and observe his behaviour. I enjoyed a drink as much as any other man, but I needed to know the kind of person I would be working with. We were, after all, on a wet contract and he was free to consume as much alcohol as he wanted to after hours. We sat, smoking and drinking for the next hour during which Stompie consumed 4 beers. I had only 2 but I watched as the tremor in his hands began to settle with every passing minute. Deciding not to say anything, I ordered a final one for myself and spoke.

"Think I'll head for the sack after this one," I said looking at my watch. "It's been a long, hot day."

"I think it was a good day," he said thoughtfully "We managed just fine."

Just then I saw the sweeping figure of Penny Riddle making her way into the dining area past the reception.

"Oh, Jesus," I muttered under my breath, "here we go."

Stompie groaned audibly as she spotted us and gave us a flamboyant wave. Penny Riddle wore a loose fitting white cotton top with flared sleeves and her usual tight blue jeans. Upon seeing us she burst into a wide smile that filled her heavily made-up face.

"Hello, my darlings," she greeted us, before bringing her finger up and pointing at us as if we were children. "Now you don't move anywhere! I have to drop something in my room and then I'll be right back to join you."

I looked at the woman with a half-smile on my face as I considered my escape options. Sadly they were few and far between and I heard Stompie groan again as he reached for his cigarettes and ordered another beer from the barman.

"Please don't leave me here alone with her, Jason," said Stompie quietly.

His face was serious but I saw the corners of his mouth turning up into a grin. It was the first time I had seen the man smile and it was only then that I realised how ridiculous our situation was. Here we were, two grown men of military backgrounds, hired and paid a great deal of money to protect a huge multinational conglomerate from a band of marauding Islamists. And there we were cowering and terrified of a drama teacher from London. I paused as I looked into his face but I could hold my laughter no longer. My mirth came in torrents and eventually I had to shake my head to stop it. Even the barman was battling to hold his decorum when I finally gave in and ordered another beer. It had been a moment that finally broke the ice between two men and both of us realised the importance of it. I knew then that this was a man I could rely on. From that moment on I regarded him as a friend as well as a colleague. Penny Riddle returned as promised and exploded with excitement as she recounted the events of her day. She leapt up from her barstool repeatedly to demonstrate how she had taught the children to mimic animals and her laughter was outrageously loud and manic.

She still managed to be condescending and roll her eyes when she asked about our day but we took it in our stride and rolled with the punches. It was 11.00 pm when I finally pulled the plug and announced my departure. I would support my friend Stompie no more and I slapped him on the back as I left after excusing myself. I made my way back down the shaded walkway to my room feeling satisfied and in control. There were no more doubts about the calibre of the men I was working with. Gone were the concerns I had had about the day-to-day running of the security operation. I had broken the ice on all fronts and I was confident at the prospect of spending a month on the site. Plus, I was being paid a fortune to do it and I was actually enjoying myself. *No worries Green, you're doing just fine.* I stood under the blasting jets of the shower and grinned at the thought of abandoning Stompie to the wicked witch that was Penny

Riddle. *You might be a tough military operator old boy, but I'd like to see how you get out of that one.* After drying off I lay down on the bed but didn't even bother turning the TV on. I was pleasantly tired and sleep came quick and easy.

Chapter Eighteen.

———————— ⚜ ————————

It was around 4.30 am when Joao Quintas sent Darwesh back to his camp nearby. Through the night they had spiked themselves 3 times as was normal, but the lovemaking had not happened. There was far too much on Joao's mind and although Darwesh had tried, he would have none of it. Instead, he had limited the doses of the bola they had injected and both men had slept fitfully, tossing and turning through the night. The great weight of responsibility that Joao was carrying was heavy on his mind and he had been unable to think of anything else. Joao had watched the sunrise sitting alone, knowing full well that it was rising over the sea at Palma, not 15 kilometres from where the men were encamped. As instructed, Darwesh brought his morning tea at 5.30 am and had begged for a snort of bola before returning to the men. Joao had granted this wish and had also sent another bag of the stuff to the waking men. At 6.00 am, Joao Quintas made his way through the forest to where the men had gathered for the morning briefing. They stood, as they always did, in rows. Fully clad in battle gear and clutching their weapons, they were a fine sight and Joao felt a measure of pride as he conducted the morning inspection. Finally satisfied, he walked to the front to address them.

"My brothers," he began. "Soldiers of Islam and revolutionaries. I am sure you have heard, that last night, after our great march, I was taken to the place where the weapons we will be using for the attack were hidden. I am pleased to tell you that our compatriots have excelled. Not only have they left what we requested, they endowed us with a great deal more. With what we now have at our disposal, we are a veritable army."

There was a low rumbling of approval and the men shifted where they stood.

"This morning, before the sun is high, we will go to this place to uplift these weapons and bring them here."

The men cheered this news and Joao's voice grew louder as he went on.

"We will distribute them among us so that tonight, when the signal comes, we will be ready and the town of Palma will become hell on earth!"

Once again he paused to allow the news to sink in and the excitement build.

"My brothers," he said with a grin. "The cache is so large that I will request a vehicle is brought here tonight to transport it all. We will march with this vehicle so we are ready when the time comes. So now, my brothers, we must go and uplift this great offering, this holy blessing that will allow us to triumph over the infidels. Are you ready?"

The men cheered louder this time.

"Are you ready?" shouted Joao.

By then the men were almost in a frenzy. The extra doses of bola had taken their desired effects

"Allahu Akbar!" shouted Joao.

The men repeated this chant, again and again, raising their weapons in the air and stamping their feet until clouds of dust gathered around their legs. Joao Quintas smiled and nodded as he sensed their fervour and blind loyalty. *Yes,* he thought to himself. *I have done my job well.*

It was 20 minutes later when the Joao and the men arrived at the old abandoned quarry. Walking in single file, they made their way down the treacherous rock sides and around to the east side of the stagnant pool. The two piles of crates under the tarpaulins and rocks were there just as he had left them the night before. The job of moving the cache was arduous and backbreaking but the men worked through the morning and finally at around 11.30 am, the job was done. The cache was neatly stacked in the forest near where they had camped. The men were tired but elated at the same time.

None of them had ever seen such a massive amount of modern weaponry. Their eyes glittered with enthusiasm as they were handed their respective armaments while the heavier mortars and RPGs were assembled, polished and oiled in preparation for the arrival of the truck. It was at midday when Joao finally called a halt to proceedings and instructed the women to bring food and drink in the form of fermented sorghum beer. The meal had the effect of calming the men and although most were raring to go, Joao ordered them to rest for the duration of the afternoon. There would be another briefing at sunset but until then the men were to recuperate and bolster their energy for what would be a very long night ahead. Joao Quintas left the men and walked back to his solitary camp to await Darwesh who would bring food and tea. As he sat down he reflected on the work of the last year. *Maybe, just maybe, the outrageous plan would work.* With the extent of the munitions the others had provided, it was now a distinct possibility. But the niggling doubts began to bubble up from the cesspits of his mind. Joao Quintas needed a dose of bola and he needed it right away. The dreadful cycle of drug-taking was inescapable and seemed to be the only constant in his life. He sat down on the steel trunk that held his belongings and pulled the plastic bag from his top pocket. Using his blade, he dipped the tip into the bag and snorted a great pile of the stuff.

Chapter Nineteen.

The following day was a blur of activity that began at 6.00 am and continued through the day until lunchtime. Stompie and I took the short walk from the JAG offices to the managers' canteen and ate together. I had noticed he had been slightly withdrawn compared to the previous night. I had not given it much thought as I had been extremely busy with the daily tasks that had to be completed by 4.00 pm. Sarge had been in and out through the day and had dispatched a crew of scouts into the outlying areas for their stint in the bush. The returning scouts had presented their reports, none of which had detailed any untoward events, and these were being typed up for my perusal later in the afternoon. It was at 3.00 pm when I had joined the crew from the surveillance office and observed them flying the drones for the first time. Using a maximum altitude, they sent the expensive machines 15 km into the surrounding areas, filming everything as they went. I sat in the shade of the launch area and watched the countryside flash by below on the screens. Occasionally I would stop them and request that they zoom into small villages or settlements. The men were well trained at using the machines and every moment was filmed as they flew, from takeoff until they returned. The footage after the flights would be studied and compared to previous flights and any discrepancies or unusual changes would be reported to me directly. The results of this study would be handed to me the following day but as far as I was aware nothing noteworthy had been spotted. I had been pleased to hear there had been an email from the JAG head office giving the go-ahead for tightened security at the gates to the facility. Now, all visitors would have to be logged into the computer system and ID cards would be recorded on entry and exit. It made for a little extra time spent at the gate for every vehicle but it added to the general transparency of the operation. It was at 3.40 pm when I called Stompie into my office to ask how his assignments were going that the phone rang on the desk. The maintenance crew who had repaired the palisade fencing had requested we go to inspect their repairs. I glanced at my watch as I spoke and then agreed to go there immediately. It would only take 10 minutes to okay the repairs and I was quite able to send off my daily email report in good time.

"Seems the repairs have been completed from the break-in last night," I said. "They want us to go check it out. Let's do that quickly, get it out of the way."

"Sure," said Stompie, standing to leave.

We made our way out of the office block and into the steaming heat of the late afternoon. It was only as we were walking down the steps that I realised I had forgotten my car keys.

"Damn," I said. "Forgot my keys. Let's go in your vehicle."

But it was as I climbed into Stompie's land cruiser that I smelt the booze on his breath. There was no mistaking the sweet smell of neat vodka, pungent and sickly. I frowned as I opened my window and he started the vehicle. My immediate thought was perhaps it was simply the residue of the alcohol from the previous night and he was simply sweating it out, but this was not the smell of beer. This was raw spirit and of that I was sure. I kept quiet as we drove out through the main gate and headed up the outskirts of the fencing up to the north east quadrant. It was there near the far corner of the site that we found the maintenance crew waiting for us to inspect the repairs.

Stompie pulled over on the grass verge on the right and opened his door to walk over to the waiting crew. Using the opportunity alone in his vehicle, I opened the glove box to take a look. It was as I had feared. Stashed there in amongst some random papers and fuel receipts was a small half jack plastic bottle of local vodka. *The fucking idiot is drinking on the job. I knew there was something up with him. For fuck sake!* Saying nothing, I climbed out of the vehicle and walked over to where the men were waiting. They had replaced the broken palisades and reattached the fencing and the other electrical wiring that had been damaged. The men had done a good job and I commended their work on seeing it. With the inspection done, Stompie and I climbed back into the vehicle and drove in stony silence back to the gate and to the JAG offices. Once again I could smell the liquor on his breath although he appeared quite normal and relaxed. With my mind in torment as to how to deal with the situation, I made a quick decision as he pulled into the parking lot. It was as he was making ready to alight from the vehicle that I spoke.

"Wait," I said, "I need to talk to you now, and it's best we do this right here."

He turned to look at me and I saw his expression turn from upbeat to crestfallen in an instant. Without hesitating, I opened the glove box and brought the half-drunk bottle out.

"What the fuck is this?" I said, "I can smell it on your fucking breath."

The man's eyes dropped as he realised the game was up. I had caught him drinking on duty and there was nothing he could do or say to change that. He took a deep breath and spoke.

"Yes," he said as his face suddenly went pale. "I don't really know what to say, Jason. I've had a bit of a rough run of things recently. My mother passed away six months ago and since then I've kinda lost it. I thought I could manage it but it just seemed to get out of control."

"It's fucking outrageous that you would even think about doing this!" I growled "What the fuck? I knew there was something up with you the moment I laid eyes on you!"

The man visibly shrunk at this reprimand and immediately I felt a pang of pity for him. Here was someone who was clearly fighting several battles, none of which I knew anything about. *But still, it's fucking unacceptable, Green. Not only that, it's a danger for you and everyone else.*

"You drinking on the job not only jeopardises your position but mine as well for fuck sake! And worse still, you are actively placing the entire operation in danger. What the fuck were you thinking?"

Stompie shook his head forlornly and I saw the tears pooling in his bloodshot eyes.

"I, I, I'm sorry, Jason," he stuttered. "You're right. I'll have my resignation on your desk tomorrow morning."

"You'll do no such fucking thing!" I exploded as I poured the spirit onto the ground out the window.

I took a deep breath and reached for the pack of cigarettes in my pocket. I lit one and watched as the smoke billowed out of the window of the vehicle.

One thing was sure, the man was aware that I was far from pleased with my discovery. But I had begun to calm down.

"Listen to me," I said quietly. "This doesn't have to go anywhere. I'm not going to report it to the brass at head office. But this has to stop, and stop immediately. If you have any problems, you come to me directly. Is that understood?"

"Yes, sir" he replied, his head hung low.

"If I ever smell booze on your breath, or find it on your person during working hours, you are fucking gone. Is that clear?"

"Yes, Jason. I fucked up big time. I'm so sorry..."

I took another drag on the smoke and looked out of the window as I felt the calm returning to me.

"I'm very fond of you, Stompie. I regard you as a friend. Let's keep this little mishap between the two of us and never speak of it again. We've only just started here for fuck sake."

"Give me a chance Jason, I won't let you down again," he said, looking me in the eye.

It was then that I knew I could trust him. The man was clearly suffering and had been harbouring a lot of trauma of some kind.

"I know you won't..." I said, "now let's get back into the office, I have a report to send off."

Chapter Twenty.

The phone in Joao Quintas' pocket vibrated at 4.00 pm. He fumbled as he brought it out and answered it immediately. The message was quick and to the point. The assault on Palma would go ahead as planned and there were no changes. Joao hung up and looked towards the east where he knew the sea to be. Now there was only one thing to worry about and that was the imminent arrival of the truck that would transport the bulk of the weapons to the outskirts of the town. The men were relaxing as instructed although he could feel their tension and enthusiasm whenever he visited them. He had instructed the women to feed them at regular intervals and also to prepare food that would feed them for the night ahead. The attack was due to start at 11.00 pm in earnest. By then the sleepy town would be quiet and with the synchronised bombardment that would commence, no one would have a clue what was happening. The use of modern technology was a wonder and was finally being put to good use by the servants of Allah. But his biggest fear was to be the one that let the other attack squads down with some stupid mishap. *What if the truck failed to arrive? What if it broke down on the way or was discovered?* There was still a great deal that could go wrong. But now he had come so far, he had a gut feeling that all would proceed as planned. This was to be a success and the time was now so close he could almost smell the cordite and hear the crackling of the flames.

The weather report had predicted a warm clear night with a light wind coming in from the ocean. Perfect conditions apart from the moon which was due to rise early in the evening. Any security forces or members of the general public on the outskirts would be killed on sight. There was no way he would allow anyone to race off and inform the residents of the town of the coming storm. Joao had tried to eat on several occasions throughout the day but his appetite was weak from the worry and pressure of the coming mission. Instead, he had dosed himself on the hour every hour and this was keeping any thoughts of food far from his mind. What he didn't know was he was now grinding his teeth and gurning his jaw constantly. It was an effect of the drug that many users do not notice. Darwesh had visited on at least 5 occasions, bringing him tea and pleading for a snort of bola. He had given the young man what he wanted and had also prepared individual bags loaded with the drug for each man.

He had made sure that the amount he had packed in each would be more than enough to carry them well into the next day should it be needed. The plan was simple. The truck would arrive at around 6.00 pm and be carefully loaded with the heavier weapons. The men would march in single file down the old overgrown quarry track until they reached the outskirts of the town. Once there, they would lie low in the shadows and darkness until the clock struck 11.00 pm. There would be another call just before which would be a go-ahead for the attack to begin. The men would start with mortars and RPG fire and would slowly move through the outskirts of the town and make their way steadily to the centre. Every man, woman and child would be killed and all major infrastructure was to be destroyed. This included power supplies, cell phone towers and any other communication equipment. No living soul would be allowed to escape. Every vehicle, including those of the police and military would be commandeered and taken by the militants. They would, in effect, take over the town completely. Added to that, all workers from the gas sites would be executed on sight. This included both foreigners and locals. The men had been trained to show no mercy at all and were to butcher every living soul. Not only that, they were to dismember and behead them and toss their bodies into the streets for the dogs and the flies. Of course there would be resistance, this was expected, but this attack would be different from the one that had failed in Mocimboa Da Praia. Now they were organised, better equipped and coordinated. *No, this time would be different.*

Joao Quintas stood up and he felt a strange tingling in his limbs. He blinked into the setting sun and looked around him. The feelings of paranoia were there along with sudden bursts of enthusiasm and fervour. He knew then that he had consumed far too much bola but the thought of going with any less was too awful to contemplate. The heat of the day had begun to subside and he took a slow walk through the tall grass towards where the men were camped. As he approached, the men sat up and looked at him anxiously. Once again he felt the terrible weight of responsibility on his shoulders. Doing his best to maintain decorum, he smiled and nodded calmly to reassure them. The first man he spoke to was Darwesh.

"Any sign of the truck?" he whispered.

"No master," the young man replied, "Not yet."

"It will be here shortly, Insha Allah..."

Darwesh looked up at him and his dark eyes were wide and filled with fear.

"I must sit with my men," he said. "Now is the time they need me here to show calm and leadership. Bring me some tea."

"Yes, master..." said Darwesh, hurrying off.

Joao Quintas sat down, rested his back on the trunk of an acacia tree and picked a piece of grass from the ground nearby. He put it in his mouth and chewed on it to keep his jaw busy. The men, seeing their leader was nearby, smiled and carried on with what they had been doing. The atmosphere was one of elation mixed with anticipation and a measure of fear.

Chapter Twenty-One.

I stood in the shower with the hot water blasting over my body and my eyes closed. In my mind, I went through the events of the afternoon and wondered if I had handled the scene with Stompie correctly. It had been clear, after all, that there had been something troubling him from the word go. It had been apparent from the time I had first laid eyes on him although I had failed to see it. Sure, I had had my suspicions but these had been clouded over by my fondness for him and the fact the two of us were new in the job and learning the ropes as we went. His apology had been sincere and deep down, I knew he meant it. The man was suffering from many personal issues, probably more than the death of his mother, but I respected that he had told me that and would not pry any further into his private life. As long as he was sober and competent during the day, I had no problem at all and I was sure that he knew this now. There was mutual respect between us and that was something to be cherished. I had driven home with him following behind me up the hill and down into the town. The streets had seemed a little quieter than usual but I had simply put this down the many unknown moods of the sleepy coastal town. Stompie and I had agreed that we would never speak of the booze incident again and that we would continue with the contract as we had begun it. I had offered him time alone but he had insisted that we should dine together that night and every night going forward. It was more of a work-related duty rather than anything else and it would allow us time to discuss any issues that came up during the day. The presence of Sarge was a blessing both for the translation he provided and the respect and fear he commanded among the men. Colonel Jackson had chosen very wisely when he had employed him and I knew he was a huge asset to the organisation. Stompie and I had agreed to meet at 6.00 pm on the upper level of the main hotel area for a beer before dinner. As I dried myself off I wondered if he would sink as many drinks as he had done the previous night. *He may do, he may not. Just try not to watch him closely to make him nervous.* After browsing the news channels and local websites, I locked my door and took the pleasant walk up towards the hotel. The reception and restaurant area had a few guests scattered around but I caught the eye of a waiter and motioned for him to follow me upstairs.

I found Stompie sitting alone near the rough pole banister. Freshly showered and wearing a tight black t shirt and jeans, he turned and looked at me as I approached. His powerful, tattoo covered arms were almost splitting the material of his t shirt.

"Evening, Jason..." he said pointing out to sea, "lovely sunset tonight."

It was true. The sun had gone beyond the thatched roof behind us and a flurry of cirrus clouds had taken on a rich purple hue above the horizon in the distance. Below us the harbour water was calm and the fronds of the tall palm trees that lined the beaches were still. It was a picture that one would hope to see on a postcard from paradise. I turned to the waiter who had come up the stairs behind me.

"How's your drink?'" I asked.

"I'll have a shandy," said Stompie.

I laughed quietly as I looked at his glass.

"You sure?"

"Yes..." he replied. "A shandy will be fine."

I made the order and took a seat with a table between us. I took a deep breath and stared out at the scene of tranquillity below us.

"Well," I said, "you're right. It's a beautiful evening."

With the unfortunate events of the afternoon firmly behind us we spent the next hour talking about the various concerns we both had regarding the security situation at the gas site. Stompie made several valid points and pointed out some weak spots that might warrant attention. I found him to be incisive and observant and we agreed to take these issues up first thing in the morning.

We were, after all, in charge and responsible for everything related to the well being of the site and its employees and were free to implement any changes we saw fit. It was a great relief that the confrontation had seemingly been forgotten and going forward would be as professional as it was pleasant. It was as simple as that. Two men, ironing out the issues with honest conversation and doing the job we were being paid very well to do. It was with a feeling that we were both fully on top of our game that we headed down to the restaurant for dinner. Although I tried on several occasions, Stompie insisted on drinking beer shandies that night and this continued when we stopped at the bar after dinner. Sadly this pleasant and very productive conversation was disturbed once again by the arrival of Penny Riddle. Seemingly in a foul mood, there was none of the exuberant and flamboyant behaviour from the previous night and instead she spent the time listening in to our conversation and scowling at us. This did not go unnoticed but we kept our cool and continued with our conversation. But around 8.15 pm she seemed to have had enough of the two of us ignoring her and burst into an unexpected and very unwelcome tirade.

"You people are cogs in a very big and very evil machine!" she said. "You don't care for the well-being of the people here. You're all just after the money! The money! That's all you care about!"

Quite taken aback, Stompie and I were unsure how to respond.

"Look at the two of you," she continued. "Sitting there mumbling to each other about your big high and mighty jobs. Sickening!"

The sudden outburst had come as a surprise to us and I wondered what had brought it on. *Had she had too much to drink? Was it simply the result of a bad day at the office?* Either way, it was an unnecessary and unwarranted attack. I cleared my throat to speak but Stompie got in first.

"Listen here, Penny," he said in his thick Afrikaans accent. "We are here doing a job. It's as simple as that. We are not the ones mining gas here and neither are we exploiting the locals or their resources. We work in security, we mean no ill will to anyone at all, including you."

Penny Riddle's eyes burned with rage but for a brief moment, I saw them soften as she stared at the man sitting on my left.

"We have tried to be civil and pleasant with you but this outburst is uncalled for," said Stompie.

The woman sat in stunned silence and I thought for a moment she would burst into tears. It was at that moment that I decided to make a break for it. I was pleased that Stompie had stood up to her bullying and I felt that now was the time to leave. He could handle the situation himself. I leaned towards him and whispered quietly.

"I'll leave you to it, buddy..."

He nodded as I stood up to leave. On my way back to the reception I saw the moonlight in the gardens ahead of me. I decided that instead of retiring, I would take the short drive down to the harbour to finish the day off. I needed some alone time to gather my thoughts and the evening was relatively cool. I smiled to myself as I jogged down the steps at the front of the reception and made my way into the parking lot. There in the parking lot was the bright orange land rover of Penny Riddle and I chuckled to myself as I thought of my friend and colleague I had so cruelly left in her appalling company. *Think of it as penance, Green,* I thought as I unlocked the door to my vehicle. The guard at the gate seemed surprised to see me leaving the hotel at that hour but smiled anyway as he slid the gate open. I made my way down the heavily treed hill then onwards into the quaint town for another 800 metres before turning left to head down to the harbour. The streets were quiet and apart from the odd stray dog, I saw no one on the way. I pulled up and parked near a tatty looking government office close to the concrete pier that jutted out into the ocean.

There were several fishing boats moored in the harbour and the surface of the water looked like gleaming silver platter with the bright moonlight above. There was a pleasant breeze coming in from the east and this helped to quell the pungent smell of fish that emanated from the place. The pier must have been built in colonial times as half of it had fallen into the sea years before and had never been repaired. Still, it was easy enough to take the short walk along the rough concrete surface that was still standing and I took a seat on an ancient steel bollard at the far end.

The only sound was that of the ocean and the occasional creak of a nearby fishing vessel as it moved on the gentle swell. I turned to look back at the town behind me as I breathed in the warm night air which was fragrant and salty. The lights of the town glowed yellow, red and white and there was a yellow halo-like haze above the brighter of them. I took the cigarettes from my pocket and lit up, watching the smoke drift back into the harbour. It had been a difficult few days but I was pleased with the progress and my initial fears and worries had abated. There would be no issues running the operations to the standard that Colonel Jackson wanted. In fact, I was confident I would improve things during my stay. Sure, there were some unusual characters, but that in some way added to the interest of the job and guaranteed my time in Mozambique would not be boring or repetitive. But it was as I was finishing the cigarette that I became aware once again of the firearm strapped to my side. It was there for a reason and a very good one at that. *It would be foolhardy to sink into a state of comfort, Green. It may seem like you have climbed the hill but there is still a month to go. Keep alert, keep watching, and don't stop. You are swimming in dangerous waters, no matter how idyllic it may seem. Don't forget that.* It was as I was about to flick the butt into the sea that I had second thoughts and stood up to make my way to the parked vehicle. I would dispose of it in the ashtray and not litter the quaint and picturesque port. I took a final look out to sea as I unlocked the vehicle and climbed in. I was tired but satisfied and I knew that sleep would come easily. Then the whole process would begin again the following day. *You have a comfortable place to stay, good food, and decent working conditions. Add to that the exceptional pay and you're looking pretty good, Green. Time for bed.*

The drive back through the town took less than 5 minutes. But it was as I took the right turn that I saw the group of men. They appeared as if they were in a hurry and as I passed them I noticed they tried to hide from the beam of the headlights. Their behaviour was unlike any I had seen since I had arrived and for some reason their actions unnerved me. I turned in my seat as I drove past and saw them duck into an alleyway down the street. *Probably just local drunks,* I thought. But the memory of the men stayed with me as I drove up the hill to the hotel, entered and parked. For some strange reason it had unsettled me and I didn't exactly know why. *Were the streets too quiet? How would you know? You've never been out at night. Forget it Green, you're tired. Go hit the sack and sleep. You're exhausted.*

I locked the vehicle in the usual parking spot and made my way up the stairs into the reception. As I made my way through the main dining area I looked to my right to see if Stompie was still being entertained by Penny Riddle. But the bar was empty and there was no one in sight except for a sleepy-looking security guard. I nodded at him as I made my way through the main building and down the covered walkway to my room. I considered a final cigarette outside my door but I was dog tired and decided against it. Instead, I made my way in, locked the door, placed my firearm on the side table and flopped down on the bed. In the cool of the air conditioning I was fast asleep in minutes.

Chapter Twenty-Two.

It was 5.30 pm when the truck finally arrived. A dented old Isuzu pickup, it rolled up through the forest belching exhaust fumes as it approached. Joao Quintas immediately sent two of his men to meet it and guide it to the clearing where the weapons were stashed. He stood as he watched it arrive and could see that the driver's eyes were wide with fear. Knowing he needed to show leadership at this crucial point, he stood and commanded the men to begin loading the mortars, RPG launchers and ammunition crates into its battered load bed. Joao Quintas paced the makeshift camp nervously as they did so and he wondered if the claptrap old vehicle would make it back up the overgrown quarry road to the town. He pulled his phone from his pocket every few minutes to keep an eye on the time. Thankfully it only took 20 minutes to load the vehicle and once done he gathered the men for a final briefing before setting off. Fully armed and heavily loaded with ammunition, the sight of the men was a source of pride to him as he walked through their ranks. Finally, he stood in front of them and spoke.

"My brothers," he said, his teeth grinding from the drugs. "We have come so far together and now the moment is almost upon us. From here we will march to the outskirts of the town and lie in wait, for the signal. I hope you are as proud of your achievements as I am. I know we shall prevail. By this time tomorrow, the gas reserves of the Afungi peninsular will belong to us!"

The men cheered, loudly and more fiercely than they had ever done before. The reality of the moment was tangible. He knew then that the men were ready.

"Allahu Akbar!" shouted Joao.

The men responded with such fervour it was as if the ground shook. The call was repeated many times and weapons were raised and feet stamped until clouds of dust formed around them. Finally, Joao walked over to the waiting driver and told him to get into the vehicle.

The back springs were overloaded and creaked under the weight of the armaments. Then, without waiting, Joao Quintas gave the command and his second in charge shouted at the men to begin their march towards the abandoned quarry road. Joao Quintas pulled the knife from its sheath as he watched the men set off into the gathering dusk. He dipped the tip into the bag of bola and snorted a huge pile of the stuff before he too climbed into the passenger seat of the vehicle. With Darwesh perched upon the piles of steel crates in the load bed, he spoke.

"Drive slowly behind the men..." he said quietly to the driver. "But stay close. They must know I am with them at all times."

The quarry road was in worse condition than Joao had anticipated. The encroaching jungle had almost overgrown it in sections and on more than one occasion he was whipped on the face by branches as they drove. There were deep gullies and boggy sections filled with stagnant, stinking water but the old diesel engine kept going as they lurched along. It was an hour later when darkness fell and Joao Quintas felt like they were marching towards certain death. The fear had returned once again. Ignoring the driver who was sweating profusely, he dipped his blade several times into his bag of powder. Time and time again he questioned the driver as to how far it was to the town. In true African fashion, he was told it was not far, they were near, but the journey was agonizingly long and tedious. It was 8.00 pm when he sent a message forward that the men should stop to rest and drink water. The driver had informed him that it was now less than 10 kilometres to the town and Joao wanted to kill some time. It would take less than an hour to cover that distance. The break was spent in electric anticipation and there was a distinctly strange feeling among the men. The darkness was complete and the shroud of jungle that surrounded them seemed impenetrable. Crouched there in the damp humidity of the night, the men dosed themselves with liberal piles of bola as they rested and prepared themselves mentally. Finally, at 9.00 pm, the signal was given and the march began one final time. The next time they stopped would be at the outskirts of the town of Palma. Then they would wait for the final call to battle. Joao Quintas was feeling the same strange tingling in his limbs that had been there most of the afternoon.

He had no idea that he was very close to overdosing on the lethal cocktail of drugs that were coursing through his veins, and the occasional metallic taste in his mouth was blood from the broken and raw flesh on the inside of his cheeks.

The final hour seemed like it would never end. The lurching of the vehicle and the prickly heat of the interior of the cab were unbearable. The repeated moaning from Darwesh who was crouched low on the ammunition crates as his body was raked and whipped by branches annoyed Joao intensely and on more than one occasion he hissed insults and curses through the open window. It was just before 10.00 pm when they found themselves climbing a gentle hill that the old track was especially rough. There were rocks and stone chippings in the road where the locals had been crushing boulders for building projects. Joao glanced at his phone repeatedly as they climbed, fearing their arrival would be threatened by a puncture. He had not noticed a spare tyre on the truck. But just five minutes later they reached the top of the hill and below them the lights of the small town of Palma glowed in the distance. Further ahead, the moon shone off the sea and the night was clear. Finally they had arrived and now there was less than a kilometre to go. After pausing for 10 minutes, the command was given and the men proceeded down the rock-strewn slope towards the lights of the sleeping town below. There were fields at the foot of the hill where the locals grew their vegetables. This was by far the most dangerous part of the mission and Joao Quintas knew this. If the men were discovered and the alarm was raised, the entire operation would be in jeopardy. Thankfully, they walked and drove quietly through the night until the nearest houses were less than 200 metres away. They had arrived at the outskirts of one of the southern high-density suburbs that surrounded the town. A whisper was sent up the ranks and the men stopped as instructed. Slowly and carefully, they spread out for 100 metres on either side of the vehicle and lay low on the soggy earth to await the final signal. The time was 10.30 pm. Joao Quintas climbed out of the vehicle and watched as the heavy weaponry was unloaded and carted out to the men on either side of the vehicle. His body twitched and he blinked repeatedly in the moonlight. The next 25 minutes were the longest of his life and he crouched near the parked vehicle sweating and panting in anticipation. *Would the call come, or would it all be scuppered at the last moment?* But the call did come at exactly 10.58 pm. The word he had been waiting for was said and he breathed a sigh of relief and terror as he pocketed his phone. Two minutes later Joao Quintas stood up and screamed repeatedly at the top of his lungs.

"Attack!" he bellowed. "Allahu Akbar!"

Chapter Twenty-Three.

T he first explosions sounded like distant puffs of air. But it was what followed that awoke me properly and caused me to sit bolt upright on the bed. *Was I hearing things? Was I dreaming?* But it soon became apparent that I was not. There was random and repeated gunfire as well as explosions. It was initially confusing as the sounds seemed to come from near and far and all at the same time. Having fallen asleep with the lights on, I quickly looked at my watch. The time was 11.00 pm, I could only have been asleep for an hour. *What the fuck is going on?* It was then that I heard the first explosion nearby. The ear-shattering blast brought back terrible memories from my war days and instantly the hairs stood up on the back of my neck and arms. I jumped up and immediately walked to the back window which was closed. Opening it only confirmed my fears as the sounds were twice as loud and were quickly followed by yelling and screaming from within the hotel grounds. *What the fuck?* There was a cold sliding feeling in my stomach as my phone began to ring on the bedside table. I picked it up, answered it, and held it to my cheek with my shoulder as I strapped on my firearm. Above the cacophony of gunfire, on the line came the shouted warning from Sarge.

"We are under attack, boss!" he yelled. "Seems to be coming from all sides! This is a code red. Repeat, code red!"

"Copied! Where are you now, Sarge?" I shouted back as the gunfire nearby sounded.

"I am at home in the suburbs to the west of town!" he shouted.

It was then that I heard the screaming in the background of the call. There was no mistaking the sound of women and children in terror. Sarge was in the thick of it all and it sounded like the attack was more intense where he was. But at that point the line began to crackle and fade. I knew then that there was no time to waste. The town was under a serious and sustained attack and it could only be ISIS Mozambique.

"You need to get here now, Sarge!" I shouted above the appalling racket. "I repeat, leave there immediately if you can and make your way here to the hotel!"

But the line crackled once again and went dead. *They've taken out the cell phone tower. Fuck!* At that moment I heard screaming coming from the staff compound at the rear of the hotel grounds. This was quickly followed by an almighty explosion and the sound of shattering glass. The situation was rapidly becoming one of chaos and confusion. *Fucking get it together, Green. And do it now! Where the fuck is Stompie? If he is drunk again, I'll fucking kill him!* I ran towards the door and ripped it open. The lights of the hotel flickered as I ran down the walkway to his room and pounded on his door repeatedly. But there was no response. Seeing no other way, I stood back and kicked at the door with my bare foot. Stompie Van Der Reit lay there on his bed with powerful headphones over his ears. His eyes were screwed closed and he was nodding his head steadily to what must have been extremely loud music. The man was completely unaware of what was happening around him. I ran forward and ripped the headphones from his head. His eyes opened and a look of horror came across his face instantly.

"What?" he said. "What's going on?"

It was a relief to see that he was indeed sober and the reason he had been unaware of the mayhem that surrounded us was the fact that he had been listening to loud heavy metal music. He leapt to his feet in his underwear and shouted in his confusion.

"What the fuck is going on, Jason?" he said, his face turning pale.

"The town is under attack!" I shouted above yet more nearby explosions. "This is real! Get dressed, grab your gun, and meet me in the dining room right away!"

I left him and ran back to my own room, passing some panicking guests who were milling around under the walkway. Some were crying while others were simply staring around them with wide eyes.

"Get into the main hotel building now!" I shouted as I ran past them.

I watched them make their way up the walkway as I put on my shoes, gathered my radio and the keys and codes for the hotel armoury. All the while the constant sound of gunfire sounded, interspersed with the whistling of RPG shells and the deep thud of mortars.

I almost ran into Stompie as I left the room and we sprinted up to the main thatched building together. The lights continued to flicker as we arrived and I shouted to the gathered guests and staff to corral themselves to the centre of the building near the bar and dining area. It was then that I saw the hotel manager, Rogerio. His usually suntanned face was now ghost like and on seeing us, he ran up to Stompie and me. That the man was in a state of panic was abundantly clear from the look on his face.

"The lights are about to go out," I said to him. "Is there a generator?"

"Yes, yes," he said breathlessly. "It is set to start immediately the power goes out."

"Help us, Rogerio," I said. "See to it that the fuel tank is full and the extra supplies are nearby and safe. The lights *must* stay on. Once that is done, tell the head of hotel security to meet us at the armoury. Do you understand me, Rogerio?"

"Yes, Jason!" he shouted as he ran off. "I'll do that right away!"

Despite the relative cool of the evening, Stompie was sweating profusely and staring at the gathered group of guests who were milling around the centre of the dining area. Many of them were trying to make calls on their cell phones while some were sitting and weeping continuously. It was then I noticed Penny Riddle. She was sitting on the floor in the centre of the group. Her eyes were closed, her face was pale and her tears had streaked the makeup on her face. She sat with her hands covering her ears to shield herself from the appalling cacophony that surrounded us.

"Try and calm them down," I said to Stompie. "Tell them to stay there in the centre of the room and not move. Once Rogerio gets back, come and meet me in the armoury."

"Yes, sir..." said Stompie as he made his way forward towards the crowd of guests.

Wasting no time, I sprinted back out of the dining area and down towards the walkway to the armoury. As I ran the lights went out briefly but they soon came on again as the generator fired into life.

Finally, there was no more flickering and this would keep the guests calmer than they would be if they had been plunged into darkness. I fumbled with the codes and keys as I battled to open the complicated locking mechanisms but finally the door swung open and I stepped inside. Suddenly, the well-stocked armoury which I had only ever seen once looked meagre and ill-equipped compared to the extensive room at the gas site. *The gas site! What the fuck is going on there?* Suddenly there was a crackle on the radio on my belt. The garbled and panicked voice confirmed my worst fears. The gas site was under attack as well as the town. It seemed as if the entire area was under siege. *How the fuck could this have happened?* I glanced around the room as I made a mental note of the equipment it held. It was fairly well stocked contrary to my initial impressions and I knew that it would all be handy in the coming hours. I intended to set up a control room of sorts. Somewhere from which I could communicate with the outside world and in particular the JAG headquarters in Durban. There was the satellite phone and the radios which could still be relied on if the entire cell phone network was taken out. I quickly cleared a desk and ran to retrieve the satellite phone from my room where it had been left on charge. It was seconds later when I returned and began pacing the room as I tried and tried again to get through to Sarge on his cell phone. *Had he made it out of the suburbs or become a victim along with the others I had heard screaming in the background in his last call?* All the while the gunfire and explosions seemed to grow closer and closer with every passing minute. My immediate thought was for the thatched roof of the main hotel building and the rooms. Any spark would turn them into a raging inferno and leave the guests and staff woefully exposed and completely open. It was then that Stompie, Rogerio, and the head of security arrived and burst into the room. Stompie spoke first.

"The guests are all gathered," he said. "I've tried to calm them down but it's not easy. It sounds like fucking mayhem out there."

"The walls of the hotel are high and we have seven armed guards patrolling as we speak," said Rogerio, the colour slowly returning to his face.

"What about the thatched roofs?" I asked.

"All the roofs are fire proofed..."

"Good," I said. "Rogerio, I need you to stay with the guests. Give them water and soft drinks from the bar and do your best to keep them calm. There is nothing good that can come from a group of people who are panicked and screaming. This is what the attackers want. We all must keep cool heads. Can you try to do that for me?"

"Yes, Jason," he said. "Is there anything else?"

"Send an urgent message to the guards at the gate," I said. "Tell them Sarge will be arriving in a JAG vehicle. He might arrive anytime now. He must be let in. We can't leave him out there alone. Is that clear?"

"I'll do that right away..." he said as he rushed out of the door.

It was then that I realised that everyone in the room, and indeed in the hotel, was looking at me to assess and control the situation we had found ourselves in. It was a role I never imagined I would have to take, let alone so soon into the contract. Still, there was no choice and nobody else would do it for me. Next I spoke to the head of security. A short but tough-looking man in his fifties, he stood there in uniform with a glint in his eye and a look of determination on his face.

"You speak English?" I asked.

"A little..." he replied. "Enough I hope."

"How many guards are there here at the hotel right now?" I asked.

"There are seven armed people including the gate guards," he replied in broken English.

"Good," I said. "I'd like to do a tour of the perimeter now. Do we need torches?"

"No, sir. The walls are illuminated."

I glanced at Stompie who stood there looking like he wanted a fight.

"You hold the fort here, Stompie. Radio me if there are any snags. I'll be back as soon as I can."

Stompie nodded grimly as the head of hotel security and I made our way out of the room.

"Where should we start, sir?" asked the man.

'We'll start at the gate," I shouted over yet more gunfire. "Then we'll make our way around the perimeter. I need to check your men are stationed correctly and have enough ammunition."

The two of us ran through the central hotel structure and I noticed that Rogerio was doing a good job keeping the guests calm in the centre of the dining area. We made our way down the front stairs and into the garden and onto the car park. We arrived at the gate to find it locked and with two fully armed guards manning the entrance. One of them stood near the small window in the guardhouse while the other was stationed near the lock on the gate. The head of hotel security had done a good job and although the men were spooked, they remained steadfast and committed despite the chaos that seemed to be getting closer and closer by the minute.

"Remind them I am expecting one of my men in a JAG vehicle!" I shouted. "He could arrive at any moment. He must be allowed in as soon as he arrives!"

The head of security repeated this to the guards in his native Portuguese. They nodded with wide, fearful eyes and it was clear my earlier instructions had been delivered.

My fears for Sarge were growing with every minute and I wondered then if I would ever see him again. Until then I'd had no time to think. The events of the night had happened so suddenly and the bombardment had been sustained, if not escalated. It was clear that this was no random or isolated incident. This was an attack on a scale never seen before in Mozambique. Wasting no time, the head of security and I made our way along the perimeter wall to the right. It was a tall and sturdy structure built from concrete blocks and heavily plastered.

There were large globe lights atop it at intervals of every 10 metres and this made our progress through the lush gardens easier. We stopped and spoke to each security guard as we went. I checked their weapons and ammunition and made sure that words of encouragement were given to each of them. It took less than 15 minutes to make our way around the entire wall but it was when we arrived at the last guard post nearest the front gate that it happened. It started as we were talking to the terrified young guard. There was a sudden whooshing sound in the air that grew louder until the blast came. The mortar exploded with a deafening roar on the other side of the wall and the impact sent broken concrete and flaming debris all around us. It felt as if the very ground had been lifted by the rippling detonation. The three of us were whirled around and thrown to the ground as the wall was ripped apart. My breath came as though I was sucking air in a vacuum as the concussion reverberated around me in a maelstrom of compressed air. I forced myself to my knees in the cloud of dust from the destroyed wall and checked my extremities as I did so. The head of hotel security did the same not three metres from where I was. But it was only then that I saw the guard. His upper body and face had been smashed by the unimaginable force of the explosion and pounded with great chunks of broken concrete. The man lay dead and barely recognisable with his sidearm still attached to his belt. The pool of blood that spread around his broken body was black in the moonlight. I coughed repeatedly as the dust settled and my back ached as I stood up. Still, the gunfire raged on and I heard screaming from the town below.

"Jesus Christ..." I whispered quietly to myself.

Chapter Twenty-Four.

Louis Santos, otherwise known as Sarge, lived alone. His beloved wife of 20 years and his three children lived in the capital city of Maputo, thousands of kilometres to the south. His contract with JAG meant he would spend 2 months on duty in the town of Palma followed by 1 month back home with his family. When the attack happened, he barely had time to dress. The gunfire and shelling had started not 50 metres from where his humble house was located on the outskirts of the small coastal town. Stark naked, he had jumped to his feet and run to the back door to take a look at what was going on. He had been lucky to survive this as almost immediately bullets were slamming into the walls around him. Beating a hasty retreat, he ran back into his bedroom and dressed while the chaos around him intensified. He had taken shelter in the front room from where he called his boss at The Hotel Cabo Delgado. The instruction had been clear. He was to make his way there as soon as possible, if he could. Already there was screaming and wailing from the surrounding houses and the sound of panicked footfalls were all around. With his sidearm in hand, he made a run from the front door and immediately jumped into the company land cruiser. It was as he was reversing that the first man came around the left-hand side of the house. Clearly after the vehicle, the man stopped and aimed straight at him rather than shooting at the tyres and the engine. The man was dressed in green camouflage with a black and white checkered scarf around his lower face. Three AK47 rounds smashed through the windscreen and Sarge ducked as he gunned the engine, smashing through the wrought iron gate behind him and into the road. There he swung the steering wheel and engaged first gear but not before sitting up and taking aim at his pursuer. He let off 3 shots from his pistol as the engine roared and he was sure he had hit the man somewhere in the lower body as the last thing he heard was a scream. The street ahead was a confusing mess of fleeing people and animals, all seemingly running in no particular direction. Sarge knew that the attack had come from the fields behind the suburb and he pitied anyone who blindly ran into the night towards what would be certain death. It was as he reached the end of the street that the first shell exploded not 20 metres from the vehicle. The force of it caused his ears to whistle and ache and for a few seconds he was blinded by the sudden flash. Almost losing control of the large vehicle, he managed to recover and made a hasty right turn to speed off into what he had hoped was the relative safety of the central part of the town.

But this was not to be as multiple bodies were lying on the streets and he had to swerve time and time again to avoid them. The power lines on either side of the street were sparking and crackling and several fires had broken out on the roofs of the reed huts and other buildings. What had once been a pleasant and peaceful suburb had been transformed in minutes into a living hell with glowing fires, howling bullets and thumping grenades. Sarge pressed on and avoided hitting the fleeing citizens who were mostly in a state of undress and all in total confusion and terror. Most were aware of what was happening and they all knew too well the consequences of being captured by the ISIS militants. But thankfully the militants had not reached there by then and he sped off while avoiding the hundreds who had stepped out of their houses to see what all the fuss was about. But it was as he was approaching the centre of town that the bullets fired once again from his right-hand side. The rounds clunked as they slammed into the steel of the doors and he winced as he expected to feel the impact of a bullet at any time. As he took a left turn past the old municipal buildings one of the shots hit his front left tyre. The speeding vehicle lurched violently and he almost lost control and slammed into a street lamp. Thankfully he managed to right the car but in the process, he had slammed his head into the sidewall and almost knocked himself out. There was little time to think. If he had stopped he would have been shot immediately so he gunned the engine again and, gripping the wheel, sped off through town with one flat tyre. The wheels howled as he took the right turn past the port and headed towards the hill where the Hotel Cabo Delgado was located. Although it had felt much quicker, the journey had taken him 20 minutes in total and he counted himself lucky to be alive. With the powerful engine revving and the ruined wheel roaring, he sped up the hill towards the gate of the hotel while leaning on the horn. Finally, he saw the heavy steel sliding gate and he slammed on the brakes as he arrived. Still leaning on the horn and breathing heavily, he waited and prayed that someone would open up for him.

Chapter Twenty-Five.

Joao Quintas screamed with the insane bloodlust of a rampaging berserker as he made his way forward through the night with his fighters on either side. The killing frenzy had overtaken the men and they moved swiftly through the night, destroying and setting fire to everything in sight. Many of the terrified residents of the small suburb had run towards the gunfire and had been mown down immediately. A large proportion had fled towards the centre of the town but Joao knew they too would meet their fate when they ran into the other groups of militants. All vehicles, be they motor cars, trucks, or motorcycles were moved to safety and parked for later use. The elderly and infirm who remained in their humble dwellings cowered and begged for mercy as the men systematically ransacked the houses. But they were shown none and were hacked to death and dismembered with the razor-sharp machetes that each of the militants carried. The body parts were tossed into the streets to ensure that any images that were taken after would convey the true terror they had unleashed. Despite the madness that enveloped him, Joao Quintas never forgot that he was to destroy all essential infrastructure as he went. This included water supplies, electricity and cell phone networks. He made sure that all communication towers were bombed and set on fire as he progressed through the area. With the drugs fuelling their blind hatred and madness, the men made steady progress leaving behind only smoking ruins and misery. Only one of his men had been injured so far. Shot in the upper leg, he had instructed Darwesh to administer first aid to the man and promised to return to collect him come sunrise. Even an injury to a comrade would not stop the mission which by all accounts was progressing well. Radio contact had been established and reports were coming through every 15 minutes that the assault on Palma was a resounding success so far. There had also been reports of Mozambican soldiers fleeing into the night. Caught unprepared, their numbers had been overcome and they too had succumbed to panic and terror and had run like animals before a bushfire. By 2.00 am the men had been called to halt and told to rest for a while. This would give them time to dose up on more bola and rehydrate before continuing their rampage. All around them, the night sky glowed with the yellow flames of destruction and there was no respite from the continuous bombardment and explosions. The streets were filled with the cries of the wounded and the moans of the dying.

The driver of the truck had stayed nearby as instructed and more and more ammunition and shells were doled out to the men. After the embarrassing defeat at Mocimboa Da Praia, this had been a resounding success so far and he could hardly wait till daylight so he could see first-hand the extent of the devastation. For Joao, this was his life's calling and finally, he felt like he was winning. With Darwesh close behind him, he shouted and bellowed his commands all the while grinning and laughing uncontrollably while gurning and grinding his teeth. His eyes were dark pools of pure hatred and his blood pumped with greed and savagery. Steadily, the men moved forward, not leaving a single living creature in their path. The screams of the terrified inhabitants only served to invigorate him further. It was 3.00 am when he pulled his phone out and noted that the cell phone network was disabled. He grinned as he thought of the thousands of desperate cries for help that were now futile. Only the very wealthy and sophisticated would have any communication with the outside world now. Soon the main power would go out for the entire town and they would close in and meet their comrades in the centre of town. The daylight would come and with that, there would be an organised takeover of all security forces headquarters and vehicles. The operation would continue through the following day and finally, the town of Palma would belong to them. Joao Quintas could smell victory in the swirling acrid smoke and for the first time in his life, he felt invincible. It was at 3.00 am when he ran back and found Darwesh who had been trailing behind him carrying the first aid kits. He shouted to his men to proceed and told them he would catch up with them in the next half hour. He pulled Darwesh behind a smoldering building and once alone, with the sound of grenades and gunfire all around, he raped the young man with such force that both men were bleeding when he was done.

Chapter Twenty-Six.

The head of the hotel security and I pulled the dead guard's body to one side. By then the dust had settled but there was a gaping, jagged hole in the wall which was a serious breach. Thankfully the light had been taken out as well so this gap in the perimeter would only be seen during daylight. The man insisted he would stand guard and I thanked him and commended his bravery before making off towards the main gate through the gardens. With my ears still whistling and my entire body covered with a mixture of sweat and cement dust, I arrived. It was then that I heard the screech of tyres from the other side of the gate and my heart sank as I feared it may be the arrival of militants. I quickly ran to the guardhouse and peeked through the window. There, parked in the darkness was the vehicle of Sarge. With the engine steaming and the pungent stench of hot rubber, he sat there in the driver's seat leaning on the horn. The sound added to the chaos and general confusion that surrounded us and I quickly opened the window and shouted.

"Sarge!" I screamed, "Get that vehicle inside now!"

The big man's blank eyes lit up as he saw me and the guard wasted no time as he slid the gate open and beckoned Sarge to drive in. The vehicle came in steaming and lurching with its front left tyre in shreds. The rim left a deep groove on the surface as he drove but eventually, he made it up the hill and parked near my own land cruiser. Wide eyed and clearly spooked, he climbed out of the vehicle and looked at me.

"What's it like out there, Sarge?" I asked, knowing what his answer would be.

"Not good, boss," he said grimly. "They're coming from all sides. I almost took a bullet. I was lucky to make it."

"Well, I'm glad you did," I said relieved. "Now come with me. We need to make contact with the outside world and let them know."

"The power is out. Is the generator running?"

"It is..." I replied. " For now at least. The cell phones network is out. Typical terror tactic. But we have power and satellite communications. The guests are corralled in the centre of the main building. You, Stompie and I need to protect them and keep the perimeter secure. A mortar explosion took out part of the wall nearby but that's being guarded."

The big man nodded, he had sensed that I was in control and ready and willing to fight. This boosted his enthusiasm and he brightened up immediately.

"Let's go..." he said.

The two of us ran up the driveway through the gardens and up the stairs into the main building.

"Try to appear calm," I said as we slowed down to a walk. "No need to spook them more than they already are."

Stompie saw us arrive and ran forward to greet us.

"Jesus Christ," he said upon seeing me covered with cement dust "What happened?"

"Mortar took out the wall near the gate," I replied, keeping my voice low. "Killed the guard but the breach is being looked after by the head of security. Sarge made it to us, just. The vehicle was shot to shit on the way. Tell Rogerio to stay with the guests, we need to go to the armoury and get busy. We need to let the outside world know what is happening here. This is fucking serious. It seems it's not going to stop either."

Stompie arrived in the armoury a few minutes after Sarge and I. Both men were wide-eyed and in a mild state of shock but I could see that they had been in similar situations before and would be useful. For that I was grateful. Wasting no time, I set up my laptop and began making calls on the satellite phone to the JAG headquarters in Durban and the authorities in Maputo.

In between these calls, I could see that Sarge was itching to do something so I sent him on a similar perimeter patrol to the one I had recently completed. I told him to reassure the guards and check on their ammunition. He picked up an AR-15 semi automatic rifle and strapped two lines of ammunition over his shoulders before leaving.

"Good idea," I said. "Be safe..."

Stompie began preparing the weapons as I made call after call to the authorities and the JAG offices. The response was quick but the message was clear. We were on our own until daylight when the choppers would start flying in. Manned with armed personnel, they would start airlifting those trapped in the gas site to the north and would attend to the rest of us in the hotel after. The instructions were literally to 'hold the fort' until then. All the while I listened for the sound of approaching gunfire. Up until then I had been completely unaware of the situation in the town itself. *Had the security forces been caught unaware? Were they launching a counterattack on the insurgents?* With a communications blackout and the total darkness of the night, we were a vulnerable and valuable target for the militants. A hotel full of rich and influential guests was sure to raise the profile of the attack and this would make newsworthy stuff should they gain entry and achieve their goals. But that was something I would do my best to prevent. The resulting notoriety and global coverage would be a solid victory for ISIS Mozambique and would be sure to make global headlines. The hours passed and we held our positions with Stompie making his way back and forth to the guests to reassure them while Sarge made his way again and again around the perimeter. All the while the barrage continued. Mortar shell after mortar shell fell onto the town and the gunfire never ceased. There was, however, a worrying lapse in the screaming and I feared the worst as this happened. *How many have died? How many butchered?* The reports I had read during my research had left no doubt in my mind as to the savagery of these monsters. They would not only kill, they would do so in the most brutal way possible to raise their profiles. I felt like an actor on a stage in a theatre surrounded by an extremely hostile audience. I only paused once to go back to my room and clean up before going through to the main area to check on the guests. Rogerio was doing a sterling job and had actually made some of the guests laugh with his jokes.

This I was grateful for although I did notice Penny Riddle, her face streaked with tears, her entire body shaking as she stared at me with blank eyes. Our situation was bleak to say the least, but we were not done yet. The thatched roof above us was an advantage given any shells and mortars would hopefully bounce off without the possibility of flames. Still, the nearby shelling and the breach in the wall were of serious concern, but that was in the capable hands of Sarge. Stompie had laid the contents of the armoury out in an organised fashion and already the batteries for the two drones were fully charged. Sarge came in on three occasions to inform us that the entire electricity network had been disabled and he had heard what sounded like a large crowd forming near the port. I glanced at my watch, wary of the fact that there was a powerful generator keeping the lights on. We had now become a target in the darkness, a fort on the hill to which the militants would be drawn like moths to a flame. I glanced at my watch. The time was 3.30 am.

Chapter Twenty-Seven.

Colonel Callum Jackson stormed along the upstairs corridor of his sprawling mansion in the wealthy suburb of Umhlanga in the city of Durban, South Africa. The time was 12.45 am and he had been awoken by a series of urgent calls to both his cell phone and his landline. The news was not good and it seemed his worst fears had been realised. Wearing a red pleated silk dressing gown and Italian slippers, he made his way downstairs to where his close security team had assembled in the entrance hallway. The faces of the men were pale and tired looking and they stared up at him with real fear in their eyes as they watched him descend the grand marble staircase.

"My study," he bellowed "Now!"

The three men followed him down the lower corridor and into the plush study that was the nerve centre of the business empire known as the Jackson Advisory Group. The walls were filled with taxidermy from hunting trips around the world and there were military antiques of every kind. A fine collection of hugely rare and expensive Purdy shotguns stood displayed in a cabinet to the left of the room. The value of the guns alone ran into the millions. Then there was the bookshelf. First editions of all the major African explorers from Livingstone to Selous. All of them signed and rare as hen's teeth. Colonel Jackson walked immediately over to the drinks cabinet on the right-hand side of the room and poured himself a half glass of fine scotch whisky from a crystal decanter. Standing there facing the wall, he took a deep draw from the tumbler and closed his eyes as the expensive liquor slid down his throat. The persistent ringing of the telephones on his desk and those of the cell phones of his team grated him deeply and this only served to infuriate him further. Doing his best to keep calm, he walked around the massive stinkwood desk and pulled out the leather padded Eames chair. Without raising his eyes to look at the men who stood expectantly before him, he sat down and reached over to flick the switch on the green-shaded desk lamp. Once illuminated, he stared at the heavy crystal tumbler in his hand and took another deep draw from it. Finally, he placed the glass neatly to his right on the expensive leather top, intertwined his fingers, took a deep breath and looked up at his men.

"Now," he said wearily, "what the fuck is going on in Palma?"

The initial briefing took less than half an hour although there were constant disruptions in the form of messages coming through from his front office. Lines of communication were established with all parties and sitreps were delivered every fifteen minutes. Not for the first time, the shrewd military tactician sat there and absorbed the information as it came through in real-time. He was already planning the inevitable evacuation of key staff and assets. But Colonel Jackson was aware of the staggering amounts of money involved in the gas extraction sites in the north of Mozambique, and already he as planning the recovery and future contracts that would be required of his company. Multiple calls were made and piles of preparatory instructions were handed out to various members of staff around the world. It appeared, by all accounts, that the attack on Palma was the biggest and boldest operation ever attempted by ISIS Mozambique, and the repercussions would reverberate loudly through the hushed corridors of the energy majors. They would be shaken to the core, but it was vital that whatever happened next was smooth and ultimately professional. The safety of the Total staff was his main priority and he would avail all of his assets to ensure that this was jealously guarded. It was, after all, his business. Sleep would not come for Colonel Jackson that night. He did not need to sleep. His military mind had kicked into gear and he would remain awake until the job was done. It was 2.45 am when he was finally able to open a direct line to the satellite phone of his head of security in Palma. He took a long sip of whisky and sat back in the comfortable chair as he waited to answer the call. Finally, he pressed the button that would connect him, and spoke.

Chapter Twenty-Eight.

"Green," said the voice on the other end of the line. "Talk to me..."

I had found the quietest corner of the armoury and held my left forefinger to my ear as I briefed him.

"The town is under siege," I said. "Seemingly from all sides. There is also a sustained attack at the gas sites but the security staff there are holding the attackers off. I am in constant communication with the Total site and am told that the critical staff have gathered in the managers' canteen and are all safe and accounted for. The situation is dire, Colonel. It's not letting up and there is no sign of the army anywhere."

"And what of your situation at the hotel?" he grunted.

"We are in a similar scenario," I said over the clatter of fresh gunfire. "The guests have been marshalled into the restaurant where we can keep an eye on them. The manager is doing a good job keeping them calm and fed. A random mortar strike has taken out a section of the wall and killed a guard. The wall has been secured and armed personnel are now monitoring the perimeter. All seem determined to preserve the status quo and I have my 3rd in charge making patrols constantly. The main power supply has been taken out plus all communication systems. The hotel and the gas sites are running on their generators."

"How long can you keep this up?" asked the Colonel.

"Not long," I said. "I'll know more at sunrise when I will send up some drones. But for now, it's not looking good at all. I think it's essential that an evacuation is planned sooner rather than later. This is unlike anything anyone has ever known in Mozambique. The gas site has the lion's share of weapons in its armoury. We here have sufficient for now but in the event of a determined attack, I'm not sure how long we can hold out."

"Rest assured an evacuation is already in the works, Green," said the gruff voice. "I will await a report from you within an hour of sunrise. For now, we will be sending choppers up to the gas site immediately after dawn. We have arranged a municipal building and medics to be ready and waiting in the town of Mocimboa Da Praia just south of Palma. We will fly in throughout the day with armed men in the choppers. I anticipate I will be able to move everyone out by the end of the day, but I need that report. There is no one else in Palma I can rely on for information. Your report will be crucial for your own evacuation and that of the rest of you there."

I glanced at my watch and gauged the time I would need to get a picture of what had happened in the town. I knew that the sun rose at 5.10 am in March in Mozambique and if the drones were not shot out of the sky immediately, I knew I could fly a grid over the town within half an hour.

"I'll have it ready for you by 6.00 am..." I said, "barring any unfortunate incidents."

"Good," he replied. "This is now a direct line to me. I'll be expecting your call then."

The line went dead and I replaced the satellite phone in its charger immediately. I took a deep breath and exhaled as another burst of gunfire sounded to the north of the hotel. *Fucking hell, Green. You've got yourself into a hell of a scrap here.*

Chapter Twenty-Nine.

Joao Quintas scaled the ladder of the cell phone tower that his men had just blown up. The remains of the electrical box were still smouldering below him as he climbed. He paused once he had reached a height of 20 metres and smiled as he watched the pink swell of the sun rising over the ocean ahead of him. Despite the racket of random gunfire and thudding of mortar shells, he gazed around him in the early morning light and marvelled at the spread of utter devastation that surrounded him. The smoking ruins and shells of burnt-out buildings. The acrid smell of cordite and the sweet smell of blood and death filled his nostrils. *This is all my work. Our work*, he thought. *What a great day to be alive.* Clinging to the steel of the ladder, with the barbed wire fence blown out and singed below him, he smiled and pulled the knife from his belt. Although his mouth was dry and his groin itchy and painful, there was nothing that could stop the intense buzz of victory. *They had done it. They had actually done it this time.* A great pall of low lying smoke hung over the once beautiful town and the screams and moans of the wounded could still be heard all around. During the night his team of men had met one of the other groups of attackers. The meeting had further bolstered their enthusiasm and the men had been spurred on to even more debauchery and savagery. The slaughter had been incessant throughout the night. Behind them lay the corpses of hundreds of men, women and children. Already the humidity and heat was starting to bloat their bodies. Soon the flies would come and continue their work. The centre of the town lay near now, perhaps only 1 kilometre ahead. There they would rendezvous with the other units and the mission would be complete. Joao Quintas grinned and the spaces between his teeth were dark with his own blood. Still, he felt nothing and he deftly dipped the blade into the rapidly deleting pack of cocaine and heroin mixture. He snorted from the blade and sneezed loudly before spitting a great globule of mucus and bloody saliva down to the sandy earth below. He turned once to check on Darwesh. The young man stood not 20 metres behind him and gazed up at him with devoted, awestruck eyes. Despite the raging bloodlust that had consumed him since the previous night, he smiled at the young man, and this did not go unnoticed.

Darwesh Gonzales waved up at him from where he stood and there were tears in his eyes. Whether this was from the thick smoke that filled the air or a sense of pride, he did not know. With his energy levels boosted once again, Joao Quintas climbed down into the pall of smoke that hung around the tower's electrical box below. He jumped from the ladder a full 2 metres up and landed heavily on his feet. Emerging from the smoke, he looked back to see Darwesh approaching, a nervous and longing look on his face. He nodded at the young man to move away to his right where they met. There he gave the young man another dose of bola and then went back to the frontline where the men waited.

"My brothers!" he shouted, grinning from ear to ear. "We are not done yet. Drink water now but be ready to move on in 15 minutes. We have an appointment in the centre of the town, and that will be a celebration you will not want to miss! Allahu Akbar!"

Chapter Thirty.

Despite the frantic events of the night, I felt no fatigue at all. Rogerio had been good enough to send multiple cups of coffee and sandwiches through the night. I had concentrated on intelligence gathering during that time and had only stopped to smoke on three occasions. I had spent the last minutes of darkness perched on the top level of the hotel at the viewing deck. I had been hoping for a glimpse of what was actually happening and had sat there willing the sun to rise. When it did, the sight was one of pure horror. The port where I had sat only hours before was shrouded in smoke and I could see hundreds of people huddling there hoping to escape by sea. The few vehicles that plied the roads did so at speed and in a panicked fashion, and still the yelling and screaming continued. The sunrise was beautiful on the horizon over the ocean but what it revealed was like a scene from a post-apocalyptic horror movie. To the west, inland, multiple fires were burning and there were random explosions happening everywhere. Whether these were gas bottles or grenades, I had no idea, but the picture was far from the idyllic paradise it had been the previous day. I watched a group of women carrying babies running past the municipal building on their way to the port. Their screams could be heard from where I was and it seemed no one was coming to assist them. Their fate was unknown and I knew it would be many, many hours before any kind of sea rescue could be attempted. Even then, the numbers of people any boats would be able to carry would be negligible. *How many*

thousands had fled into the bush? How many had died during the night? More importantly, how near were the marauders to the hotel? I stayed in this brief moment of reflection until I realised that I had become a prime target for a sniper. A white man watching from a protected fort on a hill. I quickly got up and made my way downstairs to the restaurant area where the guests were still waiting. I nodded at Rogerio to follow me so I could have a quiet word with him.

"Turn off the generator," I said. "It's light enough now and we don't want to draw too much attention to us here. Keep the guests fed and watered. Let them know we are all going to get out of here. I'll make an announcement in the next hour about the evacuation plans."

"I'll do that now, Jason," said Rogerio, his face strained and pale. "What about you?"

"I'm going to send up some drones," I said. "I need a picture of exactly what has happened here. It's also essential for our escape."

I walked out of the restaurant area and ran down the shaded walkway to the armoury. Stompie was there and had already prepared the two powerful machines for flight.

"All set, Jason," he reported. "We have eight fully charged batteries. Two hours flying time for each drone."

"Thank you, Stompie. Let's get them out and up into the air now."

Sarge arrived as we were carrying the drones out into the garden beyond the walkway. Despite the ordeal he had been through, he smiled as he saw us and seemed happy to see the sunrise.

"How's everything on the perimeter?" I asked as I laid the drone on the lawn near a flowerbed.

"Everything is fine, boss," he replied. "There seems to be a lull in the gunfire."

"Good," I said as I checked the SD card on the machine. "But don't be fooled. These fuckers will want us and want us badly. For them, it will be the ultimate prize. There's a pot of coffee and some food in the armoury. Get some of it into you and then make sure the kitchen sends the same to the guards. They must be starving and they're doing a fine job. Make sure they're looked after."

"I'll do that, boss..."

Stompie laid the second drone down near my own. I checked the machines thoroughly and glanced at my watch afterwards. Satisfied they were both charged and ready to fly, I spoke.

"This is probably the most important thing we will do today," I said quietly. "No doubt they'll try to shoot them when they see the drones but everything will be recorded here. Our escape depends on this and the Colonel is waiting for my call. I'm gonna send one of them up now."

"Good luck..." said Stompie, blinking his bloodshot, tired eyes.

There was an electronic beeping sound as the screen on the controller came alive. Wasting no time, I activated the propellers and sent the machine straight up. At an altitude of 400 feet I sent it inland on a northwesterly course. I winced as I heard the gunfire once again and expected the screen to go blank at any time. But the drone was fast and high enough to escape any potshots. It took less than 3 minutes to reach the outer edges of the town where I stopped it and flew it south along the outskirts of town. The flashing images on the screen were confusing but I would study them later in slow motion. Once the machine had reached the southern reaches of Palma, I brought in eastwards for 300 metres and repeated the process. By doing this I was building a picture of the town as it stood. The images and videos would be sent around the world and used to gauge the severity of the attack. It was vital intelligence and I was anxious to get it recorded quickly. The drone flew in this pattern repeatedly, making its way eastwards as it went. There was a point where there was intense gunfire and I was sure it would be shot out, but the flight was a success and I brought the machine back within 17 minutes. Wasting no time, I sent the second machine up and did the same until I had reached the beach. This only took 10 minutes and by the time I brought the machine down, I was sweating. The heat of the day had begun in earnest and it would not let up. I removed the SD cards from both machines and ran into the armoury to where my computer was set up and waiting. There, on the big screen, I scanned the videos, pausing and memorising the scenes below. The videos and images made for grim viewing and I shook my head as I watched. Within ten minutes I had a good idea of the damage that had been done and from where it had started. I glanced at my watch and saw that I had five minutes before I would need to make my call to the Colonel.

I took a deep breath as I stood up and walked out to smoke. Stompie arrived as I lit up and walked up to me with an expectant look on his face.

"So, Jason," he said quietly, "what does it look like out there?"

"It's not good," I replied grimly. "It's fucking carnage. There are houses with S.O.S. signs everywhere. People have used sheets and anything else they can find, even painted their roofs. The streets are littered with body parts and most of the buildings are either blown to pieces or burning."

I was not exaggerating. What I had seen in the videos was nothing short of a vision from hell.

Chapter Thirty-One.

"Speak to me, Green," said the Colonel.

The time was 6.00 am and the call on the satellite phone had been answered immediately.

"The attack seems to have come from a number of points surrounding the town," I reported. "This was highly organized and coordinated from the word go. There is mass destruction and death. I have seen hundreds of bodies from the sky and there are probably many more in and around the buildings. The militants are making their way towards the centre of town where I assume they will meet. For now, there seems to be a lull in activity but I expect it to resume any time now. I have uploaded the videos and they are on their way to you and the JAG servers as we speak. You will soon see for yourself."

At that moment I heard the first helicopter above. I looked up as I was speaking and saw immediately they were from JAG. Clearly headed for the gas extraction sites in the north, they sped past us, headed over the coast and the town respectively. Immediately I noticed armed men sitting in the cabins.

"The choppers are on their way..." said the gruff voice.

"They're here," I replied quickly. "Just flew over us now."

"Good," said the Colonel. "The evacuation has begun. I need

you to stay put and keep everyone safe. Keep them calm. We will get to you as soon we can. In the meantime, I need you to keep flying the drones. I need you to identify a landing spot where we can uplift you."

"It won't be in the hotel grounds, that's for sure," I said. "Far too much vegetation and trees."

"Find one, Green," said the Colonel. "And choose wisely. You will need to get there when the time comes. Pick a clear route to the safest place you can find. I'll expect communications through the morning."

With that, the line went dead. I took a deep breath as I walked back into the armoury and placed the satellite phone back into its cradle. It seemed the battery in the device was weak and needed constant charging. Something which had been overlooked by our predecessors. It was clear that the events of the day would dictate the conditions of our escape. The situation was fluid and would stay that way. My job was to monitor it and keep the hotel secure and safe until then. Just when that would be, I had no idea. Sure, the shelling and gunfire had calmed, the militants were obviously regrouping or tired, but I was in no doubt it would continue, and with the coming of the dawn, I expected worse. There were hundreds, if not thousands of people congregating in the centre of the town. They were a prime target for the militants and there was no way they would simply stop the assault. They wanted to kill and I was certain that it would continue. It was then that I had the idea. The vantage point offered by the viewing deck at the top of the hotel was a valuable and crucial asset. Sure, it was a dangerous place to be, but if we could remain up there unseen, it would be a place that would offer ongoing and crucial intelligence on the happenings of the day. I made my way into the restaurant area where I found Stompie talking to Penny Riddle. She appeared to have calmed down somewhat but her face was still as white as a sheet. She looked at me with a resigned expression on her face as I approached and called Stompie to one side. I told him of my idea and we both agreed it would be a valuable asset. After checking on the guests, I assured them that rescue was on its way. This seemed to boost their resolve and with that, more coffee and sandwiches were delivered. Stompie and I made our way carefully up the stairs and crawled over to the timber sides of the viewing deck. Keeping low on our bellies, we managed to shift a few of the wooden struts enabling us to peek out from the deck unseen from the town below. We repeated this on all four sides of the deck until we had created a spot from which there would be a safe, 360-degree view of the town and the port.

"That works," I whispered. "I think it'll be alright."

"I agree," said Stompie, already sweating heavily. "The bastards won't see us from down there."

"We're going to have to have someone up here through the day to keep an eye on things," I said. "You and I will be busy preparing to get the guests out of here. We need to find a pick-up point for the choppers."

"I can start the first shift while you find someone."

"Good man. I'm going to go look at the video footage again and see if I can identify a landing spot. Has to be near here and open enough while still offering cover."

"Not gonna be easy..."

"No," I said "But I'd better get on with it. I'll be back soon."

I crawled over to the stairs and made my way down. The calm in the town had boosted the spirits of the terrified guests and I smiled as I walked past them. *Pray it continues, Green.* Once out of sight, I jogged back to the armoury and set to work. Two possible extraction points were immediately clear. Both were on the beach to the north and the south of the port. The main road that ran through the centre of the town would offer access to either of these places and if there was no massive presence of militants, I saw either as viable evacuation points. Using the GPS points I worked out the distance to both spots. The logistics of moving a large number of terrified people to these points would be a challenge. I knew it would have to be done in a vehicle convoy. There would need to be armed men at the front and rear of this convoy and we would have to move fast. The events of the day would dictate whether this was possible or not. This was the big unknown which weighed heavily on my mind. It was as I was scanning the videos that I realised how thirsty I was. Apart from several cups of coffee, I had not drunk any water at all. Added to that was the stifling heat which had begun in earnest. Without the generator, there was no air conditioning and I knew then that I would have to drink plenty of water if I was to make it through the day functioning properly. I walked quickly to my room and took three bottles of mineral water out of the fridge. The water was still chilled and I drank a full litre before getting back to work studying the aerial videos again for an evacuation point. All the while I kept an eye on my watch.

The choppers came back over the town a few minutes later and I ran outside to take a look as they passed. Loaded with evacuees from the gas sites, they sped overhead and I saw the same armed men watching the town from above. *Lucky fuckers*, I thought. *They'll be sipping Pina Coladas in an hour*. I spent the next two hours working on getting the equipment and ammunition ready for the convoy. In total, I had allocated weapons and ammunition for 4 men. I figured if there were 2 in the front and another 2 to the rear, there would be a chance of getting to where we were going. There was a lot of random equipment which appeared to have been placed in the armoury as an afterthought. There was webbing, extra radios, knives, first aid kits and uniforms along with packs of dried food. I put the presence of these items down to the organisation of the Colonel. Only he could have been so thorough and even if they were never used, it was reassuring that they were there. It was at 11.00 am when the gunfire and shelling restarted. Until then I had been lulled into a false sense of security. It had been as if the attack was over for the time being. But I had no idea how terribly wrong I was.

Chapter Thirty-Two.

———— ❧ ————

Joao Quintas climbed atop a burnt-out vehicle and called his men to gather around. He waited as the men arrived. To him, they appeared fit and strong as if they had just had a full night's sleep. Although their uniforms were bloodied and dusty, the men were fired up, wide awake and eager to continue their rampage through the town. Their early success had bolstered them and they now felt invincible.

"My brothers, true soldiers of Islam!" he shouted "We have triumphed and so far there is only one of us who is injured. I am told he is doing well and will make a full recovery!"

The men cheered and one of them let off a shot into the air in celebration. All around them was a scene of total destruction. They had moved steadily through the night and the early morning, killing everything in sight. Although most of the inhabitants of the town had fled towards the port, there had been much to burn and loot and they had done this with cold calculation. Joao knew that the final push was near and soon they would arrive in the centre of the town near the port. There had been constant communication from the other militants and this pause was intentional and planned. The final salvo would be as brutal as the first and would finish the job. Glowing with the thrill of his successes, he went on.

"I know you are fatigued so I have instructed Darwesh to send more bola to get you through the final part of the day. Soon I will give the signal and we will move ahead once again and take this town as our own. Will you be ready?"

The men cheered loudly in response.

"Are you ready?" shouted Joao, his mad eyes glowing in his thin, cruel face.

The men responded with sheer elation at the news and Joao knew then that they were unstoppable. He looked behind him to where Darwesh waited and nodded.

The young man stepped forward, carrier bag in hand, and began dishing out portions of the white powder. A rest period of an hour was allowed but by then the men were raring to go once again. For Joao Quintas, it was time to finish the job.

Chapter Thirty-Three.

Colonel Callum Jackson stood up from his seat and walked up to the wide bay window that looked out onto the very same ocean where 3000 kilometres to the north, his extremely lucrative contract was in grave danger. In his left hand, he clutched a tumbler of neat whisky and although he had drunk over a bottle and a half since he had been awoken, he was still as sober as a judge. His bloodshot eyes stared out at the scene of serenity in front of him as he pictured the mayhem that must be happening in the beautiful coastal town of Palma, Mozambique. There had been constant communication with the gas site, the team in Pemba, Mocimboa Da Praia and Palma, and the evacuation of workers from the gas site was progressing extremely well. Fuel supplies had been boosted and every single person in his vast business network was working overtime to ensure that the operation continued smoothly. But time was not on his side that day and he blinked as he looked at the gold Rolex watch on his left wrist. It had just gone 12.30 pm and the attacks on the centre of the town of Palma had intensified significantly. Although the majority of personnel from the gas site had been extracted, there was still the issue of the hotel to deal with. His helicopters had made 15 trips so far and the armed men aboard had kept him updated on the situation. There was now a race against time and a race he could quite easily lose. By his calculations, he would only be able to get to the rendezvous in Palma at roughly 3.00 pm. That would not leave much time to evacuate the 30 souls who were sure to perish if he failed. He nodded, still staring out to sea, as one of his aides delivered a sitrep behind him. Without turning around, he took yet another sip of the expensive spirit and spoke.

"How long until we can get into Palma?" he asked.

"Still the same prediction, sir." replied the man.

"Connect me to Jason Green," said the Colonel. "He must have arranged an evacuation point."

"I'll try, sir," said the young man. "But the word is the attacks have intensified and are nearing the centre of town..."

"So fucking connect me now, you idiot!" he roared in fury, as droplets of spittle landed on the glass of the window.

Chapter Thirty-Four.

It was around 12.15 pm when the situation in Palma began to deteriorate drastically. Using binoculars I had found in the armoury, I watched the militants as they drove and ran into the centre of town cheering and firing into the air. It was, by all accounts, over and the town had been taken. The only token of hope that I had was that it appeared that there were still many more of them to arrive and those were still in the process of making their way into town. The sight made for grim viewing as I lay there on my belly gazing through the tiny hole in the wooden struts of the top deck under the thatched roof. All dressed in green fatigues with scarves wrapped around their heads and lower faces, the men were jubilant and the hooting of the vehicles and the gunshots only served to further terrorise the many thousands of residents who had gathered at the port. Their fate was looking very bleak indeed as there had only been two small boats arriving to take people away. I knew then that it was a matter of time for both them and us. More militants would surely arrive and continue their campaign of butchery and rape. I had seen their advance from the drone footage. The Mozambican army was nowhere to be seen and there had been a complete breakdown of order. I crawled back towards the stairs and made my way downstairs. The guests looked at me with hope in their eyes and I smiled as I fought great trembling waves of fear and apprehension. Wasting no time, I made my way back to the armoury where I had left Stompie making last-minute preparations with our equipment. It was as I was making my way down the walkway that he ran out clutching the bulky satellite phone.

"It's the Colonel," he muttered. "Doesn't sound too happy."

I grabbed the phone as I walked in to take a look at what he had done. True to form he had prepared four neat piles of equipment and weapons. I put the phone to my ear and spoke.

"This is Green," I said over the sound of yet more gunfire.

"What is the situation there?" asked the Colonel. "I am waiting for a location from you, Green. What is taking so long?"

By then the tension had become too much and I felt like smashing the phone on the concrete floor.

"I'm working on it!" I replied quietly. "The fuckers are *right here* in town. I have identified two possible locations. One to the north of the port on the beach, the other to the south. Either will depend on the situation along the main road when the time comes. When do you think that'll be?"

"We're looking at around 3.00 pm," said the Colonel. "Either of these points are fine, Green. You let me know. Just make sure you're all there by then."

"I'll keep you informed," I said before hanging up.

I took a deep breath and stared blankly at the equipment laid out on the floor of the armoury. It was only then that I realised that everyone there had more faith in me than I had in myself. The weight of responsibility was enormous and I glanced at my watch as I wondered if we could hold out until then.

Chapter Thirty-Five.

Joao Quintas drove his men relentlessly through the suburbs towards the centre of town. There were pockets of resistance in the form of some brave members of the Mozambique Defence Force but they were outnumbered and eliminated quickly enough. Their bodies were dismembered and dragged into the blazing sun so any aircraft flying above would see them. They would also take note of the uniforms of the dead and this would send a clear message. He had seen a couple of drones flying overhead and had personally tried to blast one of them out of the sky but had failed dismally as the machine was both too fast and too high. It did cross his mind as to who was operating these machines but these thoughts were soon forgotten in the heat of the moment. At one point he had stalled behind his men and taken a half-hour in a burnt-out shop. There, he and Darwesh had spiked themselves with bola. Both men had slumped in near unconsciousness for 15 minutes but were soon roused by the gunfire and grenade blasts around them. Still dazed and intoxicated, they had made their way out to where Joao had commandeered a police pickup truck that had been abandoned. With Darwesh standing in the back waving the black flag of the Islamic State, they had trundled through the smoking ruins of the town and had caught up with the other men. Now they were near the centre of town and he had already heard the news that some of the other units had arrived and were celebrating. The word was that there was a large gathering of civilians near the port who were effectively trapped there. Joao Quintas grinned and gurned his jaw as he imagined the sheer joy of that final killing spree. The slaughter would be complete and epic in proportion. Their drug-fuelled rampage was almost complete and victory was certain. It had been the greatest achievement of his life. It was as he was driving through the suburb behind the line of men that he noticed a small movement in an alleyway to his left. Immediately he stopped the vehicle and shouted to Darwesh to accompany him as went to investigate. What he expected to be simply a dog or some chickens cowering under a pile of thatching reeds turned out to be two elderly men. Both immobile and terrified, they lay there in the dirt having covered themselves with the great pile of reeds. One of the old men had soiled himself and lay there with tears in his eyes. Joao Quintas marvelled that his men had missed them and had not thought to set fire to the reeds.

The men had been unable to run anywhere and had taken their chance by hiding. But they had been foiled.

"Darwesh!" shouted Joao "Come here and look! I have found some rats hiding in the grass!"

Darwesh arrived and giggled like a girl at the old men's fear. One of them was praying and making the sign of the cross repeatedly on his chest and forehead. Joao kicked the man savagely in his chest and stumbled about laughing manically as the old man fought for breath. When the laughter had subsided, Joao spoke.

"Now, you rats," he said with gritted teeth as he pulled a cigarette lighter from his pocket. "You have a choice. You can either die here in the flames or you can come with us. What will it be?"

Neither man spoke; both remained cowering in the dust and filth. Once again, Joao lashed out with his booted foot, this time kicking the other man in the head. His body went suddenly went limp as he lost consciousness. Seeing there was no choice, the other man spoke.

"We will go with you," he whispered as he sat up.

Joao and Darwesh lifted the two old men, one of which was beginning to come around. They force-marched them to the pickup truck and threw them into the load bed.

"Keep an eye on them," said Joao. "We will take them up to the other men."

It only took 5 minutes to find their way through the deserted and smoking streets before they had caught up with the line of men. Darwesh hooted and waved the flag wildly as they approached. The men stopped their rampage and gathered to see what all the fuss was about.

"Come and see what I have found hiding in the grass, my brothers!" shouted Joao over the roar of a nearby blaze. "I have found a couple of rats!"

The curious men walked over and began laughing hysterically at the pathetic sight of the two geriatrics, skinny and dressed in rags, cowering and whimpering in the back of the truck.

"They thought they would hide from us, my brothers! They thought we would miss them, but here they are!"

One of the men ran forward with his weapon raised and took aim at the prisoners.

"No!" shouted Joao. "We cannot waste our precious bullets on mere rats! Darwesh, drag them both from the truck and take them to the centre of the street. I will show the men what we do with vermin!"

Darwesh did as instructed although his skinny frame could only manage one man at a time. The men, sensing there would be another exciting display, cheered and grinned as the terrified prisoners were dragged across the rough dirt of the street and deposited in the blazing sun. Up ahead there was more gunfire and explosions and Joao grinned as he heard this. He walked up to the young man who had been about to shoot the prisoners and took the machete that hung from his belt.

"Don't worry, my brother," he said quietly, "I shall return your blade as soon as I am done."

Slowly, and with a great show of stagecraft, he swaggered over to where the two old men knelt in the dust. Both were trembling and praying furiously. Joao Quintas took a position that would allow his men a full-frontal view of what was about to happen. Slowly he brought the razor-sharp blade up and it glinted briefly in the sun. Without warning, he brought it down with such force that it took the man's head off in one swing.

The body slumped forward as the head rolled away and the blood squirted in jets from the stump of his wrinkled neck. A roar of applause sounded from the audience. The second man had seen this and, resigned to his fate, turned and looked down at the ground as he waited. He died without a whisper, a few seconds later.

Chapter Thirty-Six.

It was around 1.00 pm when I had finished preparing the vehicles that would be used in the escape convoy. I had sent a drone up and finally decided that the southern beach would be the spot from where we would be uplifted. I had instructed Sarge and Stompie to prepare a line of the toughest vehicles to be parked and warmed ready to go. Rogerio had agreed to drive with me at the front of the convoy while Stompie and Sarge would take up the rear. I had learned that Rogerio was proficient with guns and his courage and determination so far had been admirable. The route had been agreed upon and the plan was put into action. Sarge had done a great job of securing the perimeter and arming the guards. The relevant calls had been made and all that was left was to await the instruction to leave when the choppers were on their way. Stompie, Sarge and I had dressed in camouflage and loaded ourselves with ammunition and weapons. Our combat webbing was filled with as much as we could carry from the armoury. Our path would take us dangerously close to the militants but there was no alternative and I hoped that the element of surprise would work in our favour. Should there be any incoming fire, it would be met with the same from Rogerio in the front and Sarge in the rear. The other cars would follow the leader blindly and simply hope for the best. It was a daring and brazen plan, but it was our only hope. Sitting and waiting for help was no longer an option. There was no one coming to rescue the town. At least not for a few days. Staying put would only mean one thing for us all.

Certain death.

By 2.00 pm the situation at The Hotel Cabo Delgado had deteriorated significantly. The militants who had arrived at the centre of town had realised there was a hotel of foreigners on the nearby hill and had regrouped and begun their assault. At first, it had been potshots but they soon took on a much more determined and dedicated approach. Stompie and I had watched it happen from the viewing deck and a cold feeling of dread had filled me despite the brutal heat of the day. We had watched as the initial celebrations at having reached the centre of town had begun until the inevitable had happened. One of the men had been pointing at the hill on which the hotel was built in among the trees. It soon became an object of interest and we had watched as a discussion had been held in broad daylight.

Through the binoculars, Stompie and I watched a group of them jump into a battered pickup truck and drive towards the base of the hill below us.

"Here they come..." I said quietly.

"Yup," said Stompie. "I could take a few of them out even from this distance. I know I could."

"No," I replied. "It would bring a whole lot of unwanted attention. With any luck, they haven't told the others about us. We need to lie low as long as possible. But you're right. They're coming."

It did not take long for the siege to start. Stompie and I made our way downstairs and I ran out to the guardhouse to alert Sarge that we would very likely come under direct attack within the next hour. But it happened a lot quicker than that. Minutes after the guards at the perimeter had been alerted of the advance, it started. Almost immediately the bullets started whining and ricocheting through the upper beams of the building like crazed hornets. Hidden by the dense foliage and trees on the lower reaches of the hill, the militants intensified their assault and I knew it was only a matter of time before the mortars and grenades would start landing. I ran into the restaurant to find the terrified occupants shrieking and trembling with fear. Doing my best to keep them calm, I spoke.

"Now it's important that all you all stay low. Get down on the floor and stay there!" I shouted. "We will be leaving in a convoy very soon. The helicopters are on their way and a collection point has already been arranged. Please try to remain calm. We have things under control."

But in my heart, I knew that was a blatant lie. Control was the very thing I was rapidly losing and it would only get worse. I ran to the armoury and made a final call to the Colonel. It took a minute to get through but eventually the phone was picked up.

"Talk to me, Green," he said.

"We are under direct attack!" I shouted into the bulky phone "It's a matter of time until the perimeter is breached and the bombardment begins. We need to move now! Requesting permission to go ahead with this urgently!"

I had sent the drone up 20 minutes beforehand and had decided on the south beach for the evacuation spot. With the militants now approaching and actually on the hill below us, we would effectively be running the gauntlet. Still, it was better than staying put and waiting.

"Affirmative, Green," said the voice on the line. "Go for evacuation now. I repeat, go for evacuation!"

The message was clear. The guests were to make their way into the parking lot and board the vehicles. It was time to leave Palma.

I made a quick radio call to Sarge, Stompie and Rogerio and then rushed to the restaurant to meet them. By then the guests were in a state of pure terror and some of them had wet themselves with fear. There was no time for smiles or pleasantries anymore. I shouted at the lot of them as I forced them to their feet. The majority were happy enough to move but many needed coercion. The entire group of us moved down the stairs and into the lush gardens of the front of the hotel. From there it was only 30 metres to the parking lot where the vehicles were waiting. One by one we bundled them into the vehicles. It was as we did this that the first of the mortars began landing in the garden around us. Shrieking with fear, Penny Riddle almost collapsed to the ground but I grabbed her by her wrist and bundled her into the back seat of the front vehicle.

"Hurry up!" I shouted as the last of them climbed in.

Finally, everyone was in the vehicles and I made a radio call to Stompie and Sarge in the rear vehicle.

"Right. Time to move. You confident with our route?"

"I sure am," replied Stompie. "Ready when you are."

Sarge made the radio call to the front gate and I buried the accelerator of the front vehicle. The powerful land cruiser lurched forward and sped down the hill with the other vehicles following close behind. It was strangely liberating to be on the move after having being trapped in the hotel grounds for so long. It seemed somewhat surreal and for a moment it was as if our attackers no longer existed. But they did, and the bullets came almost immediately. Within seconds the cab was filled with the deafening clatter of the AR-15 as Rogerio pulled round after round at our hidden attackers. The militants had plenty of coverage given the amount of foliage and trees on the way down the hill. I kept my eye on the prize although I could hear Rogerio shouting each time he saw a new face poke out from behind a tree. Rogerio shot and shot again and the tyres howled and crunched on the tarmac as we wove our way down the hill around the treacherous corners. Rogerio shouted again as he found one of the militants and I saw the bullet hit him in the stomach before he dropped into the tall grass. It was a battle cry of triumph and even through the manic screaming of Penny Riddle, I couldn't help but feel proud of the man. Here was a simple hotel manager who was prepared to fight like a soldier. His bravery was astounding. But the bullets kept coming and I heard them clang into the side of the vehicle as we reached the bottom of the hill. I took the right turn half expecting to hear the cry of one of my passengers but I made the corner with only the screeching of the tyres as the vehicle almost tipped over. But it was as I straightened out to run the gauntlet down past the municipal building that I heard the vehicle behind me take a barrage of bullets. It was as if they had come out of nowhere and I felt sure that many had died. My fears turned out to be true, when a few seconds later I watched the vehicle in my rear view mirror as it veered off the road and smashed into a building on the right. I forced myself to concentrate on the road ahead but I saw the explosion as it burst into flames. All aboard that vehicle were surely dead. I could only hope that the bullets had killed them before the flames. But there was no time to pause and I floored the accelerator once again.

The suddenness of our break out escape attempt had taken the attackers by surprise. I reached 90 km per hour as I sped through the central streets eventually taking a sharp left after the port. All the while, Rogerio pumped the bullets out of the front passenger window. Keeping an eye on the road ahead, I sped off towards the south beach while watching the rearview mirror to see how many had made it. We had already lost one vehicle and the true horror of our situation was becoming all too apparent. Suddenly an armed man jumped out not 30 metres ahead of us. He stood there with a checkered scarf around his lower face and took aim straight at us. There was no way Rogerio could shoot back from that angle so I feigned a leftward trajectory with my driving to give him the impression I was trying to avoid him. Although the ruse worked, he still took at least 5 shots at the front of the speeding vehicle and suddenly there were three holes in the windscreen. Tiny shards of flying glass filled the air and my vision was instantly compromised. The situation had become somewhat surreal and everything appeared to me in slow motion. At the very last moment, I swung the wheel to the right and the heavy vehicle smashed into the startled attacker. For a split second, I saw his terrified eyes he was slammed by two and a half tonnes of speeding metal and disappeared under the chassis. The vehicle lurched and jumped over his body and I almost lost control for a second. But apart from the holes in the windscreen and a lot of steam emanating from the punctured radiator, the vehicle carried on moving and finally I could see our target area in front of us.

"We're almost there!" I shouted over the hissing and screaming.

But there was no reply and I turned in my seat quickly to look at Rogerio. The man had taken a bullet to his chest. Wheezing and coughing pink froth, he valiantly held the weapon out the window although I saw the huge amount of blood that had soaked his shirt. Still, he tried to keep the gun up and aimed out to the side. There was no helping him by that stage and I knew I needed to keep my passengers calm. It was 10 seconds later when his body slumped backwards and the gun dropped into the footwell. The vehicle raced onwards towards what looked like a football field on the right. There was a huge crowd of people who had gathered near the far concrete stands and appeared to be sheltering there.

I knew then how terrified they must have been as they awaited their fate. A few hundred metres ahead was the spot where I had chosen to hunker down for the evacuation process. The site offered easy access to the beach while there was a series of abandoned buildings nearby that would give us cover while we waited for the choppers. Racing onwards while acutely aware of the vehicles behind me, I scanned the area ahead for a place to pull over. I found it in the form of an old parking lot near the front of the buildings. There were a few palm trees in the space and the sand of the beach had encroached up onto the concrete. I slowed the vehicle and skidded sideways to a halt. It was then that Penny Riddle realised what had happened to Rogerio. Her high pitched scream filled the interior of the cab and she pulled and tugged at his limp body from the back seat. I turned in my seat and grabbed her hands as I tried to calm her.

"He's gone, Penny!" I shouted. "He died protecting us! We need to leave now and get into cover. Hurry!"

Seeing she was in a state of profound shock, I opened the door and jumped out to run around the vehicle. I flung her door open and dragged her out of the vehicle as quickly as I could. By then her body had gone totally limp and I feared for her. As I moved I took a final look at Rogerio slumped in the front seat. The blood from the chest wound had covered his lower body completely but his eyes still reflected the determination and courage he had shown since the attack began. The crunching of the tyres of the other vehicles arriving filled the air as I made my way into the abandoned buildings and into safety. Panting and sweating heavily, I set Penny resting against a wall while I went back to the entrance with my weapon raised to give the arrivals cover while they disembarked from the vehicles. I held my breath as they arrived but was relieved to see the final vehicle with Sarge and Stompie in the front. At a glance, both seemed to have survived the short journey although their vehicle was peppered with bullet holes. They leapt out and got straight on with the task of corralling the remaining passengers of the other cars into the safety of the abandoned building with Penny Riddle. It was only then that I noticed that another one of the vehicles had failed to make it. Before I could ask, Stompie told me it had been shot out on the way down past the football pitch and had veered off into a ditch.

"If there was anyone left alive, they won't be by now," he said grimly.

Sad as it was, I knew he was right. I could only pray that whoever it was had died quickly. The vehicle was out of sight and there was no way to effect a rescue attempt. That would have been a suicide mission. The fact was we had made it to the extraction point but had lost two vehicles. In the theatre of war, this was a good overall result. I stood guard as the remaining guests were moved into cover. One of them had taken a bullet to his left arm. Thankfully it had travelled through the door of the vehicle so had lost much of its velocity and the wound was superficial. Sarge attended to him whilst I waited for Stompie to come out. He appeared a minute later dripping with sweat but still with the crazed look of a fighter on his face. It made for a fearsome sight.

"What's the story here?" he asked with a wheezing voice.

"Quiet for now," I said as I scanned the area. "But that'll change soon enough."

At that moment I heard the first of the choppers approaching. It flew in from the east having made a wide turn over the ocean. *Thank God*, I thought to myself. I watched as it circled above us and I saw the eyes of the armed men aboard. They had followed their instructions and knew exactly where the pick-up point would be. I watched as it slowly descended nearby, its rotors throwing up great stinging clouds of sand as it came down. I shouted at Stompie over the racket and told him to go back inside and return with 6 of the guests. I would remain where I was and offer cover in case of any attackers. The last thing we needed was a wrecked helicopter burning on the beach. The situation was beyond desperate and I was determined to avoid that. Stompie acted fast and I watched out of the corner of my eye as the huddled and crouched figures ran from the building behind me towards the chopper. He stood by as they were hauled into the cabin and ran back as it lifted off. *How many more to go?* I thought. True to his word, the Colonel had planned well and I watched as the second helicopter came around following the same path as the first. But instead of simply landing where the first one had, this one went over us and flew towards the crowd of people at the soccer pitch. *What the fuck is he doing?* I thought.

The helicopter flew to the centre of the soccer pitch and hovered there for a while before descending slightly. Almost immediately a large section of the crowd of locals who had gathered there rushed towards it. As if sensing danger, the pilot pulled away to the right and started to gain altitude. It was then that I saw the burst of gunfire from the cabin. The automatic fire sent a spray of bullets into the terrified crowd and I watched in disbelief and horror as several of the people went down. The crowd, now more panicked than ever, ran away in all directions and dispersed. I could not believe what I had just seen. I watched as the helicopter pulled up and away and headed back towards us to the landing spot.

"What was that all about?" shouted Stompie above the racket. "Those are civilians!"

I shook my head as I lit a cigarette and watched.

"I've got no fucking idea," I said. "But the Colonel and I will be having a word about that if I ever see him again."

I watched as a signal was given from the pilot of the chopper. His raised fingers indicated that he would only be able to carry four passengers. Stompie saw this and wasted no time running back into the building to get more people out. Sarge joined me at the entrance and positioned himself to give covering fire. Once again I watched out of the corner of my eye as the guests were taken out to the waiting chopper and loaded. Before long, it took off and I stood there waiting for the next one. But the vision of what I had seen on the soccer pitch stayed in my mind and refused to budge. It made no sense at all. *Had they seen something I hadn't? Surely if there had been militants in the crowd, they would have been known? Fuck knows, Green. You have a whole lot more to worry about right now.*

Chapter Thirty-Seven.

It was 3.45 pm when the radio on Joao Quintas' belt squawked. He and his men were rapidly approaching the centre of town and he was already starting to celebrate. But the news was not good and it seemed that his day would drag out a little longer than anticipated. The message had been clear. A group of foreigners had escaped from the hotel and had made their way down to the south side of the port near the beach. There was an evacuation effort taking place and these foreigners were responsible for the deaths of at least three fighters. Given his unit's proximity to this place, he had been instructed to head there immediately and stop the evacuation in its tracks. Joao Quintas knew full well that an image of a dead foreigner was a powerful message to send to the world and would be extremely valuable to their standing and notoriety. The fact that this would delay his triumphant arrival in the town angered him but he knew he must obey the order. Sulking like a child, he walked into a looted shop and poured a pile of bola onto the dirty counter. Without using his blade he dropped his face to the wooden surface and snorted loudly. His nose came up covered with white powder but the boost was unlike anything he had ever snorted. It was almost as powerful as the needle. Suddenly the irritating order was no more than a minor irritation and he decided that it may well accord him even more glory at the end of the day. He might even bag a trophy of a white person to show off to the others. Rejuvenated and boosted, he bounded out of the shop and ran to where the pickup was parked.

Using the hooter, he got the attention of the men and they gathered around, all somewhat confused. Once they were all present, Joao jumped onto the load bed and addressed them.

"My brothers," he shouted, "I have just received a message that there is a group of foreigners who have escaped from a hotel in town. They are gathered near the beach in the south, not far from here, and are being evacuated by helicopter. We have been ordered to go there and stop this from happening. I know it will come as a great disappointment and I am sure you are all tired. But, my brothers, there are many white people there. I am sure you would be pleased at the prospect of removing the head of a white man. Would you like that?"

The men cheered and one of them shot a round into the air to signify his willingness. Joao could see that there was still a lot of fight left in them.

"We must go immediately, my brothers," he shouted. "Jump in the back of the truck, as many as you can. The rest of you remain here and continue making your way to town. I will be there to meet you shortly. Allahu Akbar!"

The load bed of the old pickup was filled and the springs creaked under the load as they made off down the dirt street towards the beach. Ahead of them was a football pitch where he had been told was a crowd of civilians. But his instruction had been clear. He was to go and put a stop to the evacuation of the foreigners. Still buzzing from the effects of the drugs, Joao Quintas floored the accelerator and with the black flag of the Islamic State billowing above, they set off in a cloud of dust. The old truck sped down the dirt road at a dangerous pace and finally came up next to the football pitch. Lying in the centre of the patchy dry grass were several bodies. Joao Quintas frowned as he drove past and wondered how this had happened. The scintillating sight of the huge group of civilians cowering near the concrete stands was almost too much for him to ignore but he pressed on regardless thinking only of the order and the prize that lay at the end of the road. Up ahead he saw a jumble of vehicles parked near a roofless, abandoned building near the beach. He knew this had to be the place. But it was as he was approaching that the gunfire started. Almost immediately there was a shriek from the back of the truck followed by shouting and retaliatory gunfire. Joao Quintas had almost driven into a trap. The foreigners were armed and were actively shooting at his vehicle. Thinking fast, he made a quick left turn and headed along the far side of a low wall that ran on the left-hand side of the road. There were the remnants of a fish packing factory there but it was the wall that Joao knew would work in his favour. It would offer cover for the men whilst they disrupted and prevented the evacuation. There might also be a chance to take out a helicopter and this was something that appealed to him. Racing along the inside of the wall with the shell of the old factory to his left, Joao pressed on as far he could until he was 50 metres diagonally across from where the gunfire was emanating.

Ahead of him was the beach where the helicopters had been landing. The rough tarmac was covered with rusted tins and litter and he pulled the handbrake to bring the old truck to a halt. The men leapt from the load bay of the truck and took up positions along the length of the wall. There was the sound of gunfire coming from the abandoned building but it seemed there were only a few shooters. With his group of men, Joao felt confident he would be more than able to eliminate this threat and prevent any more evacuations. Without wasting time, and acutely aware of the risk, he jumped from the vehicle and crawled up to the wall where Darwesh was sheltering. He looked to his left and his right and noted with pride that his men were laying on the attack thick and hard. The evacuees, however, had the advantage of the abandoned building from which to take cover. Against the deafening crackle of gunfire all around, Joao heard a different sound. He glanced upwards and out to sea. It was then that he saw the helicopters. They hovered a few hundred metres out and it appeared they were awaiting a signal to approach and land.

"Helicopter!" he screamed at his men. "It must not land!"

The men heard his cry and duly commenced to focus their attention on the hovering machines. The low wall offered excellent cover and one by one, the men would poke their heads and weapons up and take random potshots out to sea. The arrival of his men had seriously disrupted the evacuation and this pleased him greatly. But it was then when despite the firefight, that one of the choppers flew in and descended to land on the beach not a hundred metres away. Raging with anger, Joao bellowed at the men to increase their fire. As if on cue, they were met with a barrage of bullets and one of his men 20 metres down the wall fell with a fatal chest wound. Their opponents in the abandoned building were putting up a spirited fight and it seemed they were a formidable enemy. The men, seeing one of their comrades killed, fell into a state of disarray and panic. Instead of taking the time to aim correctly, they fell into the typical untrained method of blindly holding their weapons over the wall and firing randomly. It was a cowardly thing he had been warned about, but now it was actually happening on his watch.

"Take aim and fire correctly!" he screamed.

But it was to no avail. The men had been spooked by the killing of one of their own and continued the panicked and useless random fire. Their opponents were not simple unarmed civilians, these were dangerous armed men who meant business. While this chaos had erupted, the helicopter had landed and Joao poked his head up to see a group of people being led from the building towards the waiting aircraft. Enraged and facing defeat, Joao Quintas raised his own AK47 and took aim at the defenders of the building. As he did so, a section of the wall less than 30 centimetres from his head exploded in a cloud of white plaster dust. He dropped back to the safety of the cover of the wall and swore loudly. By then the helicopter had flown off and the second one was coming in to land. But then there was a shout from one of the men down the line. He had jumped up and removed a rocket-propelled grenade launcher from the back of the pickup truck. His brave fighter was busy arming the deadly weapon and Joao felt a surge of pride as he realized what the man was about to do. He was going to blow the helicopter up as it sat awaiting its passengers.

"Yes!" he screamed. "Shoot the helicopter now!'

The man smiled back at him as he inserted the grenade into the end of the launcher. By then the helicopter was being loaded with yet another group of people and Joao feared it might be too late. But at that moment, the man gave him the thumbs-up signal and stood up raising the RPG launcher at the same time. Unable to control his curiosity, and not wanting to miss out on this moment of glory, Joao Quintas poked his head up once again above the wall, just enough to see the fireball that would surely come.

Chapter Thirty-Eight.

I saw the old pickup coming from a distance. Seeing the billowing black flag held on the back of it, I knew it was bad news. The militants had witnessed our escape and were coming for us. They would attempt to block the evacuation and threaten the choppers. This was something we could not allow. Sarge and I wasted no time and began firing at it before it had even parked. The driver took immediate action and moved to his left beyond a low wall near an old factory building. I saw one bullet hit one of the men on the back of the truck and watched him drop into the crowd on the load bed. This spooked them and the driving became more erratic and dangerous. Eventually, the truck skidded to a halt on the far side of the low wall, not 50 metres from where we were based. The driver had thought well and immediately the men on the truck leapt off and took cover behind the wall. With the helicopters hovering just offshore, there was no time to waste and we laid on the fire whenever we saw a head pop up from behind the wall. Sarge was an excellent shot and I watched as one of the men took a bullet to the chest. The shot would have been fatal and I spoke when there was a lull in the racket.

"Nice shot, Sarge," I said. "He 's not gonna be going home to tell his mother any stories."

The big man grinned at me and it seemed as if he was enjoying himself. He appeared to be in his element. The helicopter pilot, seeing we were giving effective covering fire, decided to come in to land. It was risky but there was no alternative. It was getting late and soon the sun would set. After that, there would be no more flights so it was vital to keep the flow of evacuees moving. This was a deadly standoff and failure was simply not an option. I knew we had limited ammunition compared to our attackers and we had to use it sparingly and effectively. But the death of one of the attackers' comrades seemed to have spooked the militants. I watched as random weapons were held over the wall and fired blindly. I grinned as I recalled seeing this during the war all those years ago. It was typical of hysterical and panicked men. They were losing control and had not anticipated the spirited defence we were giving. We kept the covering fire as I watched Stompie run out with another group of terrified guests.

Crouching down beneath the blades of the chopper, they rushed forward into the stinging sand that blasted all around them as they made their way into the waiting aircraft. But my growing confidence was misguided when a few seconds later I saw a man stand up from behind the wall with a rocket-propelled grenade launcher. My heart sank as I realised it was child's play from then on. Only an imbecile could miss the static figure of the chopper as it waited on the beach. The guests were in the process of being bundled into the cabin and once again things appeared to me in slow motion. *No, please God, no!* I knew from bitter experience the devastating power of the RPG. It would blow the helicopter to smithereens and scuttle any hope we had of escape. There were still several guests to evacuate and this was threatening it all. We would be left with a dwindling ammunition supply and would surely perish. I aimed at the man with the RPG and took a deep breath as I prepared to pull the trigger. The sights of the AR-15 were focussed on his head and I said a silent prayer as I pulled the trigger. But all that happened was a dull click. *You fucking idiot! You've only gone and run out of ammunition. Stupid cunt!* Feeling hopeless, I dropped my aim and prepared to reload. But it was then that I saw Sarge to my right. He stood deadly still with his weapon raised. It was as if he was in some sort of trance. Once again it all seemed to be slow motion but I saw his trigger finger as it pulled. Suddenly there was an almighty explosion combined with a vacuum of air and a physical blast to my chest. But it was not the chopper that exploded. The fireball came from the opposite side of the wall where the man with the launcher had been standing. I could hardly believe my own eyes. Sarge had aimed at and hit the nozzle of the grenade that was mounted on the end of the launcher. The wall exploded and great chunks of concrete and dust filled the sky. The bodies of at least 4 of our attackers were blown into the air. It was as astounding as it was incredible.

"Did you hit the rocket?" I shouted at Sarge.

"No!" he replied with a wide grin, "I hit the grenade before he could launch!"

"Bravo, Sarge!" I shouted as I reloaded. "You might have just saved the day!"

The massive hole in the wall was littered with body parts and my ears were still ringing from the concussion. I could only imagine our attackers were now in a state of shock and would be thoroughly demoralised. Those of them that were left that was. Sarge had single-handedly saved us all and for that, we owed him our lives. Stompie returned from the landing zone and shouted at us both as he ran in to collect more guests.

"Fucking hell!" he shouted as he ran in. "You made quick work of those fuckers!"

"Wasn't me!" I shouted as I flicked the cigarette away. "You can thank Sarge for that!"

By then the next helicopter was coming in to land. My spirits were lifted once again as I saw a chance that we would actually prevail and get out of the hell that we had found ourselves in.

The devastation that Sarge had caused by shooting out the RPG launcher had caused serious disarray to our attackers. It was some time before I saw any activity but even that was in the form of the random gunfire from weapons held above the wall as they had done before the explosion. More and more my confidence grew as the guests were ferried out and flown to safety by the choppers. But it was when the last of the guests were on their way to the chopper with Stompie that I saw the skinny man pop up and take aim directly at the group. I lifted my weapon and took aim at him. Through the sights, I saw that he was young and slightly effeminate looking. Still, the man was brandishing a loaded AK47 and was about to pull the trigger on terrified, innocent civilians. With my sights trained on his face, I pulled the trigger.

Chapter Thirty-Nine.

Joao Quintas shouted out as he urged the man with the rocket launcher to fire at the helicopter. In his mind, he pictured the roaring fireball that would ensue once the grenade struck the aircraft. But his vision of glory was destroyed when out of the blue, the immediate area around the man exploded in a violent maelstrom of hellfire. Joao had no time to think as he and the men around him were blown backwards and sent rolling on the filthy concrete behind the wall. The explosion had damaged their ears and singed their hair but it was the absolute carnage done to the men that shocked him. They had been ripped to shreds and there were body parts littered all around. In his slightly concussed mind, Joao counted the dead. There must have been at least 7 fighters killed. *What had gone wrong? What had happened? Surely the defenders could not have shot the missile itself?* He wiped the dust from his face as his senses gradually returned along with a seething rage. Darwesh, who had also been blown to the side by the blast coughed and propped himself up against the wall next to him. He sat there with a slightly confused look in his eyes and wiped the dust from his face. Both men picked up their guns and did their best to recover after what had been a shocking development. Joao did a quick headcount of the men left alive after the blast. There were only seven when there had been at least fourteen when they had arrived. Joao took a deep breath and his fury rose like a tsunami. Seven of his best fighters wiped out in an instant. All because of a ragtag group of escapees holed up in an abandoned building.

"Bastards!" he screamed. "Bastards!"

Joao turned around and got to his knees while still carefully keeping his head below the line of what was left of the wall. He heard the sound of yet another helicopter landing and this only served to infuriate him further. The blast had had a sobering effect on him and even through his rage, he could feel the fear and terror returning.

"Bastards!" he screamed again as he checked his weapon.

Joao Quintas popped his head up and let off a burst of fire towards the abandoned building.

At that moment he saw two men. Both were tall, one white, the other black. There was another shorter white man leading the escapees to the helicopter. In his mind, he had already blamed the two defenders as being the ones who had caused the explosion. He dropped his head and cursed again as he paused and waited a few seconds before continuing firing. He was coldly determined to take revenge for the death of his compatriots. Sensing his master's anguish, Darwesh Gonzales decided he would do something to ingratiate himself further to his master. He checked his weapon, which up till then had not been used. Seeing it was in order, he too got to his knees and prepared to fire. He waited until Joao had let off another bust of fire then popped his head up and took aim. This was the last thing Darwesh Gonzales ever did. The bullet from the AR-15 hit him in the centre of the neck, just below his Adam's apple. His body was instantly slammed backwards and he landed with a violent thud on the concrete behind the wall. He lay there staring up at the darkening sky in a state of mild confusion. *What had just happened?* He did not know. Horror filled Joao Quintas' mind as he saw his lover blown from his kneeling position onto the concrete behind the wall. He immediately dropped his weapon and crawled over to check on the young man.

The last 90 seconds of Darwesh Gonzales' life were deeply unpleasant. With his spinal cord severed, he lay there unable to move his limbs. gurgling and slowly drowning in his own blood that poured into his lungs as he stared up at the face he idolised. Time and time again he tried to tell Joao that he loved him, but the words simply would not come out. Instead, he lay there with his eyes filled with tears, blinking repeatedly, until the darkness encroached and everything went black. Darwesh Gonzales's young and unfortunate life had just ended. Joao Quintas howled in anguish and turned to see who had made the fatal shot. There was no doubt in his mind. It had been the tall white man.

Chapter Forty.

———————❦———————

The satellite phone vibrated in my pocket as Stompie was making his way back from the landing site. By then the sun was setting and darkness was starting to encroach. The number on the small screen was one I recognised immediately. It was Colonel Callum Jackson. I ran into the building to better hear what he had to say. Sitting against the wall where I had left her was Penny Riddle. Stompie was squatting near her and was busy opening a bottle of water for her to drink.

"This is Green," I said.

"Green, this Colonel Jackson," said the voice. "I regret to inform you that there will be no further evacuation flights today. Our aircraft do not have the avionics capability for night flight and none of our pilots are qualified for night flight either."

I paused as I held the chunky phone to my ear and stared at the figures of Stompie and Penny in front of me. I could not believe what I was hearing. With my voice low, I turned away and spoke.

"There are only four of us left here," I said between gritted teeth. "We have successfully evacuated all of the surviving guests and we are here with limited ammunition. Are you seriously telling me that you are abandoning us here?"

"I have no choice, Green," said the Colonel, his voice growing louder with frustration. "I repeat, our aircraft have no night flight avionics and neither are our pilots licensed."

I saw the red rage of fury clouding my vision and my stomach churned with fear.

"Your pilots saw fit to get their gunners to shoot into a crowd of civilians," I growled. "Are you aware of that?"

"Of course, I am aware of that, Green," was the shouted reply. "There were militants in that crowd. It was an act of war. You should know that!"

"Bullshit. There are four of us left here," I said calmly. "We have limited ammunition and no means of escape. What would you have us do, Colonel?"

"Green!" came the reply, "This conversation can serve no further purpose. You are on your own. Make contact in the morning and we will take it from there. Goodbye."

I hung up and turned back to look at Stompie who was still tending to Penny Riddle. Just beyond the wall, I could hear the gunshots as Sarge was still defending our position. I was as stunned as I was furious. After all we had done, the four of us would be left in Palma to defend ourselves. There would be no rescue flight for us. I stared down at my own ammunition and saw that it was woefully depleted. This would also be true for both Stompie and Sarge. At that moment, if I could have gotten my hands on Colonel Callum Jackson, I would have ripped his head off. *Get yourself together, Green. Now is not the time for those kinds of thoughts. You need to think and think fucking fast!*

"Stompie!" I called out "I need a word please."

I watched as he stood up and walked over towards me. Seeing something was badly wrong, he began to speak but I held my finger to my lips to silence him. I took him outside where I called Sarge over so I could speak to them without Penny hearing us. The news came as a heavy blow to the two exhausted men and for the first time, I saw real fear in Stompie's eyes. There was still random gunfire from behind the wall although this had calmed down somewhat since the explosion.

"So what the fuck are we supposed to do now?" asked Stompie, his grizzled face a picture of exasperation.

"We have no choice," I replied grimly. "We don't have enough ammo to last us another hour let alone the night. Soon enough there'll be another hundred of these bastards arriving and then we are *fucked*. We have to run. We have to head south on foot. We must hold off for another 15 minutes until darkness, then we must leave immediately."

The two men stared at me with wide eyes but I could tell they knew I was right. Staying put was simply not an option. It was only a matter of time before we were overrun and what would happen after that was simply unthinkable. Stompie nodded his head in understanding and spoke.

"What should we do right now?" he asked.

"Prepare your ammo and kit," I said. "Tell Penny we are going to have to make a run for it. I am going to take a look at my GPS device and decide on the best way out. Sarge, you go and find a way out of the back of this building. Hopefully the cowardly fuckers will think we are simply hiding inside and it'll take them another hour to find the courage to come in looking for us. With a bit of luck, we'll be a long way from here by then. I'm sorry guys, we did well, but now it's down to us whether we get through this night alive. We need to go, and soon."

Chapter Forty-One.

Joao Quintas howled with anguish as he cradled the head of his dead lover. In his mind, he wished he had told Darwesh that he loved him before he had been so cruelly taken by the tall white man. The blood from the hole in Darwesh's neck soaked his combat fatigues and his head fell backwards from his shattered spine. In his mind, he swore an act of bloody and terrible vengeance on the man who had done this. No matter what, he would take his revenge. He placed the head of the limp body on the concrete and closed the blank, staring eyes one last time. Seeing his obvious distress, the men afforded him some privacy as he mourned. Finally, he removed his jacket and placed it over the young man's head to stop the flies from gathering. He knelt there for another 15 minutes by which time the sky was darkening and the night was encroaching. The firefight had calmed down somewhat and the defenders were now nowhere to be seen. Neither were there any more helicopters arriving. Perhaps it was now too late. But the defenders and the murderer of Darwesh were still there. There were at least three of them and Joao Quintas swore he would make good his retribution if it was the very last thing he did. It was a solemn promise he made to himself and he would stop at nothing to fulfill it. The celebrations of the glory of having taken the town would have to wait. Now there was something far more important to take care of.

Chapter Forty-Two.

"What about Rogerio?" asked Penny Riddle, her eyes wide and mad looking. "He's still out there in the car!"

"There's nothing we can do, Penny," said Stompie. "We have to go, now!"

At that moment Sarge walked in from the rear of the building.

"I found an exit," he said. "The old door was rotten and all I needed to do was kick it in."

"Good man," I said. "Now collect everything you can carry and let's go!"

By then the interior of the abandoned building was pitch dark. We made our way through using only the light from a penlight torch. The rear of the building was overgrown with vegetation and the light was even worse there. We crept along in the darkness with me leading and the others following closely behind. I had taken a good look at the GPS device and had determined that the safest route out of town was to head south, parallel with the beach but staying well away from it. When the militants discovered we had gone, which I hoped would take some time, they would immediately assume we had headed down the beach and I knew they would send a unit of men down there to find us. They would more than likely use a vehicle and would be armed to the teeth. Going down the beach would be a death sentence. The only alternative was to head in a south-westerly direction and keep going until we met the old coastal road the pilot had told me of. Of course, we would not use that road either. The plan was to stay in the bush. The jungle would offer the cover we needed. With any luck, the men would simply give up on us and go on to join their comrades in the town. But that was something we could not count on. There was a long hard journey ahead of us and I was sleep-deprived and wired to boot. Our limited ammunition dictated that we should avoid contact with humans for as long as possible.

The GPS was a lifesaver and would guide us accordingly. If the militants did try to track us, I would make sure it would be difficult. As instructed, I would attempt to make a call to the Colonel the following day, but I was also aware that the satellite phone was already running low on battery and may not last the night. The worst possible situation would be that we would have to make the 90 km walk through the bush to Mocimboa Da Praia. Given the average speed of walking, this would take up to 3 days. This was assuming the terrain was manageable. I knew very well that there would be great difficulties and challenges along the way. Exhausted, thirsty and in a state of shock, I wondered if Penny Riddle would be able to make the journey. Still, I had more immediate worries, namely getting as much distance between the town and ourselves as soon as possible. Walking slowly but steadily, we made our way south and gradually the sound of the surf faded as we moved inland. The jungle seemed to consume us and it hindered our progress as I stumbled into vines and over tree roots. Still, we kept as quiet as we possibly could and soon there were no more sounds from the town. It was a blessed relief not to hear gunfire and explosions, although our surroundings were dark and eerie. It was surprising to note that given her previous hysteria, Penny Riddle soldiered on without complaining. I did hear the occasional encouraging whisper from Stompie behind me. For two hours we walked, groping and stumbling our way through the darkness until suddenly the moon began to rise. This was a blessed relief and it gave us an idea of our immediate surroundings. The vines and branches of the trees looked like the limbs of demons and the heat under the canopy was intense and still. It was around 8.00 pm when we reached the abandoned coastal road. The sandy soil of its surface was scattered with natural debris and leaves but I worried that we would leave a trail as we crossed it. I told Sarge to make sure our trail was covered so anyone coming down the road would be unaware that we had crossed at that point. Finally, there was a feeling that we had actually made progress and maybe, just maybe, we were safe. I paused the march so we could rest and drink a little from our water bottles. I told everyone to use it sparingly as I had no idea when or where we would find more. My bones ached with fatigue as the trudge continued. The heat was like a tangible blanket lying over the land. I pulled out the GPS device to see that we had made 8 kilometres from the town. We had indeed crossed the old road and were now at least 5 kilometres inland. There were no roads there, only a series of rolling hills that continued all the way to Mocimboa Da Praia.

No one spoke as we walked, instead, there was only panting and grunting from the crew as we bumped into vines and stepped into hidden ruts and holes. It was at 10.30 pm when I called a halt to the march and told everyone to sit down to rest.

"We've done well," I said. "With any luck, our attackers will have abandoned us and gone into the town for a party. I want to congratulate you all on your bravery."

In the moonlight, I could see that the sweat-stained and washed-out looking Penny Riddle was barely able to keep her eyes open. I nodded at Stompie to assist her and make her as comfortable as possible so she could sleep. She had been unusually quiet until then and I was worried for her. I was however impressed with her grit in getting that far. I had not expected she was capable of it but I had been proved wrong. As Stompie tended to her, Sarge came over and took a seat near where I sat.

"Do you think they'll try to track us?" I asked.

"I don't know boss," he replied, his eyes glowing in the moonlight. "But if they do, I will know."

"How will you know?" I asked.

"In the light of day, I will keep a look out behind us. There are hills everywhere and I will use the binoculars as we go. Also, they may make mistakes, and I will hear them."

I took a sip of water from the bottle and stared into the darkness.

"Let's hope that doesn't happen," I said.

"Yes, boss," he replied quietly. "Let us pray that doesn't happen."

Stompie returned a few minutes later and told us that Penny had fallen into a deep sleep. He had rummaged in his webbing and had found a pack of cereal bars. He gave us one each and we sat in grim silence as we chewed on the sticky grain-filled bars. All of us were exhausted and even the extreme discomfort of our current location could not mask the relief we all felt to be away from the gunfire and shelling. Fighting to keep my eyes open, I spoke.

"Who's feeling strong enough to take the first watch?" I asked.

"I'll do it," said Stompie.

"Good," I replied. "Wake me in 2 hours and I'll take over. For now, I just need to close my eyes."

I leant against the tree behind me on the damp earth. All around me the mosquitoes buzzed and stung but I cared not. I fell asleep within 30 seconds.

Chapter Forty-Three.

It was a full hour later by the time Joao Quintas and his men burst into the abandoned building where the escapees from the hotel had hidden. By then it was completely dark and they used their torches as they blasted their way in with grenades thrown in first. The ensuing explosions seemed to have no effect and when finally, they cautiously moved into what was left of the building, they found nothing. They made their way through the rubble to see the back door had been forced open and it became clear then what had happened.

"They have made a run for it," said Joao, his eyes burning with rage "My brothers, these men have hurt us badly and have killed many of our comrades. We must follow them, find them, and deal with them accordingly. Who is with me?"

The remaining men all made clear their willingness to follow their commander and they stood awaiting further instructions. But Joao Quintas was feeling empty and fearful and he knew both he and his men needed more bola to continue.

"Wait here," he said, "I will return shortly."

Wasting no time, he ran out into the darkness at the front of the building and made his way towards the bullet-riddled pickup truck. All around were the dead and the sight of Darwesh with the jacket over his head pained him deeply. He climbed into the truck and retrieved his bag which contained the stash of bola. Before heading back to the men, he snorted a huge amount and sneezed violently. He saw the blood in his saliva once again but he ignored this and took a brief look at himself in the rear view mirror. Satisfied, he slammed the door closed and took the run back to his men. As he went he heard the manic gunfire coming from the centre of the town. He knew that his comrades were celebrating and killing more civilians for pleasure. It pained him that he would miss this but he had some very serious business to attend to. With his thoughts racing, he made his way back through the building and called his men out into the moonlight.

"We need to go, and go now," he said through gritted teeth "It is dark and these people will be unable to move far. I am certain we will catch up with them very quickly. If you think I have shown you displays of cruelty in the past, rest assured my brothers, when we catch these men, you will witness something that you have never seen before."

Joao Quintas proceeded to hand out liberal amounts of bola to the men. He was fully aware that they had not slept for more than 24 hours and would need it. In his mind, he suspected that the escapees would have taken the easiest route possible and headed down the beach to the south. Going north would have been suicide as they would have run into hundreds of his comrades. *No*, he thought. *They will be heading south and will almost certainly be on the beach. We will track them down by the light of the moon and then I will have my vengeance.* Joao Quintas gave his men 10 minutes to rest and dose up on the bola before he called them to order and made the announcement. They would head down to the beach and make their way at speed, searching for any trails in the moonlight. Drugged to the hilt, and still fired up from the savagery of their murderous rampage, the men were raring to go. They set off in the moonlight heading back towards the pickup truck.

Chapter Forty-Four.

"Jason, wake up," said the voice "Jason..."

I opened my eyes to see the figure of Stompie above me. He held out a water bottle and I took it from him as I sat up. My body ached and I knew I could have slept for another 48 hours despite the uncomfortable and stinking hot environment we had found ourselves in. Overhead the moon shone in the sky. I was grateful for the ambient light and I looked at my watch as I handed the water bottle back to Stompie. It had just gone 12.15 pm and all around was quiet save for the rustling and hissing of the crickets.

"You must be exhausted," I whispered. "Where is Sarge?"

"He's awake, he's moved back a few hundred metres to keep an eye out for us."

"I'm not sure how he is still awake," I said. "The man is like a machine. Why don't you go get some shuteye? I'll sit up for the next watch."

"I think I can manage another half hour," said Stompie "What are your thoughts?"

We spent the next twenty minutes talking in hushed tones. Stompie was keen to hear my plan and I didn't sugarcoat a single aspect of the appalling situation we had found ourselves in. The man nodded as he took it all in. I pulled the satellite phone from my webbing and tested it. As expected, the battery had died.

"Now that's fucking useless to us. We are on our own, Stompie. We have to make the walk. It'll be at least 80 kilometres to Mocimboa Da Praia."

We sat in silence as the gravity of our situation became apparent to us both. In my mind, I wondered what had become of our attackers. *Had they given up and gone on a drinking and raping spree in Palma? Or were they determined to follow us and finish what they had started?*

It was then that I was struck by a disturbing thought. The events of the past 24 hours had given me no time to think, but I knew then I had better bring it up with Stompie. Especially as he seemed to have established a connection with Penny.

"Stompie," I whispered. "If these fuckers come after us and actually get us, you *do know* what they'll do to Penny?"

I watched as he turned to look at me in the moonlight. It was clear that he understood and he turned once again to stare into the darkness.

"Yah," he said. "I won't allow that to happen. I'll take care of her if it comes to that..."

Chapter Forty-Five.

Joao Quintas drove down the hard sand with his men walking parallel to him on the beach. Using the headlights of the old pickup truck and the torches of the men, they drove slowly for a full 5 kilometres until he called a halt to the mission. Exhaustion had caught up with him and he rested his head on the steering wheel as he gathered his thoughts. Finally, a plan formed in his mind and he shouted at the men to jump in the back of the pickup as he turned back. They arrived back at the spot where the helicopters had landed where he stopped the truck and got out to speak with his men.

"It has become clear that these men have avoided the beach," he said. "We all know there is no way they could have walked back through the town so we can only assume that they have headed south through the bush. We have trained trackers among us and I have no doubt that we can catch up with them. We have all our equipment and resources, and they have very little."

The men watched their leader and nodded in agreement.

"I am going to send one team to trail them through the bush, while the other, led by me, will make our way down the old coastal road. I am told it is rough but we will navigate it with everyone's effort. We cannot, we *must* not allow these devils to escape. They have caused us much pain, and now they must pay."

There followed a half-hour conversation with final arrangements made and instructions given. It had gone 9.45 pm when they finally set off. Using powerful flashlights, the first team followed our trail south through the bush. This was easy enough in the moonlight and the escapees had made no effort to conceal their tracks. Meanwhile, Joao and his team of three men set off in the pickup and found the old coastal road. As they had heard, it was overgrown and nearly impassable, but they persevered while staying in radio contact with the others. The news was good. The tracks were easy to follow and there had been further reports that there were 4 sets of prints instead of the three they had initially thought. The tracker had mentioned that the 4th person was small and he suspected that it may be a woman.

Joao Quintas' eyes glittered at the thought that there was a female with them. It would make their final meeting all that much sweeter. The teams made slow but steady progress through the night until there was an urgent call on the radio. The tracker team had found the point where the escapees had crossed the old road. There had been an effort to conceal the crossing point but they had seen it. Joao told them to wait and stay put until the truck arrived. As it happened, this meeting took place less than an hour later and a feeling of triumph filled Joao as he saw his men waiting in the darkness of the overgrown road. By then the motor of the old pickup was hissing and overheating and he doubted whether the tyres would hold out for much longer. But this was irrelevant. The escapees had crossed into the bush where there were no roads. The pursuit would continue, but it would have to wait until daylight. The men, including Joao, were exhausted. It was time to rest. Joao gave the orders that the men should rest, eat and sleep. There would be a watchman on duty through the night and the hunt would continue at daybreak. The men dined on dried meat and drank bush tea before settling down to rest. But sleep did not come easily for Joao. He took himself a good distance from the men, sat and rested against a tree, and spiked himself in the arm with a liberal dose of bola. He slumped into a stupor where he sat, but awoke several times during the night to repeat this process.

Chapter Forty-Six.

D awn came in the form of a pink glow on the horizon to the east. For the first time since we had arrived the previous night, I became aware of our immediate surroundings and I saw that we were at the foot of a low hill. The surrounding countryside was made up of thick clumps of jungle-like vegetation mixed with grassy glades with acacia and msasa groves. It was as I recalled when I had seen it from the air and I knew the terrain would be hard going. Stompie stirred a minute after I did and I watched as he sat up and looked at the curled up figure of Penny Riddle who was still fast asleep near him. He turned, saw I was awake, and made his way over to speak to me.

"Where is Sarge?" I asked.

"He's still back there keeping watch," came the reply. "He said he'll rest when we are all safe."

I shook my head at the man's fortitude and told Stompie to go and wake Penny. There were plenty of energy bars but our dwindling water supply was now my primary concern. Added to that, we had no idea if we were being pursued so I was anxious to get moving immediately. Sarge appeared a few seconds later. He moved silently through the brush towards us. It seemed he was relieved by the coming of the daylight although I could see the fatigue in his face. With Penny roused from her slumber, she made her way over to where we sat as the sun crested the bush on the horizon. The four of us ate a cereal bar each and drank sparingly from our water bottles. It was agreed that we would move off immediately. I took another look at the satellite phone but it was as it had been the night before. The battery was completely dead. I shook my head as I thought of the betrayal we had suffered at the hands of Colonel Jackson. That and the shocking sight of the chopper firing into the crowds at the football pitch. *An act of war, he had said. Bullshit!* But there was no time to dwell on such thoughts and I pulled the GPS device from my webbing and activated it. In the light of day, it was clearer. We were approximately 5 kilometres from the coast and 8,5 kilometres from Palma. Making it that far in darkness had been an accomplishment in itself.

Ahead of us lay a journey of more than 70 kilometres over what would be rough and unpredictable terrain. The atmosphere was sombre and quiet but there was a tangible sense of relief at being out of the town. Before setting off, I spoke.

"As you know, our satellite phone is dead," I said. "By my calculations, we have a trek of over 70 kilometres to Mocimboa Da Praia. If we set off now, we could make over 30 kilometres today alone. We don't have much food but there are sure to be wild fruits along the way. If we concentrate, and keep a good pace, we can do this and get to safety. As we don't know whether we are being pursued, we *must* keep moving. Any stopping will put us at risk. Those men have unlimited ammunition and weapons while we have very little. We must set off now. Is everyone in agreement?"

My three companions nodded somberly and I stood up to make good our exit. It was only then that I felt the terrible aching spread through my entire body. My back was still injured from the mortar blast and my limbs felt as heavy as lead. Still, the boost of energy from the cereal bar had done me well and we set off making our way up the low hill ahead of us heading due south. We walked in silence, picking our way around clumps of jungle and rocky outcrops that jutted out of the hill. The birds began to sing as the heat descended. The rising early morning temperature felt hotter than in Palma. This was probably due to the lack of wind and by 6.00 am I was sweating heavily and thirsty once again. Sarge took up the rear while I took the lead with Stompie and Penny walking between us. Penny Riddle was silent and seemed to be in a state of severe shock from the recent events. I was impressed by her stamina so far but I feared for how long it would last. This would be no walk in the park. The sun began beating down by 7.00 am by which time we had crested the hill. Ahead of us was a seemingly endless landscape of rolling hills covered with varying degrees of thick vegetation. The task ahead seemed insurmountable and once again I feared for our water situation. This was redeemed however when on our way down the hill, we encountered a spring. It had been Sarge who had identified it. He had pointed out a clump of unusually green trees near a rocky outcrop and had insisted he go check for water. It turned out he was right. Trickling out of the earth in the cool green shade of the canopy was a steady flow of clear water.

We used the opportunity to wash our faces and drink to our heart's content. Feeling refreshed, we filled the water bottles and headed off once again. With our spirits lifted, we made our way down the hill into the steaming heat of the valley below. Once again Sarge took up the rear and he used his binoculars to keep an eye on the hill behind us we travelled. The day dragged on and we stopped only once to drink in the shade of an acacia tree at around 12.00 midday. But just as we were setting off again Sarge called out to us from behind.

"Cover, now!" he hissed. "There are men behind us!"

The four of us ducked into the shade of a nearby clump of mahogany trees and I quickly pulled out my binoculars. True enough, there were men following. They had come down the same route we had taken and were wearing the green fatigues we had seen the previous day. The very sight of them caused a cold burst of fear in my chest and I spoke as I watched through the lenses.

"How many?" I asked.

"Seven men," replied Sarge. "There is no doubt they are following us. I can see they are using our exact path."

"Do you think they've seen us?" I asked.

"Difficult to tell..."

But at that moment my question was answered as by magic. The sound of multiple gunshots ripped through the still air, echoing in the hills around us. It was a sickly reminder of the hell we had just come through and a dire warning that the nightmare was far from over. But at that moment something completely unexpected happened. My radio squawked and I heard a distorted voice. I pulled the device from my belt and held it in front of me. Sarge came closer and listened as I did so. The voice was a man's, and he spoke in Portuguese.

His speech sounded manic and whoever was sending it seemed to be repeating the same message over and over again. I looked at Sarge who grabbed the device and held it closer to his ear. I watched a frown form on his forehead as he finally understood the message.

"It is them," he said in his deep voice. "They have seen us and are trying to send us a message."

At that moment I heard Penny start to weep uncontrollably. Until then, she had hoped that the nightmare was over. It was now clear that it would be ongoing.

"What are they saying?" I asked.

The message was repeated as Sarge translated the chilling words into English.

"You foreigners who are being led by the tall white man," said Sarge. "We have spotted you and we are coming after you. Escape is impossible. Be aware that there are more of us in the direction you are heading. I repeat, escape is impossible. Remain where you are and we may take mercy on you."

Chapter Forty-Seven.

The tracker had spotted the 4 escapees at around midday. Joao Quintas and his men had just crested the ridge of the low hill. The tracker had led them through the morning, carefully following the trail through the bush. They had even identified the place where they had rested and drunk water at a hidden spring. As soon as the word got to him that their prey had been spotted, Joao Quintas ran forward and grabbed the binoculars from the lead man. Sure enough, there in the distance were 4 people. The tracker had been right. One of them appeared to be female. Although they were far ahead, he could see that. Joao Quintas let out a howl of glee and shot his AK47 several times into the sky to let them know they had been spotted. For hours they had trudged through the blazing sun, seemingly to no avail, but now their prey was in sight and within reach. They would surely catch them and mete out their revenge. Feeling a strange urge to make communication and terrorise them further, Joao grabbed his radio and began making a series of random, manic broadcasts in the hope that he would be heard. The people they were following were well equipped and it was quite likely they had a radio as well. He repeated his message again and again for at least half an hour. By then the heat of the day was intense and he could see his men needed rest. In his mind he felt an uncontrollable urge to give immediate chase and catch the escapees. But he was also aware of his men and needed to maintain their morale. Their prey was now in sight and there was nowhere for them to run. They would catch them, no matter how long it took. The men rested there at the top of the hill but Joao kept watching through the binoculars. Their height gave them an advantage and he salivated with glee at the sight of them. They were trapped in a vast wilderness. The woman would slow them down, they were unused to the terrain and they would be tiring and running out of food. It was half an hour later when he gave the order that the chase would commence. It was time to kill again. Sadly for Joao, the journey downhill resulted in them losing sight of the escapees. This was deeply concerning for him but he told himself repeatedly not to worry. He had seen them with his own eyes and perhaps, just perhaps, they had heard his messages. This would have panicked them and hopefully thrown them into disarray. Harder and harder he pushed his men while using regular doses of bola. The end was in sight.

Chapter Forty-Eight.

"How far away do think they are? I asked Sarge.

"Two and a half, maybe three kilometres" he replied.

"Fuck!" I shouted aloud before realising that my outburst would only further panic Penny Riddle who was still weeping and shaking uncontrollably.

"We have a good lead," said Sarge. "I don't believe them when they say there are others. They are trying to stop us. They know we are way ahead of them."

I took a moment to think about what Sarge had said before deciding he was probably right. *It's a fucking bluff, Green. They are deliberately trying to demoralise us. There's no fucking way they would have more men out here. The focus of their attack was Palma itself. It's bullshit!*

"That man on the radio," I noted, "he sounded strange, almost manic."

"Drogas," said Sarge in his native Portuguese "These people are on drugs."

It made sense to me. The man sounded like a raving lunatic. Still, there was no time to waste and I rallied everyone to get moving immediately. It was decided that we would move on at a trot. I knew that as soon as they descended, they would lose sight of us. Sure, they would follow our trail, but we had a 3 km lead on them and we were now on flat ground. We set off in the same single file formation we had used previously. My worry for Penny Riddle was surprisingly unfounded as she ran without complaint and kept up with us. We soon set into an easy pace and kept it that way for a full hour before stopping to drink water. By then our pursuers were nowhere to be seen. I had hoped secretly that they would lose our trail but deep down I knew they would not.

The fact that we were moving in single file was an advantage but it was clear that there were trackers amongst them who would have no problem following our trail. As we ran, my mind immediately went to our remaining ammo supplies and I enquired from both Stompie and Sarge as to how much they had left. It turned out that we had roughly 120 rounds between us. Hardly enough to defend ourselves against a group of seven heavily armed men, but perhaps they were being slowed down by their own equipment. This was all wishful thinking however and I feared for us all as we pressed on. It was 3.00 pm when Penny Riddle finally collapsed and fell to the ground. Her face was red and it was clear she was suffering from heat exhaustion. I called a stop to our run and went ahead to gauge the terrain while Sarge backtracked to try to spot our pursuers. I had not gone 500 metres when I noticed the strange holes in the ground. They were randomly placed, spaced out every 30 or so metres but they were there. It was puzzling at first as they appeared to be man-made. I soon realised they were exploratory holes that had been dug by gem prospectors. Ahead of me was the next hill which lay 2 kilometres in the distance. Between us was a thick grove of trees under which the daylight was darkening steadily. I made my way back to Stompie and Penny and found Sarge waiting there. By then she had recovered and was sitting upright, her face still a bright beetroot red.

"You've done very well, Penny," I said reassuringly. "We will stop soon. We have made excellent progress but we need to move just a bit further. We have enough ammo to defend ourselves. We will be fine."

The exhausted woman looked up at me with a glimmer of hope in her eyes and I felt guilty about the blatant lie I had just told her. But it was necessary to motivate her further as I knew the closer we got to the hill, the thicker the vegetation would be and that would offer us cover if the militants caught up with us. One thing was for certain, if they tried to approach during the night, we would see them before they saw us. I knew in my heart that they would not do this. *No, they'll only try in the day, Green. You keep going for another 2 hours and you'll be able to make a stop and defend the position. What a fucking nightmare.* We set off once again and soon set into our trotting pace.

The heat was unbearable and salty sweat ran down my entire body. We stopped an hour later to eat another cereal bar which gave us the energy we needed to proceed. Once again I was aware of the strange holes that were interspersed throughout the bush. All between 4 and 5 feet deep, they seemed to be everywhere. It was difficult to tell how old they were but whoever had dug them had been thorough in their search for the gems. I knew that there were emerald deposits in northern Mozambique so I could only assume that they had been searching for these. It was 4.45 pm when the sun had moved down sufficiently for the canopy of foliage above us to create a dark hollow. The heat had not let up but the shade had at least protected us somewhat. It was then that I almost fell into one of the exploratory holes. I shouted back to the others to avoid it. They too had not seen it and thankfully they dodged it as they ran. In my heart, I was proud of Penny Riddle's grit and determination. She was making a sterling effort. We finally stopped near the foot of the hill in a thick glade of acacia trees with a clump of giant yellow bamboo to the left. Exhausted, parched and totally spent, we collapsed to the ground and sat there panting heavily for 10 minutes before I spoke.

"How do you think we did, Sarge?" I asked between breaths.

"We have done very well," he replied. "I doubt they have gained on us."

I pulled the GPS device out and checked. It came as a surprise to see we had run over 25 kilometres despite the appalling conditions. I knew that without the extra water that Sarge had found, we would never have made it that far. It was simply too hot and we would have fallen a long way back. With darkness descending above the canopy, I stood up and took a look around for a place to make camp. Ahead of us, 100 metres south, was the foot of the hill. Just above the base was a rocky outcrop with a hollow beyond it. The area was raised and would offer a vantage point should the militants be foolish enough to attempt an attack by night. With our camp identified, I walked back to the group and told them to make the last move to the camp. Wearily, they got to their feet and followed me to the foot of the hill and up behind the rocks. Stompie and Sarge nodded as they surveyed the land behind us from the new vantage point.

It was only 20 metres up but it offered a sweeping view of the forest behind us. It was then that I had an idea. Without saying anything, I left the group resting and made my way back down the hill and right towards the bamboo grove. Once there I hacked a thick stalk roughly 10 metres long and carried it back on my shoulder to the camp. By the time I arrived, Penny Riddle had curled up and fallen into an exhausted sleep. Stompie looked up at me curiously as I spoke.

"I have a plan..." I said.

Dusk came soon and the heat began to dissipate slightly.

Fighting the urge to sleep while Sarge kept guard atop the rocks, I started hacking the thick bamboo pole with my knife. I cut it into sections roughly one foot long and piled the pieces up next to me. As the darkness of night was descending, I lit a small fire and began splitting and sharpening the pieces of bamboo until I had fashioned 30 razor-sharp spikes. Once done, I turned each piece in the flames until the spikes were blackened and hardened. With Penny sleeping soundly, and Sarge on guard duty, Stompie spoke.

"I have to go take a shit," he said "I'll be sure to bury it."

"Wait," I said quietly. "Call me when you're done, I need to smear these spikes before you cover it up."

With a frown on his face, Stompie made off into the tall grass to do his business. A minute later he called out to me. Quietly, I made my way over to where he had dug the shallow hole in the earth. Once there, the two of us rolled the razor-sharp tips of the spikes in his excrement. Finally Stompie covered it up and we bundled the spikes together using some string from my webbing. Stompie knew by then what I was doing. I extinguished the fire and told Sarge to come with us while we worked. Using penlight torches in the darkness, we made our way back down our path until we came to the exploratory hole we had almost fallen into. I climbed inside and began jamming the spikes into the hard earth at the bottom. Once done, Stompie lifted me out and we lay on our bellies as we jammed the spikes at a downwards angle of 45 degrees into the walls of the hole.

Working fast, we gathered a pile of light twigs which we laid on top of the hole, concealing it from the casual observer. We then sprinkled the eroded earth that had been dug out onto the twigs and scattered the rest of it. Finally, we gathered bundles of leaves and covered the hidden trap as best we could. We had created a punji trap originally used by the Viet Cong. The trap was not designed to kill, but to immobilize a man. Added to that, once down, the unfortunate victim would be dragged upwards by his panicked comrades. This would inflict further terrible injuries as the downward facing spikes would pierce his sides and limbs adding to the ones in his feet and legs. The excrement smeared on the spikes would result in a nasty infection and it would require two additional men to return the injured one to medical care. It was a simple but effective way to disable three men in one go. With any luck, one of our pursuers would fall into it and this would delay them all. We made good our return to our lookout point where Penny slept and sat down to rest. I took first watch while Sarge and Stompie slept. I sat in the clammy humidity and fought the urge to drink water. Many people think that the jungle is silent at night. It isn't. It slithers and hisses and clicks and crawls. The mosquitoes came in great clouds and my exposed skin burned with their bites. Still, we were alive and making good our escape. They were not going to get us easily. Of that I would make sure. It was 9.00 pm when Stompie awoke and took over guard duty for me. I moved my aching body to a pile of leaves behind the rock face and lay with my head against the gnarled bark of a dwarf msasa tree. *You got yourself into a fine mess here, Green. Pray you can keep everyone alive. These savages will tear us to shreds given the chance.* I lay there listening to the sounds of the night for another 20 minutes, marvelling at the unbelievable savagery I had witnessed. Stompie awoke and came to sit near me as I was drifting off.

"What are our chances here, Jason?" he asked quietly.

"I'm not sure," I replied. "One thing is for certain, we're giving them a run for their money. We're a good team and I pity them if they attack us here tonight."

"You're right," he said thoughtfully. "This is a good spot, but there's still such a long way to go. Fuck that Colonel Jackson."

"Yes," I replied. "He knew what was going on. That chopper shot into innocent civilians and then abandoned us. One thing's for sure, if we make it out of here, I'm going to hurt him, badly..."

Stompie left me to sleep which I did solidly for the next three hours. I took over watch until Sarge took over at midnight. The night was still, but muggy and humid and the mosquitoes were appalling. It was just before daybreak when the three of us made our way down the slope to take a final look at the trap before setting off. The canopy above had scattered more leaves over the hidden hole making it invisible. Sarge nodded in approval as we set off back to the camp to awaken Penny and head off. We started the day with a cereal bar and some water and began the climb up the hill. We moved in single file in the same formation as the previous day. Sarge kept watch behind us as we walked. The slope was too steep to run and we had to pick our way around the rocks and through the stunted forests. We reached the peak at around 9.00 am and took a break to drink water. By then Sarge had gathered a bag full of marula fruits and the sweet and sour flesh was a much-needed boost to our energy supplies. There was no sign of our pursuers and this was cause for worry, but Sarge insisted they would still be as far behind as they had been the previous day. Ahead of us lay yet another wide valley although this one appeared to have thicker vegetation than the last. Sarge observed that there must be water down there in abundance as there were several riverine clefts in the landscape. I hoped he was right as we were running dangerously low and the heat was appalling. It had been three and a half hours since we had left the safety of our camp and we stood up to head off. But it was then that we heard it. It started as a strange mewing sound but as the echo reverberated and bounced off the hills we realised what it was. It was a human scream of agony. What's more, there was not only one, there were several immediately afterwards that echoed even louder. I looked at the men who smiled knowingly at me. One of the militants had walked directly into the punji trap. The subsequent screams were obviously as the other men tried to pull the victim out.

My plan had worked.

"That was a result," I said. "They'll be held up for while and we have at least 3 hours on them already. We must go now!"

But the route down the far side of the hill was not as easy as the way up. Ahead of us was a steep gorge that was partially hidden by a dense canopy of foliage. The sides were treacherous and covered with jagged rocks. It was navigable but at the same time, it would have been risky. Instead of attempting it, we took a left and headed across the ridge for 20 minutes before we found a suitable slope to tackle. But it was as we were setting off down the hill that my radio squawked once again. The familiar voice was even more manic sounding than the previous day. The man was livid and it sounded like he was spitting fire. I handed the radio to Sarge so he could translate the repeated message.

Chapter Forty-Nine.

Joao Quintas' lead tracker was the deeply unfortunate soul who had fallen into the trap. Up till then, there had been steady progress and confidence was high among the men that they were gaining ground. The trail was easy enough to follow and this came as a relief as it allowed them to move with ease as the route was already predetermined for them. After a fitful night, and feeling increasingly edgy, Joao Quintas had driven the men from daybreak through the valley towards the far hill. But it had been as they were approaching it that the lead man seemed to suddenly disappear into the ground. The shock and surprise from the agonized screaming only turned into more chaos and discord as he shouted at his men to quickly pull the man from the hole. For some inexplicable reason, he was jammed in there and pulling him out only seemed to deepen his pain. It was some time later when they discovered the reason the man was in such terrible pain. The spikes that had been placed in the hole had not only been stuck in the bottom. There were several that had been placed in the walls at a downwards angle, and these had pierced the man's sides and chest in addition to his legs and feet. Screaming in frustration and pacing the ground back and forth, he finally succumbed and instructed the men to dig the tracker out. This process took precious time and this only served to further infuriate him. The ground was hard and rocky and every strike of the field spades caused the hapless victim to scream even more. Seething with rage with his temples bulging from the blood flow, Joao

Quintas pulled his radio out and began sending a series of repeated messages to their prey. In his native Portuguese, he screamed into the radio in the hope he would be heard.

"This is a message for the tall white man," he shouted with spittle flying from his lips. "We are close behind you now. There is no escape. I repeat, no escape! We have no interest in the woman. It is you we want. You are walking into a trap far worse than the one you left. Stop now and you might live to see the sunrise tomorrow!"

Chapter Fifty.

Sarge repeated the message in English and I smiled as I heard the crazed voice repeating it over and over again. Apart from sounding like a madman, I could hear that he was rattled and this pleased me. I glanced at Stompie and Sarge before I made the decision. Both men were shaking their heads at the bizarre messages but were clearly pleased that the trap had worked.

"I think I'll send this lunatic a reply," I said. "What do you think?"

Sarge grinned and shrugged while Stompie spoke.

"Why not?"

"Sarge," I said. "I want you to translate a message to this demented freak. Can you do that for me?"

Sarge nodded as I began speaking slowly and clearly in English.

"Thank you for your message," I began. "This is the tall white man. I regret to inform you that we will not be stopping any time soon. One thing I can assure you of though is the following. If we meet, one of us will die. If that person is me, then so be it. But if that person is you, I will wrap your head in a pound of bacon and bury your body deep under a pile of rocks so that not even the hyenas can get to you. Have a pleasant day."

Sarge fought the urge to laugh as he translated the message.

Suddenly the radio went quiet but it was 30 seconds later when it burst into sound once again. This time the manic screaming was completely inaudible and scatterbrained. Stompie shook his head and I pocketed the radio once again after turning the volume down.

"Time to head off..." I said as we began making our way down the hill into the steaming valley below.

The heat intensified as we made our way down the hill. As I had seen from above, the land was heavily treed and there were problems negotiating a path through the maze of forests and glades. Using the GPS device, we continued heading south as best we could and made good progress through the morning. As we walked, Sarge collected yet more wild fruit and we ate whenever we took a break to drink water. It was during the most blisteringly hot time of day, around 1.00 pm when we stumbled across the stream. It ran from the higher grounds to our right heading to the coast. Narrow and twisting, the water appeared clean and we took the opportunity to drink and fill the water bottles once again. Feeling the need to rest, we made our way past the stream and into a forest of miombo woodland. Once there I turned the radio on again but it was silent.

"Maybe the lunatic is taking a rest as well?" said Stompie.

"Maybe," I replied looking at our progress on the GPS device. "But we must keep moving. We have only covered 15 kilometres and we need to double that. No room for complacency."

It was 30 minutes later when we set off once again. Staying in the shade as much as we could, we made our way through the steaming heat of the valley. At 3.00 pm we broke into a slow trot. An hour later, panting heavily and completely spent, we pulled to a stop under the shade of a giant clump of bamboo. We lay there with our eyes closed and waited for our bodies to recover. Finally feeling able, I lifted myself onto my elbow and looked across to where

Stompie and Penny lay in the shade nearby. It was only then that I saw the snake. Virtually invisible against the thick trunks of bamboo, it slithered silently above him not 5 feet up. It was a medium-sized specimen but I recognised it immediately as being deadly poisonous. The snake was a Green Mamba. Its bright green back and green-yellow ventral scales made it almost invisible. Its slender body moved silently along the low hanging beam of bamboo and it appeared to be readying itself to strike the intruder below. That intruder was Stompie Van Der Reit. At around one and a half metres long, I knew this was a male specimen that would strike at any time.

With nothing but the quiet rustling of the leaves around us, I spoke.

"Stompie, don't move! There is a snake above you. A mamba."

Having heard me, Sarge who had sat up nearby, eyed the stalk of bamboo and whispered.

"I see it, I know this snake well. I can catch it and kill it. We used to find them when we were young in the forests."

"What should we do?" I asked.

"Stompie and Penny should roll in opposite directions but stay down. This will confuse the beast and it will more than likely give up and move on."

"Did you hear what Sarge said, Stompie?" I asked.

"I did," he replied. "Penny, are you ready?"

I watched as Penny gave the thumbs up from where she lay nearby, not 4-feet below the slithering reptile.

The moment was bristling with tension and this was a threat none of us had expected. I looked at Sarge who gave me a nod.

"Now," I said.

Stompie and Penny acted immediately and rolled away in unison, staying as low to the ground as they could. The snake, upon seeing this sudden movement, raised its head from the trunk of bamboo and shot it downwards towards where Stompie's face had been a split second beforehand. Finding nothing to strike, its diamond-shaped head hung there with the thin black tongue flickering and the poison hung like morning dew from its fangs.

Without warning, Sarge leapt forward and swatted the creature with his rucksack. There was a scramble as both Penny and Stompie jumped up and Sarge followed the writhing serpent as it flew through the air and landed on the leaf-covered soil nearby. Before it could get moving, Sarge placed his boot on the back of the snake just behind its head. Completely calm and composed, he reached down and gripped the snake behind its head and lifted it to show us. The long thin body coiled around his arm as he did so and the hideous creature hissed in fury. Smiling from ear to ear and seemingly proud of his capture skills, Sarge held the snake up and spoke.

"I'll cut its head off now and kill this devilish creature."

"Wait," I said, climbing to my feet. "Is there any way you can keep it alive?"

"Sure," said Sarge. "If you can find a forked stick I can pin it to the ground so it can't move."

Stompie and I hurried off to find what Sarge was looking for while Penny Riddle stood nearby hugging herself silently with relief. It had been a close call with a deadly predator. It took less than two minutes for Stompie and me to find the correct stick which we trimmed with our knives. We returned to Sarge and handed it to him at arm's length. Calmly, and seemingly with no fear, he placed his hand on the ground and pegged the forked piece of wood behind the green head of the serpent. Once done, he casually unwound the coils of its body from his arm and stood up beaming from ear to ear.

"See?" he said. "Easy!"

With the long slender body of the reptile thrashing around aimlessly, I called Stompie to assist me and we began hacking at the base of one of the thicker stalks of bamboo. The long section came crashing to the ground a few minutes later. Once done, we chopped a section away at the thickest part of the trunk near the base.

Finally, we had separated a thick, half metre section of bamboo and I began cutting at the closed end. Once done, I stood up with the large open-ended hollow tube. I gauged the inner thickness of the hole in the end and began hacking at a slightly thinner piece that would seal it. Once done, I tested how it fitted into the thicker piece. It was a tight but perfect fit. We had created a tube with a resealable opening to one side. Satisfied it would serve my purpose, I walked over to where Sarge stood over the snake.

"Can you get it in here?" I asked.

"Sure thing boss," he replied as he took the bamboo tube and knelt.

I watched from a couple of metres back as he stuffed the body of the reptile into the hollow inner of the thick bamboo tube. Finally, using the forked stick to keep the head in place, he took the thinner cap and flicked the head of the snake back into the tube. With lightning speed, he slammed the cap into the larger aperture and the ghastly reptile was trapped. Next, he drew his knife from his belt and began drilling a tiny hole in the side of the bamboo. This was to ensure the captive snake could breathe while inside the tube. With that done, he tied a piece of string from his webbing around the length of the tube to ensure it would not open. The fitting was tight enough to keep the snake captive but we needed to be more than sure. The encounter had been unpleasant enough for us not to want another. With the whole episode finally over, Penny spoke.

"Why have you done that?" she asked.

"You'll see soon enough," I replied. "Now, let's get moving."

Chapter Fifty-One.

It took the men a full two hours to dig the tracker out of the spiked hole in the ground. For the tracker himself, it was an agonising experience and his screams rattled Joao Quintas as he watched the painfully slow progress. The message he had received from the escapees had only served to madden and infuriate him further and he found he had to sneak off to snort bola in order to deal with this comedy of errors. When the man was finally lifted from the ground and laid out flat, the extent of his injuries became apparent. Although none of the ground spikes had gone through his boots, they had caused terrible injuries to both his right shin and his left calf. One of the hideous spikes was still embedded in the calf muscle and it twitched with every beat of his heart. The other men held him down while it was removed and the screaming continued. Sweating, confused and rapidly losing heart, the men proceeded to tend to the horrific injuries on the man's sides, thighs and chest. Not only had the spikes caused huge damage, but they had also been smeared with some kind of poison that was already starting to cause an infection. It soon became apparent that this man was going nowhere and in his mind, Joao thought about killing him there and then. But this was a trusted lieutenant and a popular figure among the other men. Finally, he decided he had no choice but to send the injured man back to Palma in the care of two others. This unfortunate and infuriating incident had resulted in his team going from 7 men to 4. *Those fucking infidels will pay dearly for this*, he swore to himself. With the decision made, and the injured man treated as best as possible, he instructed the 3 remaining members of his crew to proceed with the hunt. They set off in the blazing heat with the grim prospect of climbing the hill in front of them. The trail was clear, the mission would continue and he would have his vengeance no matter what.

Chapter Fifty-Two.

We had made another 10 kilometres by the time we finally stopped our march. During the afternoon we passed several streams similar to the one we had crossed earlier and used the opportunity to drink to our heart's content. Once again Sarge had collected a bag full of wild fruits and berries which we ate on the go. The heat of the day was starting to subside and I looked at my watch as I called a halt. It had just gone 4.30 pm and we could move no further. Ahead of us was roughly 2 kilometres of the valley before the next hill. I knew there was no way we would make it there by nightfall so I decided to find a place to camp. With Stompie and Penny resting, Sarge and I went off to find a suitable spot. It came in the form of a giant mahogany tree. It must have been at least 300 years old and its giant, lichen-covered branches reached up high above the surrounding trees. Underneath it was a bed of dry leaves that had fallen over the years and I imagined it would be like a feather mattress compared to the rough earth we had slept on the previous night. Sarge climbed up and took a look behind us with the binoculars but could see no sign of our pursuers. Satisfied the punji trap had delayed them further, I made the decision and we walked back to call the others to our camp. We trudged in at 5.00 pm and collapsed onto the soft leaves. I lay there staring up at the branches as I fought the overwhelming urge to sleep. Jutting out roughly 12 feet above was a massive branch. It reached out at least 20 metres horizontally before rising towards the sun. I stared at it as a plan formulated in my mind. Finally, feeling rested enough to sit up, we gathered to drank water and eat fruits. The mood was solemn and it was clear that the endurance of the trip was taking its toll on all of us. Still, we were lucky to have the food and water, meagre as it was. Without it we would have perished. There was no doubt about that. Sarge laid his rucksack with the bamboo tube against the massive trunk of the great tree and slept while Stompie kept first watch. I waited until Penny Riddle had curled up and fallen asleep before doing the same. It was dark when Stompie woke me to take over at 9.00 pm. I sat there for the next 3 hours, smoking and thinking about the events of the past days. They had been as unprecedented as they were unbelievable, and although we had made progress, I was under no illusions that we were still in grave danger. By all accounts, we were being pursued by a madman who would stop at nothing to get us.

This played on my mind constantly until it was time to wake Sarge to take over. The big man awoke and took his position immediately without a word. Finally, I laid my aching bones in the same spot where I had slept earlier and drifted off within minutes.

I awoke as the first rays of light began glowing on the horizon to the east. The birds were still silent and I sat up slowly feeling the dull ache in my back as I did so. My mouth was dry and I rubbed the sleep from my eyes as I took a look around. Stompie sat nearby, still on watch, wide awake and aware of the threat we all faced. He heard the rustling in the leaves and turned to look at me, giving me the thumbs up. I stood up and walked over to have a quiet word while we waited for the daylight.

"What do you think about today?" he asked.

"We have to keep moving," I responded. "We're making progress but we cannot and must not slow for any reason. Those fuckers are determined to get us."

"We're doing well so far," he said, "Penny especially."

"Yes," I replied quietly. "To be honest, I didn't think she had it in her. It was a big worry. Let's hope it continues."

The camp came alive with the first rays of sunshine and we gathered to drink water and eat a cereal bar each. Once done, we set off heading south to cross the final two kilometres of the valley before the next hill. We arrived at the foot of the slope and immediately began climbing. This one was lower than the last and had multiple granite rocky outcrops in amongst the grass on its face. Keeping our pace, we gained altitude steadily until we reached an area of rock just ahead of us. I took a look around and saw a dwarf msasa tree that had managed to grow in a thin crack in the rock ahead. It was a testament to the tenacity of the species that it had managed to not only grow, but to thrive in its unusual location. We stopped there and sarge took a look through the binoculars behind us for the ISIS militants. As hard as he tried, he could see nothing but the long valley we had come through which was starting to steam as the day grew hotter.

I wiped my forehead and took a look ahead to decide on the path we should take for the final stretch up the hill. On either side were clumps of rocks and the obvious choice was directly under the dwarf msasa I had just seen. But it was then that I realised that this tree offered the perfect opportunity for us to lay another trap.

"Sarge," I said, "give me the bamboo tube with the snake. I think it's time to give our friends another surprise. Stompie and Penny, you continue walking ahead, be sure to walk directly under that dwarf tree and wait on the other side on the rocks."

Stompie and Penny did as instructed and sat down on the rocks to watch what I was about to do. I pulled the knife from my belt and unscrewed the back of the handle. Hidden in there were several small but useful items. One of these was a wound up length of ultra-fine fishing line. Sarge rattled the bamboo and held his ear to the hole to listen.

"The snake is alive and well," he said. "Probably a bit upset."

"Good," I replied as I grabbed the tube and stepped up to the tree. "It can stay that way."

I stood beneath the tree at the exact spot where Stompie and Penny had walked underneath it. It was the natural path that anyone would take to get to where we needed to be. Behind us, our trail was clear among the leaves and in the soil of the slope. Beyond the rocky outcrop the grass covered soil continued up the hill. If our pursuers were following us properly, as I knew they were, they would be proceeding with caution but would be following our trail exactly. They would see that we had passed here and there would be no fear of another punji trap in the surface of the rock. They would pass the exact same spot where Stompie and Penny had walked. I looked up at the trunk of the tree and saw that it split into branches roughly 7 feet up. The branches were as thick as a man's leg and covered with lichen. The tree was small but mature. Using a section of the fishing line, I bound the bamboo tube to the branch on the right with the removable opening facing downwards. As I did so, I heard the snake hissing in its prison and my skin crawled at the sound of it. It took a good 5 minutes to secure it solidly but finally, it was done and I knocked the tube with my fist to check it was fixed securely. Even with a solid strike, it would not budge.

I stepped around the tree and walked back, gauging the route the ISIS militants would take as they followed us. Against the thick grey lichen of the tree trunk, the fishing line was completely invisible as was the tube of bamboo. *So far so good, Green.* I stepped back to the rear of the tree and uncoiled the fishing line fully. Once done i bound the end of it around the plug we had inserted in the bottom of the bamboo tube. Using a good knot, I secured it and gave it a light tug. There was no way it would come loose. Next, I drew the line down the trunk of the tree and hooked it around the stump of a long-dead branch. Having done that, I pulled the line across the path that Stompie and Penny had walked and extended it to the rocks at the far side. Once there, I squatted down and tied the remaining line around a large boulder, testing the tension as I did so. Finally, I stood up and walked back to take a look at my handiwork. I made my way back to the grass and stood there picturing what our pursuers would see as they came up. The fishing line ran across the natural path near the tree at a height of 25 centimetres. Against the natural grey colour of the rock, it was completely invisible and even I had to take care as I approached it. I squatted down a final time to check the line was taut, then stood up and looked at the others. Sarge stood there grinning from ear to ear while Stompie spoke.

"Genius," he said. "Someone is gonna get a fuckin' *hell* of a fright."

"I'm hoping it'll be more than a fright..." I said. "Let's move on."

Chapter Fifty-Three.

The night had not been kind to Joao Quintas and his men. The mosquitoes had been incessant as they had chosen to make camp in the heat of the valley near a stagnant pool and Joao had been bitten by a tsetse fly on his inner wrist. The itching was intense to the point of being painful and this distraction had kept him awake most of the night. Added to that, the remaining three men were showing signs of despondency. But Joao knew he could easily remedy this with more drugs. *Food and bola will fix them and we will be good to go*, he thought. After a breakfast of bush tea and dried bread, they set off following the trail of the escapees albeit doing so a lot more carefully than they had done the previous day. The delay caused by the trap the tracker had fallen into had lost them close to three hours, but this was something he intended to make up for. *Surely the woman would be tiring and would be slowing them down? They could not possibly keep up this pace for much longer.* In his mind, he had pictured the face of Darwesh, confused and scared as he died in his arms. Trying to speak but unable to do so. The image was burned into his consciousness and it brought forth waves of anger and rage unlike anything he had ever known. The pursuit would continue for as long as it took, no matter what. The message from the tall white man had angered him to the point of exasperation. It had been an insult to his faith that would never go unpunished. *Never!* They stopped at a stream an hour later to refill their water bottles and drink. Joao used this opportunity to dose the men up on bola and they set off at a run. Their determination had been bolstered and their sights were now truly set on their prey. The heat of the day did little to stop the men and they ran for hours on end only stopping occasionally to rest and repeat this process. Joao knew they were gaining ground rapidly, they were keeping a keen eye on the route ahead in the event of another trap, and all seemed to be going well. The ground was solid and the pace was fast. In the distance, he saw the next hill they would have to cross. Gauging from his timing, he imagined that the escapees would have slept nearby. The spot would surely be revealed, and soon. A little after 2.00 pm they stumbled upon a giant mahogany tree. Underneath were all the signs of recent habitation. There were wrappers from cereal bars and clear indentations in the leaves where four people had slept.

After a quick drink of water in the shade of the tree, Joao told his lead man to pick up the trail and continue the hunt. The path led them through the forest and up to the base of the hill. It was slightly different from the last in that there were rocky patches and outcrops along the face of it. Still, the path was easy enough to follow and they slowed to a walk as they wove their way up the incline. It was at 2.30 pm, as they were nearing the crest of the hill, when the front man paused to study the tracks. Ahead of him was a section of rock with a tree growing out of a crack between the surface. He looked further ahead and saw the footprints in the earth where the escapees had continued their climb. Feeling confident he was on the right path, he set off with the others walking behind him in single file. But it was as he stepped beneath the overhanging branch of the msasa tree that he heard the strange popping sound. It was a dull and unremarkable sound, but it was distinctly unusual in the current setting. Joao Quintas heard the sound as well. He glanced up and saw the snake fall from the tree. It did so with lightning speed and immediately curled itself around the neck of the lead man. Suddenly the air was filled with terrified shrieking and once again the scene around him turned into one of complete chaos. The lead man fell to the rock surface below and wailed to the heavens above. The snake had coiled around his neck and buried its fangs deep into the man's nose. He pulled at it but it would not let go. Joao Quintas stared in horror as the head of the snake pulsated as the poison was pumped through the fangs into the man's face. At first, the men jumped away in fright at this sudden and unexpected event. Their fear of snakes was apparent and the scene rapidly descended into one of confusion and chaos as the man writhed on the ground. Joao Quintas pulled the blade from his belt and stepped forward. Without hesitating, he gripped the body of the snake behind the hands of the man who was grappling with it and severed the body from the head. Still, the body of the reptile curled and writhed but finally the man's hands came away. Joao stared down in horror as the green, diamond-shaped head continued to pulsate and pump poison into the man's nose. He stepped back as the man gradually untangled his arms from the body of the serpent and finally pried the jaws of the reptile from his face. There were two black holes in his nose, deep and filled with clear liquid venom. With the snake now dead, Joao kicked the head into the rocks to the right and reached down and tossed the body into the grass behind them. The man lay there panting and moaning as the venom coursed through his body. Joao Quintas had been fooled yet again. Once again his superiority and bush craft had been challenged.

The men, now seeing the snake was dead, gathered around their stricken comrade and began to administer what first aid they could. But there was no snake antivenom in their first aid kits. The men knew full well that the snake had been a Green Mamba and there was little chance of survival for the victim. This was especially true since he had been bitten in the face and the attack had gone on for some time. With the venom consisting of both neurotoxins and cardiotoxins, it did not take long for the effects to manifest. Almost immediately there was massive swelling to the man's face and nose. This continued until his head resembled a football and the skin on his face split open. Within 30 minutes the now delirious victim complained of dizziness and began vomiting uncontrollably. All the while, Joao Quintas and his remaining men looked on helplessly. It was less than 40 minutes later when he started having breathing difficulties and could no longer swallow. His breathing came in short, random wheezes and his chest seemed to rattle. This soon led to violent, spine cracking convulsions and respiratory paralysis. The man died soon after.

Chapter Fifty-Four.

T he far side of the hill was a lot easier and we made our way down quickly. The seemingly endless valley that lay ahead was thick with vegetation and the day was already starting to become uncomfortably hot. We stopped at the foot of the hill and I took a look at the GPS to gauge our progress. We had come a third of the way to Mocimboa Da Praia and I let the others know this before we set off. This news bolstered their enthusiasm and the pace was fast as we set off. Following our southward bearing, we made our way through the forests as quick as we could. Sarge stopped and climbed a tree every half hour to scan the hill behind us for signs of our pursuers. It was at 12.15 pm when he shouted from above as he held the binoculars to his eyes.

"I see them!" he growled. "Three men, just starting to make their way down."

I looked back at the distant hill but could see nothing. It was only when I used my own binoculars that I managed to pick them out. Sarge was right. Even with their green camouflage uniforms, I could see them clearly as they made their way down, following the very same path we had taken.

"Only three," I said as I dropped the binoculars. "Their numbers are dropping."

"Maybe one of them ran into the snake?" said Stompie with a grin.

"Maybe they did," I replied. "Either way, we must get going."

We continued through the early afternoon, stopping only to drink water and eat. By then the four of us were looking worse for wear. A ragtag group of tramps, filthy dirty with gaunt, haunted faces. It crossed my mind that to the casual observer we might look like the very people we were trying to escape from. It was at around 3.00 pm that I noticed the gradual dip in the landscape. It appeared we were headed towards a river. I checked on the GPS and immediately saw that we were. The low lying ground ahead was greener than the surrounding countryside and the trees looked riverine. As we approached, the forest became thicker and darker around us but we were grateful for the shade.

All of us barring Sarge were badly sun burnt and our exposed skin was red and swollen from mosquito bites. We continued walking, weaving our way through the tangled mess of thorn bushes and tall grass. I was grateful for the GPS as it was the only way I could ensure we were heading in the right direction. It was at 4.30 pm when we finally stumbled across the river itself. At roughly 15 metres wide, its yellow waters flowed fast from the rainfall inland and there were steep sandy banks on either side. The water was filled with scattered boulders and tangles of driftwood that had been brought downriver by the floods. We stood there panting and exhausted as we surveyed the scene in front of us.

"Looks like we'll be swimming today," I said quietly. "There's no other way across."

"The water is fast but it looks shallow," said Stompie. "Shouldn't be too much of a problem."

Sarge, Penny and I sat and rested while Stompie walked upstream to find a crossing point. He returned a few minutes later looking pleased with himself.

"I've got the perfect spot," he said. "A bend in the river with a fallen tree almost crossing it. We would only have to swim 5 metres or so to make it across."

We followed Stompie a couple of hundred metres west until we reached the spot he had identified. True to his word, the river was narrower there and it seemed a natural choice at which to make the crossing. The fallen tree spanned most of the swirling waters and would offer a buffer for us as we crossed, preventing anyone from being swept away. Using the opportunity to rest and drink water, we began planning the crossing and the logistics of getting our weapons and equipment across while keeping it dry. Finally, it was agreed that Stompie would go across first and would walk back upstream to catch our equipment as we threw it over. Wasting no time, he stripped himself of his rucksack, webbing and ammunition and made his way down the steep sandbank to the rushing water below. We stood and watched as he waded out, his body forced up against the trunk of the fallen tree which glistened black in the late afternoon sun.

It took 5 minutes to reach the end of the tree but once there, he turned around and gave us the thumbs up. We returned the same sign and I held my breath as he plunged into the fast-flowing torrent beyond. For a brief moment, his head disappeared in the raging water but it soon popped up several metres downstream. A strong swimmer, it took him less than 20 seconds for him to pull himself through the water to the bank on the far side. Staying at the waterline, he ran back up until he was opposite us and smiled as he shouted.

"It's easy!" he called. "We won't have a problem."

Feeling relieved by this, I told Penny she should be the next to cross. I had expected some resistance but was pleasantly surprised when she simply nodded and made her way down the sandbank to the fallen tree below. Slowly but steadily she waded out into the water along the trunk of the tree until she was opposite where Stompie stood. I saw his mouth move as he called to her and pointed downstream. It was clear he was encouraging her and promising to assist. Before I knew it she launched herself into the river and I held my breath as she too disappeared under the water. But as Stompie had done, she soon popped up and swam to the far bank to where he had run to receive her. The process of ferrying our equipment across the river was time-consuming. I waded out to the end of the half-submerged tree while Sarge went back and forth ferrying the equipment, ammunition and weapons. I tossed these across the narrowest part of the river to Stompie who caught and placed it all up the bank safe and dry. The process took a good half hour but finally, we had sent everything across. Feeling somewhat naked without my gun, I turned to look at Sarge who waited a few metres behind me, up to his waist in the fast-moving water.

"Are you a confident swimmer, Sarge?" I asked.

"Yes, boss," he replied. "I grew up on the coast. We spent half our childhoods in the sea."

"Good," I said, "I'll see you on the other side."

The water was blessedly cool although the current was powerful and fast-moving. I pulled myself through it until I felt the sand crunching beneath my hands and knees. Finally, I dragged myself up and stood on the sandbank. I ran and gave Sarge the thumbs up as he took the plunge. His head popped up soon enough and I reached out to pull him ashore as he arrived. We climbed up the sandbank into the forest on the far side of the river and stood in the shade as we clad ourselves in our webbing once again. It had been nerve-wracking but we had done it. It also struck me that the river might pose more of a problem for our pursuers. In any case, it was a barrier that they would have to contend with as we had done. We used the opportunity to eat some of the fruit that Sarge had gathered and we filled our bottles with muddy water from the river. With our clothes still soaking wet, we set off into the thick riverine forest heading south once again. The humidity was like a wet blanket but the slow evaporation from our wet clothes offered some relief. It was less than five minutes later when we arrived at a small open glade in the forest. Shaded and seemingly cooler, it seemed like a perfect spot to make camp. It would offer easy access to the river for whoever was on watch and there was a thick bed of dried leaves on the ground. I glanced at my watch and saw it had already gone 5.30 pm. The forest was darkening fast and the sight of my exhausted companions told me it was time to stop for the day. Stompie read my mind and spoke.

"You thinking to camp here?" he muttered.

"I think so," I said. "We have water and good cover. Whoever is on watch can wait by the river. The moon will be out so there'll be good night vision."

I turned to look at Penny who had sat down nearby. Her soaked hair was in disarray and her head was hanging low with fatigue. The sight of her was enough to convince me that we should make camp. With any luck, we would make it to Mocimboa Da Praia the following day. We were almost there.

"Right," I said. "It's decided then."

Chapter Fifty-Five.

By 4.30 pm Joao Quintas was dog tired and frazzled from the lack of food and constant drug use. His body refused to move anymore and he called a halt to the hunt under the shade of a bamboo forest. Ahead of them was a depression in the landscape that seemed to be heading towards a river. His two remaining men sat nearby but the younger of the two was still full of energy and raring to go. This disparity in their abilities seemed to be showing itself and it was a worry that would not go away. The three men sat in silence while they drank water and ate. It was 10 minutes later when the young man, whose name was Domingo Mussa, stood up and approached Joao.

"Master," he said, "I do not wish to challenge your authority, but I would like to make a proposal and I was hoping you would hear me out."

"Go on..." said Joao wearily.

Domingo shifted nervously on his feet and spoke.

"I could go ahead," he said. "The trail of these infidels is easy to follow and the moon will rise early tonight. It is not our fault that they have this lead but I can close it and do some damage. With your permission, I would like to go ahead. I can go now and will not stop until I catch up with them. That will be at night and I plan to attack them while they are asleep."

Joao Quintas picked a piece of long grass from the sandy soil near where he sat and put it in his mouth as he thought. His bloodshot eyes narrowed as he realised that this would be something the escapees would not be expecting. The young man was fast, more than able, and well trained. It didn't take long for him to make up his mind.

"I want the woman, Domingo," said Joao. "She will bring the others to us. She is the key."

"I will get her for you, master," said Domingo. "We know these people are resting every night. I will go now and run until the darkness comes. After that, the moon will rise and I will continue until I find them. I will kill or capture the woman, whatever you choose."

"No," said Joao, his jaw line pulsing. "I want her alive. If you can do this, it will be a great service to our cause."

"I will do that, master," said Domingo. "It will be an honour."

There followed a brief conversation where instructions were given to Domingo on what he should do in the event he was able to capture the woman. He was to silence her and immediately make his way back. If he was successful, they would meet on the trail the following morning. The bargaining chip the woman would offer was of incalculable value and would ensure that the man who had killed Darwesh would present himself. It was a simple but brilliant plan that would allow Joao to rest beforehand. If he failed, it would not change anything. The hunt would continue until the final victory. After everything had been discussed thoroughly, and they were all in agreement, Joao spoke.

"Go now, young servant of Allah," he said. "May the wind carry you through the night and may you succeed in your quest."

Brimming with enthusiasm, Domingo smiled and set off immediately. Joao Quintas leant back against the bamboo and chewed on the piece of grass in his mouth. It was a brilliant plan, one that could only work in his favour. After a short rest, he and the other man would continue until the darkness came. They would close the gap between the infidels and themselves and they would rest again until daybreak. With any luck, Domingo would capture the woman and finally, the cards would be in his hands. *Yes*, he thought. *This might just work.* It was at 5.00 pm when Joao and the last remaining man set off. There was still another one and a half hours of daylight left. They would continue at pace and close the gap as much as they could. With the sun going down in the west, they headed deeper into the thick green forest.

Chapter Fifty-Six.

I awoke suddenly at 3.00 am to the sound of leaves rustling nearby. My eyes opened in a flash and I gripped the gun that lay next to me immediately. I blinked as I realised it had been Penny Riddle who had stirred. Stompie had taken over guard duty from me and Sarge was sleeping nearby. I lay there completely still as I watched her sit up and rub her grimy face in the dappled moonlight. She had slept solidly through the night and had not moved since we had eaten. It was only when she stood up that I spoke.

"Penny," I whispered, "What are you doing?"

"I need to go to the bathroom," she replied.

"Don't go further than 20 metres from the camp," I said. "We must stick together."

I watched as she dropped her head and began weeping softly. It was a pitiful sight and I immediately felt sorry for her. *She's done so well, Green. Perhaps you should give her a break.* But before I could speak she walked over to where I lay. I propped myself up on my elbow as she approached.

"I need to talk to you now," she said firmly.

Fuck, here we go, I thought. Penny Riddle made her way over and sat down next to me.

"Jason," she said "I need to wash. I am filthy dirty and I need some privacy to do these things. Can you understand that?"

"Yes, I know but..." I started.

"No buts," she interrupted. "Please, take me to the river to where Stompie is on watch. It will only be a few minutes but I have to wash and take care of myself. I'm itching like crazy and I'm telling you I can't go on like this for much longer. Please, take me to the river, it's so close and the moon is still up."

I paused as I thought it through. Sarge had woken and the night was quiet. Stompie would be there to watch over her. The woman had proved her mettle beyond anything I could have expected and in my mind, I decided she deserved a break.

"Okay," I whispered. "I'll take you to the river to Stompie. He will keep guard while you wash. But I want you back here in 15 minutes. Is that clear?"

"Thank you," she replied with obvious relief. "I'll be quick, I promise."

The path to the river was clear in the moonlight and after a quick word with Sarge, we set off on the 3-minute walk. I called ahead to Stompie so as not to alarm him with our approach. We arrived to the sound of the rushing water below and the riverine scene bathed in pale moonlight below us. With Penny lurking in the background, I spoke to Stompie who nodded as he listened. Finally, it was agreed that he would keep watch from the bank above while Penny bathed. I would return after 15 minutes to collect her and take her back to camp. That way everything would remain under constant watch. It was the only viable option and I turned to Penny before I left.

"Fifteen minutes and I'll be back here to collect you," I said. "Not a minute longer."

"Perfect," she said with a smile I hadn't seen for days. "Thank you."

I nodded once at Stompie and left the two of them alone as I headed back to the camp. There I sat against the tree and lit a cigarette.

"Everything okay?" asked Sarge from where he lay.

"Yup," I replied, "I'll go back to get her shortly. It'll be fine."

Chapter Fifty-Seven.

Domingo Mussa ran through the late afternoon at great speed, only slowing when he needed to study the tracks ahead. His youth and fitness served him well and he made quick work of the distance. It was only when the light had faded to such a point that he could no longer see the trail that he stopped to await the rising of the moon.

The wait was frustrating but it was only an hour later when the surrounding bush was bathed in the pale light and he could proceed. The going was slower, however, as he needed to take great care to ensure he did not lose the tracks. In the open glades, there was no problem but it was under the canopy of the trees that care was needed. But as the moon rose, the trail became clearer and he was able to pick up speed once again.

It was 4 hours later when he became aware he was heading downhill into a shallow valley. This decline continued as the surrounding trees and bushes became thicker. It was at around 1.00 am when he finally heard the rushing water ahead of him. It could only be one thing, a river. Moving like a leopard in the night, he crept forward, staying in the shadows as he went. The tracks were clear ahead of him and finally, he saw where the escapees had stopped on the sandbank above the rushing water. He paused and waited for his eyes to become adjusted to the brightness of the open space. It was then that he saw the man. Hidden in the foliage on the far side of the water, he sat there watching the river below. The man sat perfectly still as he kept guard. Domingo Mussa had struck gold. *This was surely not some random peasant. No, this was one of the escapees.* He had managed to catch up with them and now he was very close. Slowly and carefully, he backed away, staying in the shadows until he was completely out of sight. It had been a lucky break. He might have simply run into the moonlight at the river bank and been spotted. But no, his skills had served him well and he had prevailed. The fact that he had caught up was testament to his abilities as a tracker. This was an opportunity not to miss and one which would send him up the ranks rapidly. Knowing the others would be sleeping nearby, he decided to head downriver to look for a point at which to cross. Domingo Mussa made his way through the woods until he was a full 300 metres downstream from the man on the far bank. Once there, he made his way back to the river and approached with great caution. Ahead of him the waters of the river gurgled and splashed below. But it was what he saw on his left that caught his eye.

Below him, not 20 metres away was an ancient weir. Constructed from boulders and mostly intact, it spanned the river at a narrow point and the white water hissed as it ran over it. Pinned up against it were several tree trunks and branches that had been washed downstream by the floods. With a bit of care, it would be a point at which he could cross the river and with any luck, he could do so without getting swept downstream. Slowly and carefully, he stepped out into the moonlight and looked down at the weir. He scanned the sandy soil around him but there were no tracks at all. The escapees had crossed, that was beyond doubt, but they had not crossed there. *They must have done so upriver somewhere.* With a final look around, Domingo stepped forward and began making his way down the sandbank towards the weir. As he approached, the sound of the rushing water became louder in his ears. The boulders were still there, just under the surface and seemingly in place. Fearful of slipping, he stepped onto the first one and the water rushed around his ankles. But the rock was rough and porous and the soles of his boots gripped well. Holding onto a branch to steady himself, he continued walking, stepping from rock to rock. It was at the halfway point that he saw the gap in the wall of boulders below. The force of the flow had broken through the barrier and there was a two-metre section of deep, fast-flowing water through which the river was funnelled. But there was also a tree trunk spanning the top of it. Covered with sharp, stumpy branches that glistened black in the moonlight, it was thick enough to carry his weight to the boulders on the far side. *Perfect*, he thought. Domingo placed his right boot onto the trunk and tested it. It was solid and there was no fear it had rotted and might collapse. With a final look to his right upriver, he stepped onto the trunk and walked the few metres to the far side and the safety of the boulders beyond. Once there he quickly dashed into the cover of the river bank. He crouched there for a good five minutes as he gathered his thoughts and planned his next move. The man on guard upstream was positioned above the river on top of the sandbank. This was at least 2 metres above the waterline. Domingo figured that if he could make his way up, under the cover of the riverbank, he would be able to launch a surprise attack on the guard and make a quick kill. The guard was watching the far bank and would not suspect that anyone had already crossed. The steep riverbank would offer the cover he needed. Moving inland was an option but it was dark and there was no telling where the rest of the escapees were camped. *No*, he thought. *The riverbank is the way to go.*

Domingo Mussa checked his equipment and weapons and after a final look around, he set off crouching low and hugging the sand walls of the bank as he went. He knew exactly where the guard was stationed. He would get as close as he could, surprise the man and kill him immediately. From there he would make his way inland and attempt to capture the woman. Joao Quintas' instructions had been clear. The woman was the prize with which Joao could bargain. Slowly and with great care, he crept up the river bank stopping every ten metres to watch and listen. The sound of the rushing water gave him the confidence to keep moving as there was no way the guard would hear his approach. It would add to the element of surprise and enable him to quickly kill the man and get on with the task. The tension built as he approached the spot. In his mind, he knew he was less than 10 metres from the man. The moment was fast approaching that would define the rest of his life. Ahead of him, not a metre away, was another fallen tree trunk. It lay against the bank and stood vertical with its lower roots under the water. Domingo crouched behind it and wiped the sweat from his forehead as he prepared to strike. He closed his eyes and said a quick prayer to Allah before he moved. But it was then that he heard the movement and the voices above him. Domingo froze and his body stiffened with tension. He looked around the trunk of the tree to see a figure coming down the sandbank. But it was not the guard. This was the unmistakable figure of a woman.

Chapter Fifty-Eight.

"Stompie, you don't understand!" said Penny Riddle. "A lady needs privacy."

Stompie Van Der Reit blinked and cleared his throat as he looked at the bedraggled woman standing in front of him.

"Five minutes is all I ask," she pleaded. "I'll be right here! I just want to wash and go to the toilet. That's it!"

Stompie shuffled his feet in the sandy soil and looked around nervously. The instructions had been clear but his Afrikaans sensibilities and manners dictated that a woman should be afforded privacy for these matters. The night was quiet and although he would move back a few metres from the bank, he would still be able to keep an eye on the river and the far side. *It'll be fine*, he thought. *It's only five minutes after all.*

"Okay," he whispered with wide eyes and urgency in his voice. "I'll watch you go down to the water and then I'll move back 10 metres so you can have your privacy. I'll be right here. Five minutes, Penny. If you're not coming back up the bank by then I'll come down to get you even if you're as naked as the day you were born. Is that clear?"

Penny Riddle smiled and her teeth glowed white in the moonlight. At that moment, to Stompie Van Der Reit, she was the most beautiful woman he had ever seen.

"Go, now," he whispered, "I'll watch until you get to the water."

Penny Riddle placed her hand on Stompie's arm in a gesture of gratitude. She turned and made her way down the steep sandy bank while Stompie cast a quick eye over the far side of the river. Satisfied all was clear, he stepped back and as promised, moved 10 metres into the forest to give Penny the privacy she needed.

Chapter Fifty-Nine.

Domingo Mussa could hardly believe his luck. The woman he had been sent to capture had presented herself not 3 metres from where he crouched waiting in the shadows. Instinctively he raised the AK47 and aimed but it was only then that he remembered the instructions. *Get her alive.* Slowly he dropped the barrel of the weapon and brought it back towards him. The man would surely be watching from above but he still had the advantage of the cover of the river bank. If he was lucky, he would be able to take the woman silently and disappear without anyone being the wiser. It took only a few seconds for him to make up his mind. He watched as the woman crouched and began unbuttoning her top. In his mind, he felt the urge to wait and watch. He had never seen a white woman naked so this would be the first for him. But then he realised better and decided to take action instead. Domingo Mussa sprang like a leopard with the butt of his rifle raised. But at that moment, the woman turned and saw him. She screamed as she jumped away and the shrill sound pierced his ears. Although the woman was no longer in a crouching position, he had the advantage of forwards motion. As he landed on her, he slammed the butt of the rifle down onto her forehead and she fell unconscious into the river immediately. But at that moment came the shouting from the guard on bank above. Domingo Mussa flipped over onto his back and raised his weapon. The man had run to the bank and upon seeing what had happened, had launched himself from above and was flying head first through the air towards him. He was a short but stocky man, strong and by all accounts, fearless. Without thinking, Domingo Mussa pulled the trigger and the weapon kicked in his hand. But the shot missed and this confused him as it was all happening so fast. The second shot hit the man and he watched in satisfaction as the flying body was spun around in mid-air. The man landed on the sand to the right with a thud and Domingo heard the grunt as the wind was knocked out of him. Then there was only silence and Domingo smiled as he thought he must have killed the man. He quickly turned to his left and saw the unconscious woman's head submerged in the water. Her long stringy hair was swirling in the current. Wasting no time, he lifted her by the the back of her shirt and pulled her onto the sand. There was a brief spluttering and choking sound as her breath returned but still, she remained unconscious. Domingo stood up and lifted the woman into the sitting position. Her head hung in front of her and he saw the profile of her breasts under her wet top.

He placed his weapon on the sand and lifted her using a fireman's lift. The woman was light and he was young and strong. It would be easy to move with her. Finally, he grabbed his gun and, after a quick look around, he set off at a run downstream towards the weir. As he went, he was sure he could hear distant, muffled shouting behind him, but he could not be certain. The sound of the river was washing it out and his primary goal was to reach the weir safely. He did this soon enough and began the precarious journey across the submerged boulders and the tree to the middle. It was a full five minutes later when he finally stepped onto the sand and began climbing the far bank. Once there, he laid the woman down on the ground so he could ready himself for the journey ahead. He would return to Joao Quintas triumphant and would surely be showered with praise for his outstanding work. The woman lay below him as he adjusted his equipment and he stared down at her pale face bathed in the moonlight. He crouched down and moved a thick strand of wet hair from her face. The horizontal cut on her forehead was now an egg-sized lump that oozed blood that looked black in the moonlight. To Domingo Mussa, she was beautiful. She was his prize, and he would never forget that moment as long as he lived. But the glory of the moment was soon forgotten as he realised the immensity of the task ahead. He would have to backtrack while carrying the dead weight of the woman. He would also have to ensure that she remained silent. This would be no problem as he would simply knock her out again. Satisfied he was ready to go, he crouched down and lifted the body of the woman onto his shoulder. He stared ahead into the forest and began walking. As he went he was reminded of the great Islamic hymns the troops would sing during training. He soon set into an easy gait and as he went he hummed the tune to himself. For Domingo Mussa, life was good. Very good indeed.

Chapter Sixty.

Penny Riddle's scream pierced the night. Immediately I felt a cold shiver run up my spine and acidic bile rising in my throat. *Oh Jesus, no.* I sprang to my feet after grabbing my gun and set off at a sprint towards the river. Sarge was 5 metres behind me in hot pursuit. It was then that I heard the shout from Stompie. Whatever he said was inaudible but it was clear that they had come under attack. *Fucking hell!* With the branches and vines whipping at my face I ran until I was within 20 metres of the river. Fearing a trap, I slowed down as did Sarge behind me. Crouching down low in the moonlight, we made our way forward to the spot where Stompie had been on guard.

"Penny!" I shouted. "Stompie! Where are you?"

It was then that I heard the wheezing, winded voice coming from somewhere near the waterline. It was Stompie but he was out of sight down the bank.

"Jason!" he shouted, "I've been hit! The fucker has taken Penny. Headed downstream. There's no one around, Come quickly!"

Sarge and I ran to the bank and looked down at the waterline. Stompie lay in a foetal position half-submerged in the water. His pale face looked up at me and I saw fear in his eyes.

"I'm sorry, Jason," he panted. "I wanted to give her a bit of privacy as she washed but one of the bastards was hiding down here.

I jumped down after him but he got me in my thigh."

Sarge and I jumped down to the waterline and Sarge stood on guard with his weapon raised as I tended to Stompie.

"Where were you shot? Let's have a look."

"It's just my thigh," he hissed with pain. "His first shot missed. I jumped down at them from up there."

"How many were they?" I asked.

"Only one," he replied. "Must have been hiding behind that tree trunk. He knocked her out and headed back downstream at speed. Please, Jason, go after her! I'll be okay here, it's just a flesh wound."

I looked up at the far side of the river and weighed up our options. It puzzled me that there had only been one attacker. There were three of them the last time we checked. The man had come from downstream. That meant that he must have found a crossing point somewhere. *There might well be more men lying in wait for us.* This was an unknown and a dangerous one at that.

"Okay," I said placing my hand on his shoulder. "If you're sure you're gonna be okay."

"I'll be fine," he said, his face pale and his blood running onto the sand. "I'll make up a tourniquet and stay right here with my gun."

I stood up and spoke.

"Sarge, you head downriver. Try to find the crossing point. If you find it, go ahead and cross. I'll head up to our spot and do the same. They've taken her alive on purpose. It is to draw us in. Keep your radio on but only use it if you find them. Is that clear?"

Sarge nodded and I saw the fires of battle in his eyes. It was as if he was born for this.

"Understood boss," he said. "Let's do it..."

I nodded at him and took a final look at Stompie who had dragged himself up to the sandbank and had positioned himself there with his gun at the ready.

"Right. See you soon."

Wasting no time, I sprinted up the river bank only stopping when I reached the crossing point we had used the previous day. I took one look at the raging waters and I knew there was no way I could cross with the AR-15. There was only one option and that was to throw my lighter equipment across to the far bank and retrieve it when I got there. I placed the rifle on the sand reluctantly and stood to throw the sidearm and the radio. I threw them one by one with all my might and watched them arc in the moonlight as they went. They landed silently on the sand at the far side and I made a mental note of the position. Next, I ran 15 metres upriver and launched myself into the raging water at my feet. The current was strong and my body was tossed about as I pulled myself across the river. For a few seconds, my world was a confusing mess of moonlight, darkness and the sound of raging water. But finally, I was slammed into the fallen tree trunk and I steadied myself as I raised my head to take a look around. The scene was one of serenity and calm and I crouched there in the gloom for a moment. There was no one in sight and I cautiously pulled myself along the tree trunk towards the river bank. Once there, I gathered my breath and began making my way back down the far side to the spot where the sidearm and radio had landed. I found them immediately and quickly scaled the banks into the forest above. I knew that our trail had initially come out of the forest roughly 50 metres downstream. The attacker must have followed us through the night to get to that point. The great unknown was whether there were more of them lying in wait for us.

Running blindly through the forest would make us sitting ducks who could be picked off with ease. The moonlight was sufficient for that to happen. There would only be one way to do this. I knew I had to backtrack along the way we had come in but parallel. I would need to travel at least a kilometre north and then come back along our original tracks. I had no idea if Penny was alive or dead. Further to that, there was no way of telling if her attacker had crossed the river once again. The fact that there had only been one of them was puzzling but it was all we had to work with. *There is no choice, Green. You must head into the forest, and do it now!* I placed the sidearm in its holster and checked my knife was still attached to my belt. It was. After making my way 40 metres upstream, I climbed the bank and set off at a trot into the forest. I ran as quietly as I could, swerving here and there to avoid thorn bushes, branches and anthills. I kept my breathing to a minimum and used the moon above to guide my course.

I gauged my pace and calculated the distance as I went. All the while I beat myself for making the fundamental mistake of letting Penny go out alone. *What a fucking stupid thing to do Green. You fucking idiot! This is your fault! Imagine what they might be doing to her right now! How could you have allowed that? What were you fucking thinking?* Stompie had said there was only one man. I knew that if he had crossed the river he would be carrying or dragging Penny with him. That was if she was still alive. I knew that if she was conscious, she would be putting up a fight. But till then there had only been silence. Silence since the terrible scream I had heard. Carrying her would slow the man down considerably. *If he has crossed the river, you now have the advantage, Green. Make your way back to the trail and head back towards him. It's all you can do!* I touched the radio on my belt. It was the assurance I needed. Sarge would only make contact if he had found something. That would either be Penny's dead body or worse. Our escape that had been going so well was rapidly becoming a disaster. *And it's all your fault,*

Green. Fucking idiot! I slowed down and paused to gather my breath and take a look around. A quick look up at the moon told me I had come in the right direction. All around me the forest was quiet save for the hissing of the crickets and the sound of my heart thumping in my chest. My mouth was dry and my wet clothes clung to my grimy body. I set off heading east in search of the original tracks we had made heading to the river. It took less than five minutes to find them. I shook my head as I realised how easy they were to follow, even in the moonlight. For a trained tracker, it was child's play. I had been far too comfortable in our lead and the distance I thought we had put between them and us. I cursed myself as I began walking slowly back towards the river. Staying a couple of metres to the side of the main trail, I lurked in the shadows, moving silently from tree to tree, stopping regularly to listen and wait for any unusual sounds. All the while I pictured the savagery these monsters might be inflicting on poor Penny Riddle. It was almost too awful to imagine. *You fucked up big time, Green.* The feeling of defeat and gloom continued for the next 15 minutes as I made my way south. But it was as I was pausing in the shadows of a mopane tree that I heard it. At first I thought it was leaves rustling the canopy above, but as I waited it became clearer. It was the sound of a human panting. Panting and humming a tune. I stood still and my body tensed up as I pressed it against the tree.

Staying in the shadows I listened as the sound grew louder and louder. Unable to control my curiosity, I poked my head around and took a quick look up the path. There, making his way steadily down the trail, was a man. Clad in the familiar green camouflage, he was almost invisible in the gloom. On his shoulder, he carried the body of Penny Riddle. The man was using the most efficient way to do this. A fireman's lift. It was the extra weight that was causing him to pant as he walked. I paused in morbid curiosity to watch him approach. His eyes were focused on the path ahead and it was clear he was not expecting any company. *No, he's clearly happy with his prize and making his way back to the others.* As he approached I slowly pulled the knife from my belt. I held it in my right hand and adjusted the handle until it felt comfortable in my hand. My limbs tingled with adrenalin as the man got closer to where I stood in the shadows. I waited until he had passed then sprang from my hiding place and in one leap, I grabbed him from behind and brought the sharp edge of the blade to his neck.

"You make a sound and I'll cut your fucking throat," I hissed through gritted teeth. "Down, now!"

I had no idea if the man spoke English but my message was clear in any language. He froze and slowly dropped to his knees. All the while I kept the blade firmly on his throat. It was razor-sharp and would easily cut to his spine.

"Drop the woman," I whispered. "Carefully..."

The man did as instructed and slowly lowered Penny's body to the ground. Her body fell the last few inches and landed with a dull thud and the crunch of dead leaves under her. With my left hand, I pulled the sidearm from the holster and slammed the butt as hard as I could into the man's temple. His unconscious body slumped forward as he fell face-first to the ground.

Chapter Sixty-One.

"Sarge!" I said into the radio. "Sarge, come in..."

The small device squawked in my hand and I heard the familiar voice.

"Boss!" came his voice. "I read you."

"I have them both," I said. "I am on the far side of the river about 500 metres down our track. Where are you?"

"I have just crossed the river," came the reply. "But I'm downstream."

"Make your way upstream and back down the tracks," I said, looking around in the darkness. "It seems we are alone for now. Hurry!"

"Yes boss, right away," he replied. "Is Penny okay?"

"She took a hell of a knock to her head. But she'll live. Hurry, Sarge!"

I crouched down once again and put my ear to Penny's mouth. Her breathing was slow but steady. *Fuck that was close, Green. No more fuck-ups!* Next, I moved to the ISIS militant and began going through his pockets and webbing. The man had been travelling light. AK47, a few hundred rounds around his body, some paperwork in Arabic writing, and two Chinese copies of M26 fragmentation grenades. Commonly known as lemon grenades due to their small size and shape, the devices were deadly if a little unstable and unpredictable. Chinese copies of weapons usually are. The grenades carried 146 grams of Comp-B filler and had an effective blast range of 15 metres. I held one of them in my hand as I waited and an idea formed in my mind. Soon enough I heard Sarge approaching and I called out to him. He arrived looking relieved that I had found Penny and disabled the insurgent.

"Let me kill this bastard now, boss," he growled as he removed his knife from his belt. "It will be my pleasure."

"No," I said. "We need information from him. You must make him talk."

"Oh, he will talk, boss," said Sarge, his eyes glowing and a smile forming on his face. "I can promise you that..."

Sarge busied himself tending to Penny while I pulled the unconscious man up to a nearby mopane tree and placed him in a sitting position against the trunk. Still completely unconscious, his head hung forward and blood dripped from the lump on his temple. I quickly removed his belt and cut it along its length into two pieces. The tough green canvas was thick but after a few minutes, the job was done. With my mind on Stompie, I acted as fast as I could and set about binding the man's hands around the tree behind him. I pulled the knot as hard as I could and once done, I knew there was no way in hell he would ever get out of it alone. Next, I did the same with his feet which were out in front of him where he sat. Finally, I squatted down in front of the man and began slapping him on the cheeks to rouse him from his slumber. It was at that moment that Penny Riddle came round and she immediately began moaning and weeping. Her first query was for the well-being of Stompie. Sarge comforted her and quickly told her that he was alive and well. This seemed to calm her somewhat and she soon sat up with her head in her hands as she nursed what must have been the mother of all headaches. It was a minute later that the militant became fully conscious once again and sat there staring blankly at me. I stood up and spoke.

"Sarge. Have a word with our friend here. Ask him where his comrades are. Make sure he tells us the truth. Oh, and Penny, you might want to block your ears..."

Sarge's first question was responded to by a gob of spit in his face. This did nothing to deter him and he quickly walked around the tree and broke one of the man's fingers. His scream would have travelled far had I not muffled his mouth with my hand. I winced as the second finger was broken with the sound of a dry twig underfoot. By then the man had had enough and immediately broke into a babbled monologue in Portuguese. Satisfied, Sarge stood up and spoke.

"There are two others left as we expected," he confirmed. "They are hours behind us but they are coming. They will be leaving and following our trail at first light. This man was sent to get Penny."

"I thought so," I said. "They figured she'd be a good bargaining chip. Well, I think we should leave them a bit of a surprise."

I went to work immediately with Sarge looking on as I did so. First I removed a strip of material from the man's shirt. At five inches wide, it was long enough to wrap around his face as a gag. Next, I threaded the material through the eye of the pin on one of the lemon grenades. Finally, I stood up and spoke to Sarge.

"Open his mouth," I said. "Wide..."

Sarge said a few words to the man. Fearful of another broken finger, he complied and opened his jaws so his mouth was gaping. Knowing what I was about to do, Sarge gripped him by the teeth of his upper and lower jaw and pulled. I immediately shoved the back of the grenade into his mouth and pushed it in. Finally realising what was happening, the man began to wriggle and scream but the sound was muffled by the large, lemon-shaped device that was now jammed in his mouth. With Sarge forcing the man's head against the tree trunk, I squatted down once again and tied the strip of material twice around the man's lower face. Once done, I stood back to inspect my handiwork. To any onlooker, it appeared the man had simply been gagged. Unable to spit out the grenade and completely immobilised, the man would sit there until he was either discovered or he died. Before leaving, Sarge and I gathered a pile of fallen mopane branches and made a fire a metre in front of where the man sat. His terrified eyes followed us as we worked. The slow-burning wood would burn for at least 24 hours and the pleasant smell of it would drift through the forest drawing the other men in. With the fire burning and the dawn approaching, Sarge and I stood and took a final look at our work.

"Beautiful..." said Sarge with a broad smile.

"Yup," I replied as I stooped to lift Penny to her feet. "Not too bad. Let's get moving. We need to cross that river and get Stompie out of here."

Chapter Sixty-Two.

Joao Quintas and his last remaining man awoke before dawn. Immediately he felt he had made the right choice in sending Domingo ahead. He had been exhausted and badly needed the rest. The night had been spent mostly asleep with only two injections of bola. The fact that he had had so little of the drug meant that he felt somewhat refreshed and confident in the day ahead. After a quick breakfast of dried bread, fruit, and tea, the two of them set off at a good pace following the clear tracks ahead. As they went Joao wondered what had become of Domingo. The young man was keen and capable and would have made quick work of the distance. Either way, he was expendable and even if he had perished, there were still two of them to continue the pursuit. The sun rose soon after and the heat of the day began. But that day it seemed even more brutal than before. Joao realised it was because they were slowly descending into a shallow valley. On the few occasions they stopped, he could see the greener belt of forest in the distance. They were headed towards a river. It was at 11.20 am when, soon after a bola break, they made their way into a particularly dense area of the forest. Instinct told Joao that they were nearing the river. There was a different atmosphere and even the bird song was louder. The humidity was almost unbearable and sweat poured from every pore. His compatriot was faring better, staying in the lead, scanning the forest ahead and following the well-beaten trail. It was then that Joao Quintas smelt it. It was the unmistakable aroma of mopane wood burning. Somewhere nearby was a fire. He called a stop to the march and watched as the lead man turned to look at him.

"Can you smell it?" said Joao "A fire..."

"Yes, master," said the man. "The smell is strong. The fire is close by."

"It could be Domingo," said Joao. "Perhaps he has succeeded in his quest and has the woman. Proceed, but do so with great care. These devils have fooled us twice already. We must not fall into another trap."

The front man nodded and turned to stare into the forest ahead. The two men set off albeit at a slower pace.

The forest became thicker and greener as they went but the trail was still easy to follow. Both men scanned the forest ahead minutely and cast their gaze from left to right as they went. The tracks were clear and there appeared to be nothing out of order so far. It was 10 minutes later when the lead man raised his right hand in a silent gesture to halt. Instinctively, he squatted down on his haunches and paused.

"Can you see it, master?" he whispered, his voice taut with tension.

"No," replied Joao. "What can you see?"

"Up ahead, on the trail, just to the left. A man is resting against a tree. Looks like Domingo..."

Joao Quintas took his pack from his back and brought out a battered pair of binoculars. He raised them to his eyes and looked in the direction the man was pointing. His hand shook uncontrollably from the continuous drug use but eventually, he saw it.

"Yes," said Joao. "I see him. It looks like Domingo. He has made a fire and as you say, appears to be resting. Perhaps he has the woman and is waiting for us as instructed."

"If so he has done well," said the front man. "Praise be to Allah."

"Move on," said Joao, his eyes narrowing with suspicion. "But slowly..."

The two men moved along the trail stopping every 10 metres to pause and look again. Soon enough it became clear that it was indeed Domingo who was sitting at the tree trunk. His head was hanging low and it was difficult to make out his face. He sat there completely still and motionless.

"What is he doing?" asked Joao.

"He is just sitting there in front of the fire," whispered the lead man. "Perhaps he is asleep? He appears to be alone. Perhaps he has the woman tied up somewhere nearby?"

"Hmm..." said Joao. "Let's move closer, but with caution."

It was a good ten minutes later when the two men had made it to within 30 metres of their sleeping compatriot. Until then he had sat there completely motionless. Still, Domingo's face was out of sight as his head was hanging low. *But he has made a fire, surely he is okay?* But before moving ahead, Joao Quintas decided to call out to the man. The scene was confusing and his senses told him something was amiss.

"Domingo!" called Joao. "Domingo, are you okay?"

It was then that the young man's head jerked upwards and they saw the gag around his lower face.

"See," hissed Joao. "He has cloth around his face to silence him."

"Domingo," called Joao. "Are you alone?"

The gagged man's eyes were burning with passion and the sweat poured from his forehead. But there seemed to be a sense of relief on his face. The fact that had not responded by calling back was puzzling.

"He is nodding at us but not talking," said the lead man. "Something is wrong."

"You are right," said Joao. "And it seems his hands are bound behind the tree."

There was a further 5 minutes of one-sided conversation between the men, with Domingo only nodding frantically.

All the while Joao and the other militant scanned the surrounding forest for signs of a trap. But in the end, it seemed there was none. They could sit there all day or they could simply get on with the task at hand. It was then that Joao made the decision.

They would move ahead and approach their comrade, but they would do so slowly and methodically. The two men crept forward, their guns raised and their gaze flicking from left to right. All the while Domingo sat there with wide eyes, silently moving his head in all directions. It was a confusing and unsettling situation. Finally, they arrived within 5 metres of Domingo and only then did they see the true terror in his eyes. There was a huge lump on his right temple that was caked with dried blood and his hands and feet were bound with thick green canvas. They could hear his repeated muffled shouts and Joao frowned as he stood up and looked down at him.

"He cannot speak," said the lead man. "He is gagged. Let me help him."

"Go ahead, but be careful," said Joao. "I will stay here and keep watch."

The lead man placed his gun on the dried leaves below and crouched down as he approached the sitting figure of Domingo. At that moment a waft of mopane smoke drifted into his eyes and stung them. Still, he moved forwards and watched as Domingo began to thrash and twist in his bindings. Finally, he arrived at Domingo's feet and stared into his face. It was clear he had been beaten, but praise be to Allah, he was at least alive. The lead man reached forward and grabbed the soaking green material that had been bound around Domingo's lower face. With a quick tug, the material came away with a dull clicking sound and he stared in momentary confusion at what he saw underneath. Protruding from Domingo's mouth was a rectangular piece of metal. The lead man frowned as Domingo thrashed his head from side to side in a blur.

Chapter Sixty-Three.

Stompie Van Der Reit lay where we had left him on the riverbank. His usually sunburnt face was pale and drawn in the dawn light. Sarge and I had left the man tied to the tree and made our way back down our original trail to the river. Instead of crossing upstream, Sarge had led us down to an old weir where our attacker had crossed. We had helped the slightly concussed Penny across the stones and the fallen tree to the far side. Once there we had made our way back upriver through the forest until we reached Stompie who was still propped up against the bank below. It took less than 10 minutes for Sarge and I to carry him through the forest to our camp. Once there, Penny treated his wound with antiseptic ointment and a tight bandage around his thigh. The AK47 bullet was still lodged in his flesh and would require an operation to remove. In the eerie dawn light, Sarge and I walked off into the forest and hacked a series of bamboo poles from which to make a stretcher. We carried the poles back to the camp and I began building it while Sarge distributed fruit he had gathered the previous day. Although in great pain, Stompie was overjoyed to hear we had caught up with our attacker and had immobilized him. He grinned from ear to ear when Sarge related the simple trap of the lemon grenade I had stuffed into his mouth.

"I'd pay a year's salary to watch that fucker go off!" he said with a wince as Penny tended to his wound.

It was just after 6.00 am when Sarge and I tested the crude stretcher that I had built. Bound together with flexible vines, it would be desperately uncomfortable but would it would do the job. By my calculations, it was only 25 kilometres to Mocimboa Da Praia. A distance we could cover if we set off immediately. But there were still the militants who by all accounts were relentless in their pursuit. It puzzled me as to why they had continued after so many setbacks. They were now straying into an area that was purportedly controlled by the Mozambican army. Regardless, we knew they were determined and it was for this reason that we could not stop. The march would continue with our wounded and nothing and no one would stop it. The tragedy we had luckily managed to avoid was burned into my mind forever.

We set off at 6.25 am and began the trudge through the dense forest heading south as always. With the added weight of Stompie between us, Sarge and I stumbled our way through the morning until 9.30 am when we stopped to rest and drink water. By then my hands were badly chaffed and my arms were burning from the effort. Stompie was stoic in his pain and only grunted and gasped when one of us stumbled. He was constantly apologetic for the fact that he had been shot but Penny attended to him constantly, much to his embarrassment. Even the slow journey out of the low river valley did nothing to abate the intense heat and by 11.00 am we were all shattered. Up ahead in the distance was yet another low hill. But it was not just any hill. It was the final one before we would reach safety. The town of Mocimboa Da Praia lay just beyond it in a bay on the coast. The sun blazed above us and the filth of the journey was sticky and itchy on my skin. We stopped once again at 1.00 pm and ate some fruit and the last of the cereal bars. By then there was a feeling that the march would never end and a kind of solemn acceptance had set into the group. I did my best to lift the mood by reminding my companions of the many victories we had made. At each stop, we laid Stompie down and Sarge climbed a tree to take a look at what was happening behind us. There was no sign of any living creature, animal or human. This was a relief to us all although I knew the danger was far from over. We had no idea what to expect, the past few days had taught us that very well. I was sick with exhaustion and by the time we reached the foot of the far hill every single step had become a monumental effort. I had to concentrate on the ground ahead of us and it felt like we would never get there. My arms were on fire and my hands had long since gone numb from gripping the thick bamboo poles. By then we were all walking dead and the prospect of pushing up the hill seemed like an impossibility. We laid the stretcher down in some tall dried grass and sat in full sunlight, our heads hanging low and our breathing laboured and rasping. If our pursuers had seen us at that point they would have known that they had beaten us. But there was no way that I would allow that to happen. The astonishing atrocities we had all witnessed would haunt us for the rest of our lives. It was 10 minutes later when I called to commence the march. My back screamed at me as I lifted the stretcher once again. By then Stompie had fallen into some kind of delirium with the pain and blood loss. I had checked his breathing however and it was steady.

But it was another reason to keep moving. We made the climb for the next 20 minutes until stopping at the foot of a rocky outcrop. Behind us lay the valley we had just emerged from. I took a moment to squat down and check on Stompie who lay in a semi-conscious state on the crude stretcher with his rifle beside him. Penny fussed over him like a nurse. A minute later Sarge climbed a fever tree and brought the binoculars to his face.

"Boss!" he called out, a note of excitement in his voice. "We have company..."

Chapter Sixty-Four.

Domingo Mussa's desperate thrashing only served to confuse the lead man further. It was only when he stopped moving did the man recognise what it was he was looking at. And only then did he realise what he had done. He had pulled the pin from the grenade that had been stuffed in Domingo's mouth. Unable to spit out the bulky lemon-shaped device, he had been sitting like that for hours. Joao Quintas had seen it however, and took immediate action.

"Nooo!" he screamed as he threw himself to his left to escape the blast.

There was a split second of realisation before it blew. Domingo Mussa's head exploded as the heavy fragments of steel tore through his skull. The blast blew a large chunk of the tree to which he had been tied and the lead man's face was ripped off in the process. He stood up briefly and stumbled around blindly for a few seconds before falling to the ground to die. The proximity of the blast ruptured Joao's eardrums and fragments of bark, grit and bone tore into his exposed flesh. But he lay there and slowly began testing his extremities as he recovered from the shockwave. *My arms and legs are there*, he thought. *At least I'm alive*. But the pain in his head was intense as was the feeling of defeat at having been tricked once again. The men he was following were no amateurs. *No, they were skilled soldiers*. It took another 20 seconds before Joao sat up and took a look at the scene of devastation in front of him. The headless body of Domingo Mussa was still bound to the tree and the front man was writhing in his death throes. Shell shocked, numb, and in great pain, Joao Quintas reached into his pocket and brought out the bag of white powder that had sustained him for so long. With a quivering hand, he opened it and stuffed it into his face as he inhaled. The smell of the mopane smoke made him sneeze and when he removed the bag, his lower face was coated with the powder. A deep sense of rage filled him as he stared at his dead comrades lying before him. The escapees were nowhere to be seen. He had been tricked yet again. Now he was alone. It was only he who could avenge the death of his beloved Darwesh. Joao Quintas screwed his eyes closed and his breathing came in great ragged wheezes.

The pain in his head intensified as he drew a large breath and screamed at the top of his lungs. It was an ugly and inhuman sound that echoed through the forest, silencing even the birds.

"Noooooooo!" he screamed repeatedly. "Noooooo!"

He sat there in a semi-catatonic state for 15 minutes until the drug began to take effect and his thoughts became clear once again. He took his eyes from the dead men that lay before him and looked down the trail that by then was well beaten and clear. *That fire has not been burning long. They are near. The trail is easy to follow and I must go now. I must continue and avenge the death of Darwesh and the other men. Joao Quintas will never allow these infidels to get away with this. Never!* Joao got to his feet and once again felt the unusual tingling in his limbs. He spent a few minutes gathering what he could from the dead men and set off at a trot through the forest. It was 5 minutes later when he arrived at the banks of the river. He scanned the many footprints and trails that had been left. There were two sets of prints. One leading upstream, the other downstream. Joao Quintas decided to head downstream. Moving at pace, he ran until he saw the crossing point. The old stone weir was partly destroyed but it was clear that people had crossed at that point recently. With a quick look across the river, he made his way down to the water and across the raging waters that covered the rocks. Once there, he saw the tracks leading back upstream. They were as clear as day and he followed immediately. The sense of bravado the drug was giving him went unnoticed as by then he had only one thing on his mind. Revenge. Soon enough he reached the point opposite where he had arrived. He looked at the prints below him. There had been a scuffle and a lot of movement there. He squatted down on his haunches and fingered a dark patch of sand. He brought his finger to his nose and smelt it. *Blood!* he thought. *One of them is injured. Good!* Joao Quintas stood up and cast his eyes up the river bank. The tracks were clear and there had been much traffic. In his mind, he pictured the scene that had occurred there not long ago. *One of them was injured and was helped up the bank by the others. I can see it in my mind. I am a genius! The injured one will slow them down. I will catch them easily if I move now.* Wasting no time, he scrambled up the sandbank and cast his eyes into the forest ahead.

There was no sound other than the rushing water behind him and the birds in the trees above. The trail was once again well beaten and clear to see. Joao's mad eyes glared around for a moment and he pulled the water bottle from his webbing and drank. He screwed the green plastic top back on the bottle and set off at a fast run following the trail into the forest. Fueled by the obscene quantity of cocaine and heroin, he ran without stopping until the forest began to thin and the landscape ahead opened up. In the distance, he saw another hill. *Not far. Perhaps 20 minutes running. But this is open country. Must be careful.* After another drink of water, and with the blood pounding through his body, he set off once again at a swift pace, dodging anthills and leaping over gullies as he went. The continuous defeats and setbacks he had suffered were now totally forgotten and he ran with the madness of a berserker. Risk was no longer a factor as there was now only one thing on his mind. He would kill the tall white man if it was the last thing he did in this world. The man who had caused so much pain and suffering and who hoodwinked and shamed him. The blind run continued for another hour but to Joao, it felt like a matter of minutes. By then his heart was strained and the tingling in his limbs was intense. It was as if he had been endowed with some kind of superhuman strength. But in reality, Joao Quintas was close to death and his body was about to give up. A minute later, still at mid-pace, his right leg stopped working and he tumbled forward and rolled over multiple times. The fall created a small cloud of dust and winded him. He lay there with the blazing sun beating into his wide eyes. The burning on his retinas caused weird shapes to appear in his vision and he blinked repeatedly. They were not unpleasant shapes. Not the stuff of nightmares. Rather like amoebas seen through a microscope that swam in his vision, turning red and black as they moved. Joao Quintas blinked again and he felt the dust and grit in his eyes. *What is happening to me?* he thought. *I feel strange.* He sat up and looked around him. All was quiet and the dust had settled. Now recovered from the winding, he looked down and massaged his right leg. There was still the unusual tingling feeling in his limbs but he felt he could stand. Slowly, and with great care, he lifted his body and stood. But once again his legs failed him and he stumbled off to the right falling over again with a grunt. *Bola,* he thought. *I need more bola.*

Chapter Sixty-Five.

I stood up immediately and turned to look behind us at the valley below.

"How many men?" I asked.

Sarge paused with the binoculars to his face in the tree above.

"Just one," he replied. "Running fast, following us."

I watched as he leapt down from the tree and walked up to me.

"Come, boss," he said pointing at a ridge just below us. "I will show you."

I followed Sarge down a few metres and stood on a rocky protrusion from the hill. Once there he pointed back down our trail and spoke.

"Use your binoculars," he said. "But soon enough you will see him without them."

I pulled the binoculars from my webbing and looked down to where he had indicated. It took less than a second to see the man. He was running like a man possessed, seemingly with almost superhuman speed. Fully armed and clad in the familiar green uniform, it seemed crazy and brazen to do so in the appalling heat of the day and I wondered if the man was sane. I watched in fascination as he dodged the anthills and sprinted through the undergrowth, following our trail doggedly and precisely. Sarge did the same and both of us were silent as we watched. Soon enough it was no longer necessary to use the binoculars and we both raised our weapons and lay down on the rocks to ready ourselves to shoot. Both of us knew it would be a matter of minutes before he would be in range and it would be relatively easy to take him out from where we were. My breathing calmed as I followed his progress and I did my best to keep him in the sights of my rifle. But the man was moving so fast it was difficult to do so. It was when he had come to within 200 metres and was in the open area at the foot of the hill that I saw him tumble.

He rolled over several times and I frowned as I watched him do so as I could see nothing that had tripped him up. Both Sarge and I watched in silence as he lay there, his chest heaving from the effort as he stared up into the sun above. Soon after, he sat up and shook his head as he made his recovery. The man got to his feet but stumbled again and fell heavily. Feeling confused, I took my eyes off him and turned to Sarge who lay next to me watching the man through his gun sights.

"What the hell is going on, Sarge? Is this a fucking mad man?"

"Drogas," he replied in his native Portuguese "These devils are all on drugs..."

Sure enough, we watched as the man brought a plastic bag from his breast pocket and lifted it to his face. It was clear he was snorting the white substance as when he was done, his lower face and beard were covered with the powder. He sat for a minute before getting to his feet with ease. But it was then that I heard the deafening crack of the rifle firing behind me. *What the fuck? Have we walked into a trap as they had warned us?* Both Sarge and I rolled over immediately but what we saw was the last thing we had expected. Penny Riddle stood not far behind us with Stompie's AR-15 raised, its barrel still smoking. At first, I could hardly believe my eyes, but it was real. Penny had taken Stompie's rifle and had taken a shot at the man below. I watched as she slowly lowered the rifle and placed it back on the stretcher next to the comatose man. Her face, a picture of impassive calm. *What the fuck?* But there was no time to waste as both Sarge and I rolled over to take a look at the man below. It came as yet another surprise to see that he had indeed been hit. The man was down in a sitting position clutching his stomach which was bleeding profusely.

"I don't fucking believe what I have just seen," I whispered with a shaky voice. "Penny just shot the fucker!"

Sarge chuckled and shook his head.

"Neither can I, boss," he replied. "She's a good shot too. Got him in the stomach..."

The force of the shot had blown the man's weapon out of his hands and it lay in the dirt two metres from where he sat dying. But it was then that something equally unbelievable happened. The man pulled a radio from his tatty webbing and spoke into it. Both of our radios squawked simultaneously and we heard the rasping, breathless voice speak in Portuguese.

"Esta é uma mensagem para o homem branco alto," said the man. "Você não joga limpo."

Sarge chuckled once again as he understood.

"What did he say?" I whispered.

Sarge turned and looked at me with a wide grin on his face.

"He said, this is a message for the tall white man. You don't play fair..."

I turned and looked at the dying man below us once again and I pictured the horrors of the last few days.

"Tell him he's right," I said. "And I don't lose either..."

Chapter Sixty-Six, Umhlanga Rocks, Durban, South Africa, 10 days later.

The midday sun glinted off the thick chrome bull bar on the front of the Ford Ranger pickup truck. I had rented it an hour before at King Ushaka Airport having landed from Mozambique after several days of recovery in Mocimboa Da Praia and subsequent transfer to Pemba. After the surprise shooting of our pursuer by Penny Riddle, Sarge had gone down to check the man was dead. He was. We had pressed on in the heat of the day finally cresting the hill and seeing the tiny port town below. Exhausted, we had stumbled into the outskirts of the town and collapsed in a straggly maize field on the outskirts of the town. Our unexpected arrival caused a huge response by the police and security forces who congregated around us en masse within 20 minutes. Once it was established who we were, we were rushed to the medical facility that had been set up by JAG. Stompie had been admitted to the field hospital and had the bullet removed from his thigh. The rest of us were treated for dehydration, shock and exhaustion and discharged two days later. I had parted company with Penny, Stompie and Sarge soon after and had caught a private charter to Pemba where I had booked into a hotel and had been following the events in Palma. During the attack, there had been a total of over 70000 people displaced. Most had fled into the surrounding bush, lucky to have escaped with their lives. Over 300 had perished in the town and that number was rising as more deaths were being reported daily. The town had since been reclaimed by security forces and negotiations were underway for regional governments to send troops to stabilise the situation. The events in Palma had brought the conflict in northern Mozambique onto the world stage and finally, people were starting to notice. There had also been a major investigation launched into the killing of civilians by JAG operatives that had been initiated by Amnesty International. So far they had gathered 43 witnesses to testify to the indiscriminate shootings. The situation was changing daily and I would follow it until its conclusion. The insurgency had so far displaced over 700, 000 people in the region and the hundreds of reported attacks were only now being noticed. However, the actual objectives of these rag-tag groups of insurgents were still under debate. The true toll of the insurgency would probably never be known as the country remained one of the most difficult places on earth to operate in and gather intelligence effectively.

The midday sun blazed through the windscreen and I took my sunglasses from my pocket as I pulled off the highway and entered the plush, leafy suburb of Umhlanga Rocks. I was there for an appointment with Colonel Callum Jackson. He didn't know about it but I was going to make sure that it happened. I had found his address after much research and had entered it into the SATNAV on the hire vehicle after picking it up from the airport. The device told me I was 15 minutes from arrival and in my mind, I prepared what I would do when I arrived. I had been through it a thousand times since arriving in Mocimboa Da Praia. One thing was for sure, I would confront him that day, without fail. The manicured streets wound through the wealthy suburb finally rising up a hill that I knew would offer a sea view on the far side. My prediction was correct as I crested the hill and saw the vivid blue spread of the Indian Ocean below. On either side were the houses of the super-wealthy. Many of them modern homes with stylish geometric designs and infinity pools. Here security was tight and there were tall brick walls with cameras, and armed response vehicles parked at the ready on the corners to protect the affluent residents. The SATNAV told me to take a left near the ridge of the hill and I did so onto a small but immaculately maintained road. The road was lined with mansions on either side, all with expansive gardens, tall walls and electric gates. *Yes*, I thought to myself. *This is just the sort of place old Jacko would choose*. The road wound its way along the ridge for another 2 kilometres until the SATNAV announced I had arrived at my destination. I took a look to my left but the property was hidden by a tall wall made from cream coloured brick. The property was large as it was at least another hundred metres until I reached the main gate which was equally tall but fairly nondescript apart from an intercom unit that rose from the brick driveway nearby. I turned the powerful vehicle into the driveway and pulled up next to the intercom. Above me, on the wall was a closed-circuit camera that was positioned to focus on the driver of any visiting vehicle. The electric window buzzed as I opened it and I took a deep breath before pushing the button. There was a short bell sound from the intercom followed by a long moment of silence. It was thirty seconds later when I heard the voice.

"Hello?"

"My name is Jason Green," I said clearly. "I have come to see Colonel Jackson."

"One moment please..." came the reply.

My anger built as I waited and I pictured the hushed conversation that might be taking place behind the tall wall. I drummed my fingers on the steering wheel as I waited and sweat began to form on my forehead. It was a full two minutes later when the man on the intercom spoke again.

"Mr Green," said the man. "The Colonel is busy and cannot see you today. Can I suggest you make an appointment through the JAG offices?"

My fingers gripped the steering wheel as my knuckles turned white from the force of my anger. I had anticipated some resistance to my impromptu visit, but all of a sudden I found my rage impossible to control. I took a deep breath and spoke calmly.

"You tell the Colonel that if this gate doesn't open in exactly 30 seconds, I will reverse my vehicle and smash it down. As you can see, I have a large bull bar fitted. The damage will be to his property, not mine..."

The intercom went silent and I took a quick look at my watch to begin the countdown. It came as no surprise to see the gate begin to slide open after only 20 seconds. Ahead of me was a neat brick driveway that wound its way up the hill through a manicured garden filled with rare tropical plants. Giant birds of paradise bloomed among variegated bromeliads, palms and succulents. There were short brick pillars with lights every ten metres going up the driveway to the massive building above. The two-storey house fronted by massive windows was a grand example of contemporary architecture. The wide expanse of the house would offer unrivalled views of the Indian Ocean below and the house would not be out of place in the millionaire playgrounds of Palm Springs or The Bahamas. I buried the accelerator and the massive wheels screamed as the vehicle lurched forward and began climbing the hill. It took less than 30 seconds to reach the top where I skidded to a halt in a large parking lot to the left of the house. Wasting no time, I jumped out of the vehicle and walked down the pathway to the front door which was set to the centre of a large pool at the front of the house. My anger grew steadily as I walked. *Control yourself, Green.*

The wide door was made from horizontal slats of textured wood that stood in contrast to the concrete, steel and glass that surrounded it. The door swung open as I approached and I saw two burly looking young men standing there waiting for me with nervous looks on their faces. *Hired muscle, no doubt.* Saying nothing, I bounded up the steps and attempted to barge my way in. Both men gripped me by my arms and immediately a scuffle broke out.

"You can't just barge in here, Mr Green!" shouted one of them in a thick Afrikaans accent.

But it was then that I heard the familiar voice of the Colonel booming through an intercom at the reception desk.

"Let him in!" he growled. "Show him to my office! You monkeys stay where you are!"

The two big men let me go reluctantly and I shrugged out of their grips.

"Where is it?" I said calmly.

The man on the right pointed down a wide corridor that led off from the main reception and spoke with a sneer on his face.

"Third door on the right..."

I set off across the marble floor making my way past a wide stairway that led to the upper floor of the huge house. The corridor was clad with wood and illuminated with subtle lighting. The air was crisp and cool courtesy of hidden vents and climate control. I reached the third door and pushed it open to reveal an expansive office with floor to ceiling windows that looked out onto the pool and the ocean below. The walls were filled with books and hunting trophies and the floor was covered from wall to wall with grey carpet. Colonel Callum Jackson stood with his back to me at a drinks cabinet on the right. In front of him were two heavy tumblers and he was busy pouring two healthy measures from a crystal decanter.

"Jason Green!" he boomed as he turned to look at me.

The sight of him standing there wearing cream slacks with a sports jacket and cravat, his cold blue eyes staring into my soul only served to infuriate me further. This was the man who had abandoned us in a Mozambican hell hole and left us to die. With the door wide open behind me, I continued walking toward him with my fists clenched. Seeing this, he placed the tumblers back on the tray and turned to face me. I watched as his body tensed as I approached. But by then I had lost any sense of control I might have had when I had arrived. Stepping up to him, my right fist swung out like a piston and connected squarely with his lower jaw. It sounded like a cricket bat slamming into a joint of meat. The force of the blow was enough to break two of my fingers and send lightning bolts of pain up my arm. Everything seemed to happen in slow motion. The Colonel's face seemed impassive at first but a second later I watched as a thin dribble of blood ran from the corner of his mouth down his chin. The big man stumbled backwards and fell onto the carpet below. The drinks cabinet rattled as he did so. Testament to his toughness, he never stopped watching me although his eyes glazed over slightly as I turned to leave. But it was as I reached the door that I heard him speak.

"What the hell was that Green?" he growled.

I stopped in my tracks and turned around to look at the man who sat on the floor behind me.

"That," I said quietly "Was an act of war."

Chapter Sixty-Seven. London, Three Months Later.

The kettle rumbled in the kitchenette and I stepped through to make myself the first coffee of the day. I carried it to the bay window in the front room and pulled the curtains open. Outside the summer sun shone down onto the sprawl of North London 5 floors down. I stood there silently smoking a cigarette and thinking about the day ahead. Once done, I took my mug and sat down at my desk to check my emails. There was the usual list of work correspondence and promotions that arrived every day, but one of them caught my eye instantly. It was from Stompie Van Der Reit. I clicked it immediately and could almost hear his voice as I read it.

'Dear Jason.

I hope this finds you well. I thought I'd send you a quick email to let you know what happened after you left us in Mocimboa Da Praia. My wound healed up nicely and I was discharged a week later. From there I travelled to South Africa for a rest and have since moved to the UK. I have set up with Penny at her London flat and have taken a job as a security guard at the Tate Gallery. It's a far cry from my usual line of work but it's a lot safer. I'm sure you will agree. I wanted you to be the first to know that Penny and I are engaged to be married. I have been in contact with Sarge who is still employed by JAG and working on a new contract in Mozambique. He sends his best wishes. Penny and I would both like to thank you for getting us out of there, Jason. I will never forget it and I owe you my life. For now, we are both very happy and would like to put it all behind us and move on. I know we will probably never meet again, but I remain,

Your friend

Stompie.'

The End.

Dear reader. I guess if you are seeing this you have finished this book. If so, I really hope you enjoyed it! There are many other books in the Jason Green Series which you can find by clicking here: https://geni.us/QCVsT24. I would like to ask you to PLEASE leave me a review on Amazon and Goodreads. Your review helps me to reach new readers and is a vital form of social proof. It really does help! Please come and say hi on my Facebook page which you can find at the link below. I love hearing from readers!

https://www.facebook.com/gordonwallisauthor

Thanks again and rest assured, Jason Green will return soon...